Elton Hall Chronicles:

THIRD WHEEL

By Sarah Fischer

Elton Hall Chronicles: Third Wheel

Limitless Publishing, LLC
Kailua, HI 96734
www.limitlesspublishing.com

Formatting: Limitless Publishing

ISBN-13: 978-1-64034-202-6
ISBN-10: 1-64034-202-8

Dedication

This book is dedicated to my friend, who ditched the perfect guy for the bad boy because she was following her heart. Here is the story of the time she stopped listening to her head and decided to live with her heart.

Chapter 1

"So we're officially on a break," I told Annabelle. We were sitting on the grass outside of her new campus apartment. I begged my parents to let me live on campus with her, but they refused. After they heard about Violet's attack, I was lucky let me on campus without my father holding my hand. Though, I wouldn't be surprised if I had a bodyguard hiding somewhere in the bushes, or if one of the kids in my class was really a trained army ranger or something like that.

"What does that mean, exactly?" Annabelle took a big swig of water and opened her bag to get her sunglasses.

"It means I'm free. I can do what I want, who I want, and how I want. We'll reevaluate in a few months and see what we want." It felt amazing to say, but weird at the same time. I had no idea what the future would hold for me. Goosebumps broke out on my arm as I pondered the idea of the unknown, but it was hard to even imagine a future other than the one my parents and Rob had planned out.

He'd graduate from Holt's Military Academy down in South Carolina in May, and then be shipped to basic training in June…but not before we had a spring wedding at the plaza. I'd be twenty years old, living in military housing by myself while my husband bravely fought for our country. I wasn't sure which part of that life scared me more.

Most people would consider themselves lucky to have such a clear and happy future ahead of them. Rob would be able to support me and his family's money would keep me in the designer clothes I liked. By twenty-three I'd have two beautiful children who would be brought up in a traditional Irish Catholic home. I'd drive a minivan and Rob would have his fancy sports car in the garage for weekend trips. Between the PTA, charity events, and being a stay at home mom, I'd have no time for anything else, but I also wouldn't have to worry about money, or conflicting career goals. In fact, I really wouldn't have to worry about anything. Yes, this was the American dream for some people, but I felt trapped.

"Is there anyone you have in mind, or are you just basking in the glory of singledom?" she asked, bringing me back to reality.

"That's the beauty. I don't know, and I kind of prefer it that way. I mean, I'm not about to go work the corner or pick up johns in some ritzy hotel. But I'm going to enjoy the next few months while I can. Once we're married, my fun will be a lot more subdued."

"When is Rob back?"

"November. We have a deal to be on a break until Thanksgiving. He'll be back from this big secret senior project where he goes off into the wilderness and works on those macho survival skills, and I'll have had a little fun before I settle down with a baby in one hand and a 1950s style vacuum in the other."

"Well, I guess it's time to have a little fun. But first, show me your schedule. I want to see if we have any classes together." She pulled her phone out and pulled up her calendar. Of course she already had all the classes set for each day, the time, and the professor. Annabelle was quite possibly the most organized person I'd ever met.

I took my phone out and went to the school's website to pull up my schedule. I wasn't as ready for our first day of sophomore year. As I reached to hand her my phone, something hit my leg. I dropped my phone out of surprise and looked down to see a football.

"Sorry, guess I didn't see you there," my assailant said. I instantly recognized his voice. It had haunted me all summer. Even when I was in England with Annabelle and Violet, his husky voice filled my dreams. Not that I'd ever let him know that.

Shane Choi was standing about thirty feet from a couple of his friends and he wasn't wearing a shirt. His pecs glistened with a sheen of sweat and his abs looked flawless. I'd felt them last semester when he'd given me a ride on his bike, but I hadn't gotten a look under his leather jacket. I was thrilled to know they lived up to my expectations.

"Maybe you should get glasses," I sneered, standing up and walking over to him.

"Can't, they'll ruin my swagger."

"Does that line work on anyone? Are there people who actually think you have 'swagger'?" I asked, putting air quotes around the word.

He stepped up closer to me and leaned down so he was inches from my face. "I don't know. You're here, aren't you?"

I smiled sweetly at him and then shoved the football into his stomach, causing him to fold over. "I guess you're right." I turned around and walked back to Annabelle.

"Do you serve fries with that shake?" he called after me.

I spun around, flipping my hair in the process. "Depends on whose askin'. Know anyone?"

"I think I know a guy who may be interested, but he's not sure if you could handle his huge, uh, personality."

I looked him up and down, trying to pretend his perfect body didn't impress me. "Well, seeing as you don't seem to have that problem, why don't you send your friend my way? I'll try not to eat him for lunch."

He laughed and waved his football at me. "I would, but you didn't give me your phone number." Shane took his phone out of his pocket and waved it at me.

I picked mine up off the blanket and made a big show out of putting it away in my purse. "Probably because you didn't ask."

He walked over to me slowly and stopped right

in front of me again. My breath caught in my throat as I waited for him to ask, unsure what I would do if he actually did. I know I said I wanted to have some fun, and Shane looked like he knew exactly how to play the game, but that didn't mean I wasn't nervous. I'd kissed the same guy for four years. I was comfortable with that...but nothing about Shane said comfort. Maybe that was why my heart was racing. I also may have been a little scared of rejection.

"Hmm." He appraised me, leisurely taking me in. "I guess I haven't. Usually, girls are beggin' me to call them."

"Funny, I don't see a line of them fawning over you."

"Probably because they know it'd be a waste of time."

"And why's that?" I asked in just above a whisper.

"You'll have to wait to find out." He backed away slowly, and then went back to playing with his friends.

I sat back down next to Annabelle and cursed under my breath. That boy was too much. It'd been about a month since Rob and I had shared a bed. Now, my hormones were raging as I watched his back muscles flex when he tossed the football to his friends.

"So, I'm gonna guess that he threw the football at you on purpose," Annabelle managed to say before she started laughing.

I rolled my eyes at her and gave her arm a little shove. "Let's go get some food." We gathered our things and headed to the cafeteria.

***

Jason was sitting at our usual table by the windows with his roommate, Kyle. Annabelle and I sat down, and instantly, we knew something was wrong. Violet always sat between us, and now that seat was empty. We talked about our upcoming classes and which comedian we hoped would come to perform at the school in October. Kyle gushed about his latest trip to Hawaii and where he wanted to go over winter break. We talked about everything but the fact that we missed Violet.

She was studying abroad in England. Her boyfriend was a twenty-seven-year-old professor, David Berneli, who worked at the university last year. He'd gone back to finish out his contract in London, and she went with him, but only for the semester. Well, we hoped it'd only be for one semester.

"Are you going to the Welcome Week event next weekend?" Annabelle asked me.

"Wait, I thought it was this weekend? Why is Welcome Week after school has already started?"

"Originally it was. During the E-board's summer meeting, we changed things. We got this crazy illusionist, but he was booked this weekend, so we decided to just do it next week. This guy has some videos online and he put an entire crowd under hypnosis. I'm really excited," she explained.

"I can tell, but I'm not sure if I believe in that kind of thing. His tricks all have to be set up," I insisted, ignoring the look of disappointment on her face when I said it. "Besides, what happened to the Casino Night plan? Isn't that what we talked about at the last meeting?"

Casino Night last fall was where Violet met Berneli. Clearly, the event had its merits. Maybe I'd meet my own professor and begin a torrid affair.

"We originally decided on that, but the executive board met over the summer and we wanted to splurge a little." Annabelle was practically bouncing up and down with excitement.

"What she means is that she wants to get hypnotized," Jason told me. "She saw the video online and has become a little obsessed with it. But even I have to admit it sounds pretty cool." He smiled at Annabelle, and then gave her a little kiss on her nose.

I looked at Kyle, and we both acknowledged the awkwardness. Those two, now that they were finally together, were a little too cute sometimes.

"I'll go, but just to prove to you that it doesn't work."

She rolled her eyes at me. "Of course it won't work. You have to be open to it. That's what Gerry says in the video. If you aren't open to it, then it won't work."

I felt that this was a little silly. If it worked, then I'd be a lot more open to it. It seemed to me that it should work the other way, but what the hell did I know about this shit, anyway? "Fine, I'll open my mind to it and then prove it doesn't work."

We hung out a bit longer, and then parted ways. Annabelle and Jason were going to have a date night, Kyle was meeting up with some friends, and I guess I was going home.

***

I pulled into my driveway and my mom greeted me at the door. Her pink frilly apron was wrapped around her waist and her blonde hair was pulled up in an elegant bun. She really was from a different time. My mom was raised in Georgia with a traditional family. She moved to New York to go to art school and met my dad one day when he had volunteered to model. He needed the extra cash since he was putting himself through school. They dated for six months and were married four months later. She quickly dropped out of school and began managing our home.

Every now and then, she'll get her supplies out and paint a still life, or she'll go to the park and sketch couples she sees. But she never does anything with the paintings. Sometimes she'll hang one on the wall, but they never stay up long. She insists that her work isn't good enough and it ruins the award winning décor of the house.

While she seemed to be happy, I wondered how she felt about giving up on her dreams. I don't know. Maybe her dream changed when she became a mom. I'm sure that would happen to me. After all, I didn't have any grand dreams or aspirations. I was studying business with a concentration in marketing. I figured that would be a good skill to have, but I didn't really have a dream to go along with it. I thought it'd be great to run a charity, and marketing would obviously help out with that. I guess it was hard to have a family ruin your dream when you didn't have one in the first place.

"So, darlin', how was school? Did you see your friends?" Mom asked when I walked in the door.

"Yeah, it was weird that Violet wasn't there, but it was nice to see everyone," I told her.

"I know. I can't imagine you going off abroad like that. I'd miss you so much. Besides, how safe can you really be? Do they even screen those host families? You could be living with a murderer or a rapist. No, I'm much happier with you here at home."

"Right, but I'll be leaving at the end of next semester. When Rob and I..." I couldn't even say it. That was probably a bad sign. "After June, I'll be following him around the country."

"Yes, but I know he'll take good care of you, and you'll be living in such a safe area. It's probably safer than our house," she said and started to laugh.

I chuckled along with her, because I knew that's what she wanted me to do. But I was a little tired of being safe. I needed to make a list of some crazy things to do before I settled down. Annabelle would be so excited if she heard me talking about making a list. Though, it probably wasn't the type of list she typically worked on.

"There are some leftovers in the fridge if you want some dinner. Those school dinners probably don't fill you up. Too many carbs."

"Thanks, I'll check it out later."

I looked at her for a second longer. She had started scrubbing the counter with her yellow rubber gloves like she did every night after dinner. My dad would come in after the news, grab a beer, and watch some television in his office, and then they'd watch *Jeopardy* together. When that was over, Dad would do whatever to do list Mom had come up with and she would start laundry or vacuuming.

It had been their routine for as far back as I could remember and they seemed to love it. Seeing them like this made me have hope for Rob and me. If my parents could be happy like this, then so could we. But I had several months before I'd be starting that life. This was my first Saturday single in four years. However, I had no idea what to do. Instead of living it up, I just headed to our basement and watched television before falling asleep. Clearly, I was the life of the party.

***

I parked my car in the school's parking lot for my 9 a.m. class. Before getting out of the car, I checked my makeup and hair in the mirror. I rarely left the house without a full face done up or my hair styled. If I tried, my mom would probably have a stroke because, as she would say, "The world gives you what you give it, so always give it your best side." I smiled at my reflection and climbed out of the car with my designer tote bag filled to the brim. As I slung it over my shoulder, I looked to the left and couldn't help but feel a little disappointed

The motorcycle spaces were empty. Last semester, Shane had given me a ride on the back of his bike when I was having a bad day. It was exhilarating and I'd loved it. Part of me really wanted to do it again. In fact, it was going to be the first thing on my list, but I would change it a little. I ripped a sheet of paper out of one of my notebooks and started my list.

1. *Drive a motorcycle*

I was done sitting in the passenger seat. It was time for me to take charge. I smiled and packed the list away in my planner. With a little pep in my step, I put one high heeled sandal in front of the other and continued across the lot. Then I heard a loud motor and it sounded too close…way too close. Spinning around, I saw a guy on a motorcycle driving straight at me. Too shocked to move, I stared and prayed he'd stop in time.

A few feet from me, the driver dropped his foot to the ground and kicked the back tire around so he stopped just short of me. He lifted the visor on his helmet, and Shane smiled back at me.

"Did I impress you yet?" He raised his eyebrows suggestively, but didn't wait for my response. He climbed off the bike and walked it over to one of the reserved biker spots.

"No, you almost killed me," I shouted as I stalked over to where he was standing. He had a leather jacket on and ridiculous driver gloves. When he took his helmet off, his usually perfectly gelled hair was mussed, but there was a spark in his almond eyes as he met my glare. It was nearly impossible to keep the fury in my eyes as I stared back at him. Something about Shane's face was just so animated it distracted me and I almost forgot why I was annoyed with him in the first place.

"Oh, please, I had it under control. I've been riding one of these since I was fifteen. At this point, it's practically second nature."

"Will you teach me to drive it?"

"What?" He looked at me, shocked, and if there was a mirror, I probably would have had the same expression. To be honest, I didn't expect to say that. It just came out. But I wasn't sorry that it did. The thought of learning to ride a motorcycle, with Shane's hands wrapped around my waist, sounded awfully appealing. Besides, even though my dad had one, he'd never allow me to drive it. Shane was my only chance. Well, my only chance if I didn't want to go to a biker bar and ask some guy named Bubba.

"I mean it. You want to know what will impress me? Well, that's it."

"All right, let's go." He swung a leg over his bike and patted the seat behind him.

"I have class now. But maybe later?" I asked him hopefully, nervous he'd back out if I gave him too much time to think about it. He probably didn't want me messing up his bike. Though, that was possibly a good thought on his part.

"Sounds good.

"I guess I'll see you around." I was about to turn when he grabbed my hand.

Shane pulled a pen out of the pocket of his leather jacket and scribbled something on my palm.

"Just in case you feel like getting a little reckless. Give me a call." Shane climbed off the bike and headed into school, leaving me to stare as he walked away.

What the hell was this kid doing to me?

Chapter 2

The first week of classes went by, but nothing really exciting happened. I didn't run into Shane again, and I hadn't called or texted him. I started to a couple of times, but I wimped out. I should have given him my number so that he could make the first move. But I did manage to work on my "livin' it up" list. So far, I'd managed to add four other things I wanted to do.

1. Learn to drive a motorcycle
2. Take an exotic cooking class
3. Go skinny dipping
4. Spend the day watching movies with my girlfriends. Eat too much junk food, no makeup, and enjoy no worries.
5. Have sex with someone I shouldn't, somewhere I shouldn't (Just to get it out of

my system for good)

I figured this would be a good way to start, but it was by no means the end. Tucking the list away, I went to get ready for the EET event. I still wasn't really feeling the idea of an illusionist. To be completely honest, it kind of freaked me out. There was no need for anyone to mess with my mind. It was a dangerous enough place for me to live in as it was, but I didn't want to let Annabelle down. She told me she had her eyes set on Vice President next semester, so she had taken the lead on this event to start proving to everyone she could handle it. I knew she could do it, but I wanted to help out any way possible.

But if I was going to go, I'd need to get dressed first. Initially, I put on some faux leather leggings and a red blouse, but when I looked in the mirror, I had to laugh. If I showed up like this, Annabelle would definitely start calling me Magician's Assistant Barbie, or something like that.

So I grabbed a pair of shorts that showed too much leg, but no ass, a light pink tank top, and added a grey sweater in case it got cold. Then the real work began. I rolled my hair in curlers and started the strenuous task of contouring, perfecting my cat-eye liner, and applying my favorite red lipstick. I took the rollers out of my hair and ran my brush through it gently. Slipping on a pair of pink sneakers, I left and headed to school. I was dangerously close to running late and having to answer to the wrath of Annabelle, who showed up everywhere twenty minutes early.

I made the fifteen minute drive in about nine minutes, thanks to my lead foot and quite possibly running a red light. I pulled into a parking spot when my phone went off. I almost didn't look at it, knowing it was probably Annabelle complaining that no one was there to help her.

I was half right.

"I just parked. I'm on my way," I said in a rushed voice.

"Oh no, it's okay. I, uh, I got caught up and I'm running a little late too," she responded, a little out of breath.

"Really? Is Jason the reason for that?"

"What? No, I was…"

She tried to come up with an excuse, but we both knew she was full of it. Since she and Jason got together, they've been going at it like rabbits. I was both jealous and excited for her. It was actually nice seeing her and Jason together. He clearly cherished her and she adored him. As cheesy as they were together, I was really happy for them. I wasn't exactly a true love kinda girl, but it seemed to suit them.

"Anyway, come meet me at my apartment, and then we can hand out some flyers on the way. Ticket sales aren't what we expected."

"Okay, I'm on my way. Wait, are you guys sure you're done?"

"Shut up."

I thought about getting back in the car to drive over to the apartments, but the sky was clear and I wasn't in heels. So I hiked my cream purse over my shoulder and started walking. The bugs were chirping and it smelled like heavy pine. It was peaceful. There weren't any other students shouting or any skateboarders trying to impress their friends. It was rare to see the campus this quiet, so I tried to enjoy it.

The problem with peace was that I could hear my thoughts. Like the ones telling me to text Shane. Here it was, another Saturday night, and I still wasn't doing anything exciting. At the very least, maybe he could take me for another ride on his bike. I needed Violet. Annabelle would tell me to leave him alone because he's trouble and she didn't want to see me get hurt, physically or emotionally, but Violet was a hopeless romantic.

I sent her a message through Facebook and asked if she was available to chat on Skype. Almost a minute later, she video called me. I sat on a nearby bench with a street light illuminating it. I needed to keep this spot in mind. The lighting made me look incredible.

"It's so good to see your pretty face," I said as she came up on the phone.

"Hey! What's going on? Everything all right?"

I explained to her quickly that I had taken a break from my relationship with Rob and was looking to let loose before we decided to settle down.

"Are you sure that's a good idea? Don't you think it's a bad sign that you don't want to be with him right before you get married?"

"I get what you're saying, and it's not like that. He's away on some survivalist mission. They have class for two weeks, and then a mission for one week, and then it repeats. He said he didn't have the time to focus on our relationship like I deserve, and I want to have the real college experience before I become Homemaker Barbie. We're probably going to get back together when he's back for Thanksgiving."

"Um, all right, so I still think it's a bad idea, but I'm not going to judge your relationship. So, is that why you called, you wanted to talk about Rob?"

"No, well, kind of. There is this guy, Shane, and he's a bad boy, and sexy, and has a motorcycle, and I've always wanted to learn to drive one. So, he said he'd teach me and gave me his number. I haven't texted him or anything, but I want to."

She smiled in a way that showed all her teeth and then she giggled. "I know who Shane is. I met him through Trent. He was a real charmer."

"Yeah, he pushes my buttons, but I think I like it."

"So do it. You wanted to sow your wild oats. Hop on the back of his motorcycle, feel the wind in your hair, do whatever makes you happy…hell, do him. Really take advantage of this break to make sure that this future you have planned is what you want."

"You're right. What's the worst that could happen? I fall off the bike and die? Then at least I'll have died trying to really live."

"And your hair looks great, so you'll look good at the funeral."

"Well, that's what really matters," I replied, laughing a little. "How are you and Berneli doing?"

"We're good. Our classes start a little later, so I

spent the day in the kitchen with David's mom, Marlaya. She's an amazing cook and is determined to teach me."

"Does she know what she's getting into?" I asked, teasing her. Violet was a notoriously bad cook. I had tried to teach her a few things, but she had, like, a magic touch that burned everything.

"Shut up. It's getting better. I only burned the lasagna a little bit, and David chipped that part off. He even asked for seconds. I think he actually liked it." She looked at me desperately.

I think we both knew he didn't like it, but I wasn't going to clarify that. But I did make a mental note to bring her over when she gets back to try again with the cooking lessons. David was too good of a guy to die early.

We talked for a few more minutes and I promised to keep her updated about Shane.

"Here goes nothing," I said to myself.

Christie: Hey, it's Christie.

I slipped the phone into my purse, got up, and started walking—almost running—to Annabelle's apartment. I needed something to focus on or I'd stare at my phone and will a text to come through. Five minutes later, I was in front of Annabelle's dorm and itching to check my phone. Instead, I knocked on the door and she opened it almost immediately.

"*Finally*, and you're not even wearing heels," she chastised.

"Sorry!"

"It's okay. Here." She handed me a stack of flyers and we started passing them out to people hanging out around the dorms, along the path to the main buildings, and in the cafeteria. We grabbed some drinks and sat down at a table to hydrate for a few minutes before we had to be up in the green room to meet the illusionist.

"He's going to play tricks on you. I have no idea why you want to meet him," I insisted, a little nervous myself.

"Oh, don't be such a sissy. It'll be entertaining."

"At the very least it will be entertaining for me to watch you fawn over him." I snickered at her and she forced a fake laugh.

Then my chair vibrated violently and I almost fell out of it. It must have been my phone. I grabbed my purse off the chair and dived in to try to find it. Naturally, it was buried underneath a whole lot of crap that I didn't need but would never take out.

Shane: *Took u long enough.*

I rolled my eyes.

Christie: *I had nothing better 2 do.*

"Is that Rob? You're blushing! Did he send you a dirty text?"

"Uh, no. Rob and I aren't talking right now. It's that guy who chucked the football at me."

Annabelle opened her mouth, as she was about to say something, but then closed it. Instead, she raised her eyebrows at me and pursed her lips.

Luckily, she didn't have a chance to say anything else as the biggest distraction in her life appeared.

"Those flyers must have done it, we just sold sixty more tickets," Jason said.

"Well, Annabelle and I flashed the soccer team and they bought a bunch of tickets," I teased.

"Thanks for taking one for the team, ladies. Maybe next time, get the freshmen to do it. You're sophomores now, you shouldn't have to do the grunt work," he said, and leaned down, kissing her on the cheek.

They talked a bit more and I returned to my phone.

Shane: If ur bored, I've a few ideas.

Trying to keep the excited smirk off my face, I pressed my lips together and looked up at Annabelle. She was too busy staring into Jason's eyes to notice that I was playing with fire.

Christie: Care to share with the class?

Shane: Where r u? I'll pick u up and u can see for yourself.

Christie: Nothing dirty.

Shane: Only if u ask nicely.

Christie: I'm at school. Pick me up in an hour.

Shane: Whatever u say.

21

I put the phone away and sent Violet a message, telling her we were going out tonight.

"Ready to meet the illusionist?" Annabelle asked, completely oblivious to what just happened.

Part of me wanted to tell her Shane was coming to pick me up. I'd never hidden anything from her since we met last semester. Okay, I had played a few games to get her closer to Jason, but nothing else. And besides, that was for a good cause. This…this was definitely for a bad one. Also, I didn't want her to be disappointed I wasn't going to stay for the whole show. She didn't need my help when the show was going on.

"Yes, let's meet this guy." I plastered on a forced grin and headed out of the cafeteria with her.

I looked over at her. She was practically skipping, she was so enthusiastic, and it was contagious. The way her face beamed as she started telling us about one of his latest tricks she'd seen on YouTube won me over. Before I second guessed it, I linked arms with her and we bounded up to the green room together, with Jason rushing to keep up with us.

"Promise me you'll try to be open?" She looked deep into my eyes, and I saw the pleading. Well, that and I saw her pouted bottom lip.

"All right, I surrender. For you, I will keep an open mind."

"Oh, I forgot to mention something else about him," she told me with a wicked grin on her face. Annabelle leaned in and spoke softly so Jason couldn't hear her. "He's frickin' hot. Like movie star level hot."

"Is that the real reason he's here? You wanted to see him in person? You knew if I saw him, I'd have to give him a chance?" I looked over at my meek, innocent friend and she winked at me. I couldn't help but be proud. Clearly, Violet and I had a good effect on her.

"It certainly wouldn't hurt."

We walked in the room, and the illusionist was standing with Nat and Clarissa, the president and vice president of the entertainment club. His back was to us so I couldn't get a full look at him, but what I saw would make any girl swoon.

"Maybe that's his secret," I whispered to Annabelle. "He can't actually hypnotize anyone but he's so damn good looking that girls just fall into like a coma thing and guys get so jealous they can't function."

"That would make complete sense to me," she said and we both giggled like school girls with a crush while Jason rolled his eyes at us.

All the EET members started lining up and the phones came out so they could get a picture with him. Initially, I was just going to get a picture to make Annabelle happy, now I wanted one where I was practically groping him.

We got to move toward the front of the line since Annabelle and Jason were on the executive board. She walked up to the illusionist, whose real name was Karl, and he wrapped his arms around her. Annabelle turned bright pink and smiled so big it looked like it hurt. He then signed her ticket and gave her a nod as he handed it back to her.

I elbowed Jason gently. "Got some competition,

bro. I think Annabelle would leave you for him."

"Nah, I know the way to Annabelle's heart." He leaned in to whisper in my ear. "Cookies, as long as I keep buying her cookies, she'll keep coming back."

I looked back at him for a second, scrunching my face up. "Is that meant to be a code for something kinky?"

"Nope, she frickin' loves cookies. Before we got together, I knew she liked them, but now I know about all the places she hides them so people don't know about her obsession. You didn't hear this from me, but she almost always has at least two cookies in her tote bag, and there's a package in her glove box at all times."

Seeing as how Annabelle never went anywhere without her bag, I guess she never went anywhere without a cookie. Girl after my own heart, but chocolate was my kryptonite, and I carried it around in my purse on the regular.

"So when you want a blow job, you just bring her a cookie and she gets so excited that she does it right then and there?" I liked teasing Jason about sex. His ears always turned bright red but he was such a good sport about it.

"No, for a blow job I need to bring a package of cookies. You should see what I have to do if I want sex."

I stared at him open mouthed as he gave it back to me. I nudged his shoulder a bit and then walked up to the illusionist to take my picture.

Karl took my hand and gave me a little spin. He dipped me and then smiled for the picture. I, on the other hand, panicked a little. I couldn't dance as I have absolutely no rhythm, As if I needed to prove that to myself, I tripped when Karl tried to pull me back up from the dipped position. He caught me, but I was pressed up against his chest and his hands were a lot closer to my butt than my shorts were.

Turning bright red, I quickly stepped away from him and ran over to Annabelle and Jason before anything else happened.

"That's crap. You have such a cute picture," she complained. Jason had taken it on his phone for me and she was looking at it.

"Well, I just made a fool out of myself and he copped a feel trying to make sure I didn't fall over."

"Like a creepy copped a feel, or it was really an accident *how did your butt end up in my hands* kind of feel?" Annabelle asked, her serious face returning. "Is this another Finn kinda thing?"

Finn was a campus security guard who had stalked and attacked Violet. He'd done a number on all of us, kinda leaving us feeling a little vulnerable, but Annabelle seemed to take it the hardest. She'd never gotten over the fact that if she'd forced Violet to report his actions earlier, she never would have been attacked in the first place. Now, she was an advocate for the police station in her spare time.

"No, it was an accident. As soon as I was stable, he moved his hand away like it was on fire. No worries," I assured her. I didn't want her worrying and I didn't want to ruin the rest of the show for her. I wanted her to enjoy it. But I definitely was going to use this as my excuse to leave and meet up with Shane. "I'm gonna go. I wasn't big into this whole thing in the first place, and I'm just really embarrassed."

"Oh, no one cares," Annabelle insisted, but she did relent. "Fine, thanks for helping me pass out those flyers. I'll see you Monday?"

I nodded, and then gave her and Jason a quick hug on my way out. As I started walking toward one of the main hallways, I made a mental note to add learn to dance to my list. I didn't need to become a back-up dancer for Beyoncé or anything, but it might make life a little easier if I had some kind of rhythm. Actually, I'm changing it. I want to sneak into a club and dance all night. I needed to think bigger and really live it up, just like Violet said. Hell, just like what Violet was doing.

I still had about fifteen minutes before Shane was supposed to show up, but I didn't feel like waiting. He liked to play with me so much, it was his turn.

Christie: I'm free earlier. Get here in 10 or it's a no go. Parking lot 2.

Phone in hand, I walked a little faster to the parking lot and made it in six minutes. I leaned against my car, trying to be casual, but really, I was antsy. What would it be like for us to hang out? When I rode on the back of his bike, it was different than all our other interactions. He was quiet for one, and there were no games. It was just him, the bike, and me. I wasn't worried if I looked pretty enough, or if I said the right thing. With the wind ruining my perfect curls, I finally had the chance to just be. I wanted to feel that freedom again.

I heard the rumble of an engine and turned to look for his bike. An icy blue sedan with a giant spoiler on the back and a giant vent on the front pulled up next to my car. I stood up, ready to tell some creep to back off when the window rolled down.

"I made it with two minutes to spare," Shane said, proud of himself.

"Where's the bike?" I was really confused. How was I going to learn to drive a motorcycle when he brought a car? I was a good driver, we didn't need to work on that.

"If you really thought I'd teach you to drive my baby in the dark, then you've got another think coming," he informed me with a lot of sass.

"So then what are we doing?"

"Get in and find out." Shane leaned over and opened the passenger side door for me.

I jumped in before I chickened out entirely. Besides, I had my pepper spray in my purse.

Chapter 3

Shane pulled out of the parking lot driving way too fast with only one hand draped loosely over the wheel. True, I tended to drive fast, but he brought a whole new meaning to the word. When he took turns, I felt like at any second we'd be on two wheels. I should have felt scared, but instead, I felt alive.

At no point did I think he was out of control. He actually had a really good handle on what the car could do and how to control her. It kind of turned me on. Strike that, it completely turned me on. If he could make a car do this, what could he make me do? I glanced at his big firm hand gripping the steering wheel as he navigated a deep curve and felt a hot flash coming on. I tried to keep it together, but it just made me shiver a bit. Shane noticed and turned the heat on. I should have told him that wasn't the case, but I didn't want to talk just yet. Instead, I slipped out of my sweater and placed it on my lap.

"So that's all I have to do to get you to

strip...turn the heat up?" Shane reached for the temperature control and I swatted his hand.

"Shut up, it's the beginning of September. It's supposed to be hot."

"Then why did you bring a sweater?" he asked, turning the heat off.

"Because girls always get cold in weird places. We almost always have a sweater with us or wish we did." I reached over to his radio to switch it on and then he swatted my hand away.

"No, no. My car, my radio."

"Aren't we supposed to be having fun?" I asked in a bit of a huff.

"Yeah." Shane stepped on the gas and the car flew forward. I panicked for a second, looking around for a cop or a car we might hit, but it was an empty road. "Can you keep a secret?"

"Depends on the secret," I responded, trying to remain cool, but I really wanted to know what he had to say.

"Next Saturday is the start of the street racing season. This is the car I plan to take there. I was giving her a test drive when you texted me."

"So that's what we're doing? Going on a test drive?"

"Isn't it?" He looked over at me for a second and held my eyes. Shane didn't look at the road but stayed focused on me. I was almost too scared to move, but I stared straight back. I knew what he was saying. It wasn't just a test for the car. We were testing each other out. Trying to see if there was any spark. As his speed increased, so did my adrenaline, and so did my libido. I wanted him, and from the look of lust in his eyes, he wanted me just as bad.

It must have only been seconds, but it felt like minutes. Shane returned his gaze to the road in time to make it around another nasty curve. If I had to guess, I would say he knew that was there, and looked back at the road just in time.

"Do you need a good luck charm? When you're racing, I mean." It was ballsy to ask. He probably had a million girls all over him when he raced. I didn't know much about cars, but I knew this one was sexy and I probably wasn't the only one to figure it out.

"I'm defending champ from last year. I don't need luck," Shane said, jutting his chest forward.

"Well, then forget I said anything."

"Hey, calm down. I could use a cheering section."

"A whole section? Isn't that a little cocky?"

"Nothing little about it."

I rolled my eyes and snorted. Then I leaned over the gear shift and whispered in his ear. "Do you know what they say about guys who are over confident?" I asked while sliding a hand up his firm chest. "They tend to have..." I paused a moment and gave his ear a little nibble. "...really small feet."

I leaned back in my seat and Shane pulled the car over to the side of the road. He reached over, wrapped his hands around the back of my head, and pulled me into a deep, unapologizing kiss. He gave me everything he could and I tried desperately to keep up. Then, he broke away, started the car up again, and smiled at me.

"See, no one likes a tease." He sped up, the car revving so loudly that he wouldn't be able to hear my response had I been clear headed enough to come up with one.

For the next twenty minutes, we drove in silence. It was like the bike, but his hand had managed to rest on my bare thigh, every now and then sliding just under the hem of my shorts. To my surprise, I didn't brush it off. I leaned the seat back a little and stared off, taking in the rush that came from driving too fast, and the thrill I felt with his hand on my leg.

By the time Shane pulled back into the school's parking lot, I felt like I was intoxicated. The adrenaline had left me feeling light headed and a little dazed. But then Shane stopped in front of my car and it was like icy water was thrown on me. The spell was broken. We climbed out and he walked me to my driver's side door.

"So how did the test drive go?" I asked as I swayed a little. I had this terrible habit when I was nervous. There was just no way to keep me still.

"She's good. I felt a few kinks in there, but I can definitely see the potential."

"Glad to hear it."

"Did you really want to come with me next weekend? To the race with me?"

"Hell yeah, it sounds like a shit ton of fun." He wanted to see me again. It wasn't like I doubted it, but the validation was nice. I bit down on my lip to keep my smile from spreading clear across my face. I didn't want him to know how much I was looking forward to seeing him again. But the truth was, I knew I'd be counting the days.

31

"Great, but just know, once you enter that world, you're stuck. You'll never want to leave," he warned, taking a step closer to me.

"I'll take my chances," I purred, and took a step closer to him, placing my palm on his chest. I could feel his rapid heartbeat and that made me feel better about my own. I wanted him to want me. The look in his eyes, the look that screamed danger, didn't disappoint.

"I guess I'll see you around school until then," he whispered, placing his hands on my hips.

"Looks like it." I dropped my hand from his chest, a little disappointed about the brush off. I started to turn around but Shane spun my hips so I was facing him again.

"Not so fast," he warned, and reached out to brush some hair out of my eyes.

"Why?" I asked, pressing my chest into him.

"I just wanted to grab a piece of ass," he growled and grabbed my butt with both hands, picking me up and placing me on the hood of my car. Then he pulled me in for a kiss, laying me down against the hard metal. I wrapped my arms around his neck, dragging him closer to me so there was no space between us, just clothes and desire.

Pulling away slowly, Shane looked at me and smiled big. "Now you can leave."

I rolled my eyes at him and pushed him away so I could slide off the car.

"I noticed we didn't do that on the hood of your car," I said to his back.

He turned his head to look at me and gave a smile.

"If you wanted another kiss, all you had to do was ask."

I rolled my eyes and climbed into my car. One more kiss wouldn't be enough. Instead, I drove home that night, thinking of Shane and his street racing. Just sitting in the car with him speeding down the road, I got a secondhand high. I wondered how it would feel to actually drive like that. Stepping on the gas, I sped up and ran through the red light as it changed from yellow. My pulse raced and I could hear my heart beating in my ears again, but I couldn't calm it down. Alarms were going off inside of me and I forced myself to ignore the voice telling me to slow down.

My street came up and I took the turn fast, my tires screeching on the street. I pulled to a stop in front of my house and headed inside while experiencing one of the best natural highs I've ever felt, though, if I was being honest, it may have had more to do with Shane than speed.

***

I woke up the next morning to the sound of my mother singing in the kitchen. She was in an extremely good mood.

"Hey Mom," I greeted her, and then sat down at the dining room table. I helped myself to the eggs and bacon she put out.

"Hello darlin'," she replied in sing song. "I am so excited. I was talking to Heather, and she told me that Rob called her to get the ring out of the safe deposit box to have it cleaned."

She looked at me expectantly, almost bursting out of her skin.

I forced a smile and nodded. "You're talking to Mrs. Arnold?" I hadn't told her about the break, and I guess Rob hadn't told his mom, either. I grabbed the cup of juice she handed me and took a big sip to try and force down the lump forming in my throat.

"Of course, why wouldn't I?" She gave me a curious look, but then sat down next to me. "No reason. Rob is just really busy with school so we haven't talked much."

Mom's smile faded and she covered her mouth. "Oh no, did I just give away a surprise? Have you two not been talking about getting married? I just assumed you knew that he was going to be asking about the ring. I wanted to give you some finality with it. Oh darlin', please forgive me if I've ruined this surprise for you." She reached out and stroked my hand, covering her face with the other one.

"No, you're right. I know Rob is getting ready to propose. I just won't see him until November, so you know, I'm just trying to enjoy college before…" I still couldn't say it.

"Right," she said, cutting me off. "That's exactly what you should be doing. Spend time with your friends, and in the meantime…" she cooed, getting up and grabbing something off the counter. A magazine came sliding toward me.

It was a bridal magazine.

"In the meantime, we can start to plan your wedding." She clapped her hands together and screamed a little in glee.

"Wait, let's not get ahead of ourselves. I'm not

engaged yet." My mouth grew dry and my breathing came quick. I took another big sip of juice, but it wasn't helping.

"At this point, darlin', you might as well be. We know he's going to propose, I know you're going to say yes. And I know you want that big June wedding at The Plaza. Well, to make something like that happen, we're gonna need to start planning early. Tomorrow, I should call someone at The Plaza and talk about possible June dates. It's not like they're going to stick around, and I want to have the best one for you." She laughed her high pitched giggle and opened the magazine in front of me.

Before I knew what was happening, she was pointing to dress styles that would look good on me, and centerpieces that she liked. It was all becoming too much, and it felt like the room was closing in on me.

"Uh, Mom, why don't I go talk to Annabelle about bridesmaid dresses?" I suggested, hoping that she would let me leave.

"Well, what about Mindy? Isn't she going to be the maid of honor?" Mindy was my childhood best friend. I've known her since I was about five, and I've liked her since I was about seven. We call those two years before that the lost years. She thought I stole her "boyfriend" in kindergarten, so she hated me. But then I pushed another girl who was being mean to her and we'd been friends since.

"Yeah, of course. But you know, I've kinda been thinking of making Annabelle, like second maid of honor. Mindy is, like, three hours away at school, and Annabelle is up the street." Really, I needed a back-up. Mom and Mindy together were too sugary and romantic. I needed someone to keep everyone level headed before I ended up in a gown covered in bows, lace, and tulle. Annabelle voiced her opinion, but never disrespected or ignored mine. She was perfect.

"That's such a good idea." She handed me the magazine and then stroked my cheek gently. "Here, take the magazine with you so you can show her my suggestions. Toward the last few pages are a collection of dresses I like for the bridesmaids."

I nodded my head and rushed to get dressed before she took me to a seamstress to get fitted for my one of a kind dress that she's been dreaming of.

Chapter 4

"So what's this ring look like? Didn't you say you wouldn't say yes unless the ring was your shoe size?" Annabelle recalled.

"Okay, so this is a super vintage ring from his great grandmother. The center stone is three carats, perfectly clear, without a single flaw. It's surrounded by a collection of sapphires that Rob has always said reminds him of my eyes. The band intertwines itself, so it is very baroque feeling. It's basically the most beautiful ring I've ever seen in my life," I said a little glumly.

"It sounds a bit like Kate Middleton's ring."

"Yup, it's a ring meant for a princess. Apparently, his family was super rich in Ireland and they bought the ring off a British royal who owed a lot of money in gambling debts."

"I can't tell if you're kidding."

"Oh, I'm one hundred percent serious." My face fell and I examined my perfect nails for imaginary flaws. "The ring is perfect."

"You know, there is something to be said for

imperfection. It keeps you honest," Annabelle said softly as we sat down on her bed.

I looked up at her and saw that knowing look again. I didn't want her to probe, and as much as I wanted to agree with her and say I wanted a different ring, maybe one with a less checkered past. Or if I was being honest, I'd say I wanted a two carat halo princess cut diamond with a plain band so I could get an elaborate wedding ring set to go around it. This way, I didn't have to be fancy every day. I could leave the wedding ring at home and just wear the engagement ring. Somedays, you didn't want the princess ring. It was great for going out, but what about when you were lying on the couch? I couldn't picture it. Instead of saying all that, I just said, "It's fine. I should consider myself lucky, right? Rob is a great man, with a promising career. And he will be able to support my kind of lifestyle."

"We do need to keep you in designers. I'd hate to see you break out if you had to put on a dress that came from the bargain bin," she teased, nudging me gently.

"Right, I wouldn't even know where to find the bargain bin." I laughed, glad she was here for me to talk to.

"You can always say no. Would it really be so awful if you broke it off with Rob for good?"

"I could say no. It's not like an arranged marriage or anything. When we're together, I'm happy. He treats me well, he doesn't take my jokes too seriously, and he's sexy as hell. Besides, I love his parents. How often do you get in-laws who aren't crazy?" I smiled, remembering that time my mom and my dad's mom got in a screaming battle at Christmas. Mom chucked a glass ornament at Grammy for insulting her cooking.

"I don't know. I haven't met Jason's parents yet, and it's not like I told mine about him."

"Why not?"

"My mom is a worrier. She worries about everything. Next thing I know, she'll be taking Jason to the clinic to get tested. It won't matter that he's never had sex before."

"Well, that's fun. It could be like the ultimate test of his love for you."

"Um, maybe not. My mom's a nurse, so the chances she'll suggest doing the test herself are way too high."

We laughed but it didn't seem pure. Annabelle was the first person who'd ever told me I could say no to Rob. Everyone else just assumed I'd say yes. It's funny that the people who have known me all my life don't seem to know me as well as the girl I met nine months ago.

"So, anyway, um, on to some more fun things. Will you be one of my bridesmaids?" I asked, hoping she'd agree. I needed someone on my side, since I decided I was going to have to deal with this.

She jumped off the bed and hugged me tight. "Absolutely, this is going to be so much fun." Then Annabelle's face turned solemn and she looked me straight in the eyes. "Promise me this is what you want. I can't do this if your heart isn't in it."

I grabbed my purse and pulled out my list. "My heart is in this. I made this list of all the things I want to do before I settle down. When I'm done with this, I will be ready for the big white wedding my mother has already planned in her head."

"Seriously, the sex one?"

I shrugged my shoulders, trying to play innocent. "We're on a break," I insisted, feeling a bit like Ross from *Friends*.

"The movie one sounds fun, we should do this next weekend. We can wear yoga pants, baggy shirts, put our hair up in messy buns, and eat food that's going to be so greasy, we're going to break out."

"Yes. All the yes!"

"Great, now, if I'm going to be a bridesmaid, we're going to need more magazines and definitely some junk food. This one magazine doesn't give us enough choices to even attempt to make a list." She grabbed her keys and we headed to the store.

We spent the next several days poring over bride magazines. Well, Annabelle pored over them, I nodded politely when appropriate. I just hadn't found my ideal wedding theme, colors, or dress style. There were so many choices, and it just seemed like every time I found something that looked great, I'd flip the page and be enamored by something else. What happened to a good old fashioned church wedding with a nice reception afterwards? I mean, obviously everything would be covered in crystals, but I don't think I wanted a giant scene. More like a group of fifty or sixty people I loved and some really good food.

On the bright side, my classes were doing a good job at distracting me. Accounting was not as simple as it sounded, and I was not impressed with the professor. But my marketing class was going quite well. It made me think that I'd actually like to find something like this to do. Maybe one of the charities at whatever country club we joined would need some promoting. I liked the idea more and more. But Saturday finally rolled around, and there was a skip in my step for a whole other reason. Tonight, I'd be going to see Shane street race, and I didn't know what to expect. All I knew was that it would be a whole new world for me, and I was desperate for the adrenaline rush.

I told my parents that I wasn't feeling good after dinner and went to my room. Mom checked on me once and then I was good to go. She and Dad would start their nightly routine and that didn't involve me.

I plugged my curlers in and quickly put my make-up on. But clothes-wise, I had no idea what to wear. I spent the day watching racing movies and a couple episodes of a street racing show to get an idea of what to expect. In it, the girls were all wearing outfits that didn't appear to fit anywhere. The shirts were too tight, the skirts too short, and the heels too high. I walked into my closet and realized I was far too preppy for that world, so I'd have to make something work.

I had a mini skirt that I'd worn with a Halloween costume once. It was faux leather, also known as plastic, and too short. Slipping it on over my narrow hips, it looked perfect. I added some black panties in case the skirt was a little too short, so at least I'd match. Then I grabbed one of my red lace bralettes, and a white tank top. I topped the look off with a pair of black heeled boots. Looking in the mirror, I couldn't help but think of Vivian from *Pretty Woman*. I think it was the boots.

I closed my closet door so I wouldn't second guess myself by staring in the mirror. Shane was due to pick me up any minute now. He'd texted me earlier, saying he'd get me at nine-thirty, but I had to figure out how to get out of the house. I walked over to my bed and tripped, falling onto the chair next to it. The sweatpants I had on earlier had fallen on the floor and blocked my path. But looking at them now, I had a whole new idea. I slipped the pants on over my skirt, slipped some sneakers on, and then pulled a sweatshirt over my head, making sure the hood was up so my mom wouldn't notice my hair. Then I grabbed one of my big bags and tossed my boots in it.

"Mom," I called down the hall from the laundry room. "Annabelle and Jason got in a big fight. I'm gonna go check on her. I know I don't feel well, but she's been so good to me with this wedding planning that I think it's only fair I check on her. She's picking me up in a few minutes." I held my breath, hoping she bought my story.

"Aw, you're such a good friend. Send her my love. Oh, and there are some extra cookies in the tin. Why don't you bring those?"

"I will," I called, forcing the guilt from my mind. I grabbed my purse from off the side table and took my wallet, keys, and lipstick out and placed them in my bag with my boots before walking outside.

As if on cue, Shane pulled up with his deafening

motor, sexy race car, and mischievous grin. "You look comfy," he teased as he rolled the window down, giving me a once over.

"Shut up, I just needed a way to get out of the house. Drive down the street a minute and then stop so I can change." I climbed into the passenger seat and he revved the engine. I felt a small rush of adrenaline fly through me. Hopefully it was just the beginning.

Shane was silent as he made a quick U-turn and made his way down a couple side streets.

"Okay, this is good," I told him and climbed out of the car and slid my sweatpants off slowly, giving Shane a bit of a show.

"Wait, what are you wearing?" he asked, rolling the window down.

"What's wrong with it?" I slipped my sweatshirt over my head and shook my hair out.

"Not a damn thing. Your ass looks great in that skirt."

"So what's the issue?" I asked, getting back into the car and putting my boots on.

"You just can't show up there like that. No one dresses like that in real life. You've been watching too many movies."

"Well, it's not like I can sneak back into my house, so I'm wearing this."

"I have a better idea." Shane leaned over and pulled my sweatpants out of the bag. "Come on, let's get out of the car." He opened his door and I quickly followed. "Take the skirt off."

I raised my eyebrows at him and shook my head. "You just want to see me in my underwear."

"Yes...yes, I do. But if you show up there dressed like this, no one will take either of us seriously, and this is important to me." He held the sweatpants out and I reluctantly took them.

"Fine, but turn around." I stood still, waiting for him to cover his eyes or spin around.

"Not a chance in hell." Shane crossed his arms and stared at me, as if challenging me.

"I could just put the sweatpants on over the skirt," I reminded him.

"You could, but if you were going to do that, you would've done it already."

Rolling my eyes, I unzipped the skirt and slid it off, twirling in a circle so he could admire the ass I worked so hard for three times a week doing aerobics.

"You do realize that I'm going crazy here, right? Maybe you can wear that skirt again for me later?"

I pulled the sweatpants up and over my underwear, and picked the skirt up off the ground. I walked up to Shane and whispered in his ear. "Only if you win, and even then, I'm not promising anything."

"Oh, I'll win, don't you worry about that. Worry about what I'm going to do to you the next time you show up in an outfit like that. Let's just say restraint isn't one of my better qualities." He clicked his tongue and looked me over again. "You still manage to look sexy," he said, and rolled the top of my sweatpants so they weren't dragging on the ground. His fingers grazed my bare skin and little shots of electricity shot through me.

"Are we going to stand here teasing each other,

or are you going to race?" I asked when he didn't move straight away.

"You don't have to ask me twice." He slapped my ass and opened my car door for me. "After you."

Shane walked around to the other side of the car and started the engine.

Chapter 5

"So, the races are pretty simple. All the drivers show up and call someone out. There is a race commissioner who is basically in charge of all the races. He won't let the same one guy call out the same driver week after week. We like to keep it a little fair."

"Okay, so how do they keep score of who is the best?"

"The commissioner has a sort of assistant for that, but really it's not hard to do. We just keep track of who has the best racing record." He reached his hand out and stroked my thigh gently. "Right now, that person is me. I hold the title as top racer in this area. Last year I only lost one race, and that was due to a mechanical error. Just shitty luck."

I looked over at him and couldn't help but notice the beam in his eyes as he said this. "You said you didn't need a good luck charm? If you'd had one, maybe you wouldn't have screwed up."

"No, I said I didn't need you to be my good luck charm. I'm Korean. We're crazy superstitious." He reached into his black shirt and pulled out a gold necklace with a rectangular gold talisman hanging from it. There was all kinds of red swirls and lines everywhere. "This is my good luck charm."

"What's it say on it?"

"It's just a protection prayer. My grandma sent it from South Korea when I was born. I never used to wear it, mostly because I've never even met my grandma, but so much crap happens at races, I just started wearing it, and the one time I lost is the one time I didn't wear it."

"That's a crazy coincidence." I decided not to ask him about his grandma. I wanted to, and it almost came out, but I didn't want to turn the mood sour. But I did notice a bit of sadness in his eyes when he mentioned her.

"I told you, I'm superstitious. I don't believe in coincidences."

"Okay, what else are you superstitious about? Do you hold your breath when you go past a graveyard, or do you have the number seven tattooed on your ass?" I wasn't the least bit superstitious, and this really threw me off guard. But then again, I'd been around Violet long enough to know that she had her own ridiculous superstitions, like holding her breath when she drives over a bridge. Come to think of it, a lot of these superstitions seemed to involve holding your breath.

"Seven isn't a big deal for us. The number four, we don't touch. That's worse than the number thirteen. If they sign me up to race fourth, I'd flat out refuse. It's just a bad sign."

"Well, what happens if you refuse? Isn't that like

losing a race?" I asked, noticing that there were goosebumps up his arm even as he discussed talking about the possibility of racing fourth.

"Nah, you can chose to wait until next week when a new line up is created. But then if you refuse, it counts as a loss. I never worry too much about that, though. I have an in with the commissioner, so he never sets me up fourth." He turned to me and flashed that wicked grin.

"What, do you bribe him? Maybe flash a little leg in his direction?" I didn't like the idea of cheating. It kind of took all the excitement out of the race. Why watch him if I knew he was going to win?

"No, nothing like that. I've just known him a while. He likes a good race, and he knows if he puts me fourth, he won't get it. So he just puts me in another slot because I'm pretty much a guaranteed good race."

"Oh, okay. Well, I guess we'll see," I responded as we pulled up to a row of cars in an open field. "Are we here?"

"Yeah, that's where the spectators park," Shane told me, pointing to the field. "A true racer would never leave his car in a field like that, so we park over here." He pulled in next to a couple cars that were parked on the shoulder of the road. Their front ends stuck out a little, since they were parked perpendicular to the street, but this was a wide road, and Shane insisted that they only ever used the middle two lanes to race.

"I can't believe they just shut down a whole strip of road for you," I marveled, looking at the half mile track where no other cars were driving.

"Oh, they don't. But we have guys on either side, about a half mile out that put up fake construction signs to reroute people and warn us if the police are coming. This is highly illegal."

"If I get thrown in jail and end up someone's bitch, I will come after you," I warned him, grabbing the front of his shirt and pulling him close.

"You're sexy when you're serious. But don't worry, I won't let anyone else touch that sweet ass." He leaned in and gave me a peck on the cheek, and then climbed out of the car.

I rolled my eyes and went to open my door, however, Shane was already there, extending a hand to help me out. "Stop pretending you're a gentleman," I teased as I took his hand and got out of the car.

"Fine." Shane pushed me against the car and kissed me fiercely. His hand slid down my back and played with the sliver of exposed skin between my shirt and my rolled up sweat pants. With the other hand, he tangled it into my hair, pulling just enough to keep my attention on only him.

"Shane, are you gonna do her now, or wait until after you lose and you need a pick me up?" someone shouted, bringing us back to reality.

"At least I didn't have to pay her to come. Heather, how much did Chuck give you this time?" he shouted at a couple about three cars down. Apparently, Chuck wasn't amused and flipped Shane the bird. Heather pursed her lips, but a smile managed to escape as Chuck pulled her away from the cars.

"I take it he called you out," I said, as I watched them walk away.

"He hasn't yet, but there's a pretty good chance he will. Chuck had the second best record last year. Rumor has it that he's been busting his ass to pay for all new parts. I heard that he didn't propose to Heather this year because he didn't want to spend the extra money on a ring," Shane told me and slid an arm around my neck.

"How long have they been together?"

"Um, I don't really know. I've been racing here for three years, and they've been here since then. So at least three years."

"I'd cut him. Spending my engagement ring money on car parts. What a jerk move."

"Don't worry, babe, I win enough money to do both." He slapped my ass as we walked up to a group of people.

Chuck and Heather were there, along with three other guys, and one badass looking chick. She had long, fuchsia hair tied into a tight braid that almost touched her elbows. Her black tank top sat firmly above the serpent belly button ring that shown in the moonlight. She had on tight black leather pants and a pair of sky high black boots that went up over her knees. I didn't know who she was, but part of me wanted to go shopping with her.

Shane introduced me to everyone, and the girl, Emma, smiled through her purple lipstick at me and pulled me into a hug.

"I'm a hugger," she explained in my ear as she gave me a tight squeeze.

"I'm not, but I'll make an exception for you

because of those boots. I want them in like four colors, some with fringe, and maybe a suede pair."

She laughed and looked me over, and I was a little embarrassed. I really didn't think it was possible to feel under dressed at a street race, but then again, I would've felt a little ridiculous in my tiny skirt. "Thanks. I change to sneakers to race, but I just get a boost of confidence when I wear these babies."

"Oh, you race?" I was a little surprised. I thought she was someone's girlfriend. Maybe I should get my mind out of the 18th century.

"Yeah," she said, and pointed to a bright red car. "That's my Camaro over there. I was ranked third last year, so I'm hoping Betsy and I can make a dent and hit number one."

"Betsy? Why did you name her that?"

"That's what my grandmother said when she saw the car. 'Oh, heavens to Betsy.' She's against me racing, but supports me anyway, so it's like a little tribute to her."

I was about to respond, but some guy was calling everyone over. He was about two hundred pounds and it all looked to be muscle. This was definitely not the kind of guy I wanted to mess with, but then a tiny guy came walking up behind him. The big guy stepped to the side and the other guy stood front and center. He must have been one hundred and ten pounds soaking wet and maybe an inch or two taller than my five four. Him, I could take.

"So, that's enough chit chat and catching up. I'll be by my van for the next twenty minutes taking call outs. You can call out whoever you want, but that doesn't mean I'll set up a race for you. I want to see good, competitive races, so try not to take on someone who will cross the finish line as you leave the starting line." He waited a beat for some kind of argument, but none came. Instead, he and the muscle man walked over to a van that looked straight out of *Scooby Doo*, and opened the door.

Shane took my hand and we made our way over to his "office." Inside the back of the van, the commissioner had statistics on what looked like at least ten different racers and their cars. There were car manuals, a couple of those red gas containers, and a crap ton of tools. Plus, he had set up the car bench so that it faced out toward the street and looked like a little cubicle. It was a moving racing office and I loved it.

The muscle man stood next to the car, arms crossed, and collected money.

"Do you pay to race?" I asked Shane.

"Sort of. You have to bet something to race. We don't do it for free. So, I'm gonna call out Newbie Troy over there," he explained, pointing to a skinny looking kid, maybe our age or younger. "He started racing last year, but rumor around the garages says that his car is no joke, so I want to test it out. It's our first race, so I'm gonna put down five hundred dollars on it. If Newbie Troy accepts the call out, then he puts his own five hundred down. If not, Frank keeps the money and I can either use it as money to accept a call out, or I can ask for it back at the end of the night if I didn't race."

"Sounds complicated. The commissioner must keep some crazy books to deal with all that."

"Well, actually, Frank does it. He went to MIT and has a bachelor's degree in mathematics. During the day, he works for the State helping to develop aircraft and monitor what models work best and shit."

"That's kind of hot," I said, looking at Frank a little different now.

"Calm down, sparky. He and Emma have a thing right now and she'd slice you if she even heard you were looking at him."

"Oh, yeah, and what will you do if I were to go over and talk to him?"

"Well, I'm certainly not going to break up the fight if Emma attacks you. That'd be one hot chick fight."

"Shut up. Emma seems nice. I don't think she'd kill me."

"No, never kill, but I can't make any guarantees she'd leave your pretty face intact."

"Aw, you called me pretty," I teased, nudging him in the shoulder.

Shane rolled his eyes at me and walked up to the van to talk to the commissioner.

"Hey, what's up, Max?" Shane and Max did some weird handshake thing that looked cool but was probably really nerdy.

"Not much. You gonna make me some money this year? I could use a new engine in my Nova."

"I've got the Subaru with me, so no stress. I should have no problem lapping Newbie Troy."

"Okay, I feel you there. How much?"

"Five hundred," Shane responded and handed a wad of cash to Frank.

"You sure there isn't any extra cash rolling around on the floor of that car? Your girl might not be impressed by only five hundred dollars."

Shane shrugged his shoulders and looked at me. I smiled big, with a hint of mischief in my eyes, and turned to look at Max. "I'm not his girl yet. That's why he bet so little. If I was his girl, he'd know exactly how much would impress me."

"Well, if you're looking for the big man on campus, come find me after call outs. I know how to throw money around for a pretty lady." He reached out and took my hand, placing a little kiss on my knuckles.

"I just might do that."

Shane sighed heavily and raised his eyebrows at us. "So, five hundred for Newbie Troy?"

"Yeah, I got it. Get out of here so I can finish up." Max dismissed us and we walked away.

Shane dropped his arm from my shoulders and walked toward the car. "Okay, I have a couple things to check on before I race. Why don't you hang around or see Emma? I just need a couple minutes with my boys." He pulled the hood of his car up and leaned under it.

"Seriously, you're irritated about that little comment to Max?" I asked, ignoring his request and also leaning under the hood.

"No, I know you were kidding, but I need to get into race mode. Just give me a couple minutes and I'll be back to the playful idiot who brought you here to impress you. I take racing really seriously, because if something goes wrong, someone could die."

"All right," I said and backed away from the car. As I turned around to go find Emma, I heard Shane call my name.

"Just wait. When you see me race, you won't be thinking about anything other than me. I'd even bet on it." He had spun around too and was leaning against the side of the car.

"What are we betting?" I walked back over to him, and stood in between his legs.

"If after I race, your body doesn't burn for me, I'll let you drive the car home and I'll teach you to drive my motorcycle tomorrow. But if after I'm done racing, you do want to jump my bones, then give me one night to rock your world any way and every way I want to."

His hands were holding my hips, his thumbs slid just inside the waistband of my sweat pants. This was obviously a dangerous bet. Just feeling the slightest touch set me on fire. Sitting in his car as he sped down the road excited me. Add competition to that and there was no way I wouldn't be a goner. But then again, maybe that wouldn't be the worst thing.

"Deal. But just know," I started and leaned in to whisper in his ear. "Losing will definitely be a turn off, and I don't do sympathy bangs." I walked away fast before he could respond and made sure to wiggle as I did it, so I could captivate his attention and give him something to fight for.

Emma was actually done with her car when I walked over to say hi, so we talked for a little while. She explained a little to me about the difference between a car that ran on nitrous, and a car that ran on turbo. I didn't really understand, but I nodded like it all made sense.

"So, how long have you and Shane been going out?" she asked me out of the blue.

"We aren't together. I mean, we've been hanging out a little bit, but nothing serious."

"Sorry, I just assumed. He's never brought a girl here before, so I thought you guys were getting serious or something."

"It's a long story. I have a boyfriend and he wants us to get married, but I'm not sure if that's what I want just yet, so we took a break from the relationship, and then Shane happened."

"Well, just don't play games with Shane. He's good people." She fixed me with a serious look and, though her arms were by her side, she ground her hands into fists. Then, without another word, she went back to her car.

I took this as a dismissal and went back to Shane's car, a little more afraid of her than I'd been earlier. I couldn't help but wonder if there was something going on between the two of them before.

When I showed up at Shane's car, he and his boys, which were actually just two guys we went to college with, had just closed the hood and were closing up a laptop. I recognized one of the guys from my history class last semester, and the other one was playing football with Shane when he tossed the ball at me.

"Ready for the call outs?" Shane asked, his same goofy smirk back on his face.

"Yes," I replied, trying to push the guilt away.

What Emma had said shook me up. Shane and I weren't anything. There was no promise of more, or exclusivity, so technically I wasn't doing anything wrong. Besides, Shane had even only asked for one night. He knows this is a temporary thing. But then again, it's not like I was being completely fair to Rob. It was probably time to figure out what I wanted in life. However, tonight I just wanted to live in the moment. And in this moment, Shane had on a racing jacket and his jeans were clinging to him in a way that glorified his ass.

I walked over to him and he slung his arm over my shoulder as we headed to the group of drivers. With heat radiating from his touch, I didn't think I'd have the power to turn away from him even if I'd wanted to.

Max called out the races and decided that Shane would be going second. He'd honored Shane's call out and the race would be against Newbie Troy. Chuck was pissed, but there didn't seem to be anyone who wanted to listen to him complain except Heather.

The rest of the call outs were presented, but Shane heard what he'd wanted and started to briefly explain how the race worked. "It's a straight line race. We're just trying to see who can go the fastest from point A to point B. We pull up to the line they'll draw on the street and drive a quarter mile to where a flag will be set up in the middle of the yellow lines. If you cross, you lose. If you go too early, you lose."

"Oh, does some hot chick stand in the middle of the street and pull a scarf out of her bra to start the race? Or does someone shoot a gun?"

"No, I feel like the hot chick would be a major distraction, and the gun would draw too much attention to us. Frank shines a flashlight and that is how we know to go. Someone stands just behind the cars, and at the finish line, and takes video so we can tell that all the rules were followed."

"There are a lot of rules," I complained as we headed back to his car.

"Well, I have another one for you. There is no way you can ride with me while I race. I'm not gonna put you at risk. When I pull up to the starting line, you need to climb out of the car and go watch the race with everyone else." He sounded serious and any playfulness was long gone from his eyes.

"You're no fun."

Shane blinked, and just like that, the goofball was back. "Remember our bet? I'll be a lot of fun then," he promised, and opened the door to his car for me as I rolled my eyes.

The first race went down while Shane was pulling his car into position. He told me that they liked to get the races moving so they didn't have to spend a lot of time on the road. The engines were loud and could draw the wrong kind of attention.

One of Shane's boys motioned for him to pull his car forward and I climbed out, as promised. I stood off to the side and Emma walked over to me.

"Ready to see your first race?"

"Yes, I feel like it's gonna either be crazy intense or a huge let down."

"The only way it'd be a huge let down is if one of their engines stops. If the race goes down, usually it's a good time."

As she said that, the flashlight turned on and the cars were off. Shane's car barreled down the road, easily overtaking Newbie Troy. But that didn't seem to matter to me. He flew like he was on air, and a rush hit me with the power of a hurricane. The moment he took off, I knew I wanted Shane to win. I wanted that one night with him. The adrenaline of cheering him on when he crossed the finish line settled in my core and he was right. I wanted to jump his bones right there. He'd just won $500 bucks, but he'd won a lot more with me. Crap.

Shane pulled the car around and parked it back in the spot from earlier. He climbed out and picked me up, spinning me around. "Did you see me? The car was at her best. I've never gone that fast that quick. You have to be at every race, I'll buy you a frickin' motorcycle, if that's what it takes." He put me down and kissed me, both hands grasping the back of my head, teeth nipping at my lip lightly.

I slid my hands under his unzipped jacket and felt up his back. In the bottom of my heart I knew what I needed to do. I needed to be at all of his races too. But I needed our night together first.

Chapter 6

The rest of the night went pretty well. Shane won a stupid amount of money betting on the other racers and I really saw him loosen up. He was in his element, spouting facts about the cars like he was a horse race gambler, surrounded by people who seemed to hang on his every word. This was him having fun, and I desperately wanted to feel this connected to something or someone. As he drove me home that night, I hoped I would find my own world where I fit in like this. Maybe the charity world wasn't as good of a fit for me as I wanted it to be.

"So, about our night together..." he brought up as he pulled up in front of my house.

"What about it?"

"You say when, and I'll have the place all picked out. Maybe a cabin in the woods so no one will hear you scream," Shane pondered out loud.

"Why, are you going to try to murder me? Way to take all of the sexy out of it."

"You don't think I'll make you scream? I'm

deeply offended." He brought his hand to his heart and sighed loudly.

"Well, I guess we'll find out on Friday. But I really hope you're as good as you think you are. Otherwise, it's going to be a long night, and I can only fake it so long," I said, and opened the door to get out of the car.

Shane grabbed my arm and pulled me back in. "Don't worry, I'm better than that boyfriend of yours."

My mouth dropped open and I silently cursed my big mouth. Emma and Shane were friends. Of course she had told him.

"Look, he isn't…"

"You don't need to explain it to me. The way I look at it, it's his loss and my gain." He clicked his teeth and then let go of my arm.

I thought about trying to explain it to him, but I decided I was done trying to make people understand. All they did was judge me. I guess the truth was, I was judging myself even harsher than they all were. It was finally time to do what I knew I needed, but could never get the courage to do.

I headed into the house, tiptoed quietly as my parents were sleeping, and then went to my room. I closed the door and sat on my bed, willing myself to dial Rob's number. Holding my breath, I hit the send button, and then quickly the end.

Damn, now he is gonna see the missed call and know I tried to reach him. I stood up and started pacing the room. Going over tonight in my head, I'd never felt more alive, had more fun, or been so turned on as I had with Shane. If I felt that way about another guy, I couldn't leave Rob hoping that I'd come back to him. To be honest, I think I knew things were over with Rob when he didn't fight me when I suggested the break. There was no passion in our relationship anymore, and it was all just responsibilities, and plans. I didn't want to settle down, and even when I do, I wasn't sure the dutiful wife and mother was a role I wanted to play. It worked for some people and I was happy for them. But I wanted the chance to find out what ignited my soul. I needed to find my dream, and I needed a man who respected that to find that dream, I'd need time. For some reason, that was the one thing Rob wasn't willing to give me. He wanted to get married in June, and I couldn't change his mind.

I dialed Rob's number again and waited breathlessly for him to pick up the phone. Just before his voicemail chimed in, a tired voice came over the phone.

"Hello," he answered, half asleep.

"Rob, it's me. I can't do this anymore," I confessed.

"I know. This break is killing me too, but we'll be together again soon. It's just another two and a half months."

"No, I mean us. I don't want to get married in June, or try and make this work. I'm too young. Why do I need to give up school to be with you?"

"Honey, you aren't giving up school. You're going to finish your degree online. We've gone over this. Why are you reneging on this now? I thought we agreed."

"We did. But I'm not happy with it. I don't want

to leave my friends, and I like school. I'm actually doing really well, and—"

"Christie," he said, cutting me off. "I know you're doing well. I wouldn't be with a stupid woman. This is just cold feet. I have to be up early for training tomorrow, so I can't go over this again."

"You don't have to, I'm done," I said, with as much finality as I could.

"I'll talk to you at Thanksgiving," he promised, and hung up the phone.

This man was infuriating. I hopped in the shower and decided to sleep on this. I didn't want to fight with him anymore. He made it seem like my feelings didn't matter. No, if anything, this phone call confirmed that we really had drifted too far apart.

After a night of restless sleep, I went over to Annabelle's. Coffee in one hand, I knocked on her door. There was some shuffling and she called out to wait a minute. She opened the door in her robe and quickly stepped outside.

"Do you and Jason do anything else?" I asked, handing her a coffee.

"Yes, sometimes we sleep," she teased. "What's going on?"

"Remember how we said we'd do the movie next week? What are you up to today? I need some girl talk and a distraction."

"Sure, is everything okay?"

"No, I broke up with Rob…well, I tried to, but he didn't seem to hear me."

"Right, movies in my room or in the theater?"

"Theater, because I need some greasy popcorn, and I'm afraid to sit on your sheets."

"Shut up," she said, glaring at me, but still managing to blush bright pink. "Let me get dressed and I'll kick Jason out. Why don't you head over to the cafeteria and I'll meet you there? We can get some breakfast in us before the junk food."

"That's probably a good plan." I said goodbye and headed to the cafeteria. London is five hours ahead, so I knew that Violet was up. Instead of going to the cafeteria, I sat on the bench outside Annabelle's apartment and messaged Violet to see if she was there.

"Hey beautiful," she cooed when she called me almost instantly.

"Hey, you look cold," I responded, taking in her heavy coat and scarf.

"London thinks that September is almost winter. They are a little confused about summertime here."

"That sucks."

"I know, but now I just have a really cute scarf collection. But I'm pretty sure you didn't call to talk about my fashion sense. What's going on?"

I told her everything and she politely listened without interrupting, though I saw her fidget every now and then as she fought her will power.

"Well, he might have thought that when you said you were done, you meant like done doubting or something. I think you should maybe send him a text message, just be super clear that you want out of the relationship."

"Right, I didn't want to be the coward who did that over text message, though."

"I know, but you tried by phone, and that was a hot mess. So try text. Maybe it will be better because he can't interrupt you."

"That makes sense. I'll try that and let you know what happens." She nodded her head and smiled at me sweetly. I saw the pity written over her face and I couldn't help but dread it. I didn't want the pity. I wanted to be strong, but there were doubts circling my mind. "Do you think I made the right decision? What if I screw up my future with Rob? Is it so wrong that he wants to take care of me? Maybe I should just let him do it."

"No, I think you're right. If you feel that way with Shane, then you shouldn't be with Rob. It's not fair to anyone. This thing with Shane may be over after next weekend, but another man still made you feel alive. If Rob doesn't do that anymore, you're going to spend the rest of your marriage looking for it. Besides, if Rob loved you as much as he says he does, he'd want to make you happy. Clearly, this rushed proposal and wedding aren't your dream of wedded bliss, so why is he forcing it?"

"You get all these perks in the military if you're married. He's trying to make our lives a little easier."

"But he's trying to make them easier at the risk of taking away your happiness."

"It's complicated. I feel like he's trying to fill this out like a to do list. Graduate, get a good job, get married, have babies, buy a house, retire from the military, work at family business, retire. All that junk. There's no diverging from the plan. I want to stay in school. I want to struggle to get a job out of college, and I want to pay my dues while I get coffee for some big shot executive in a lucrative marketing firm."

As soon as it came out, I knew it was what I wanted. I liked marketing and numbers, and I didn't want to do it for a charity. I wanted to do it for a big company. I wanted the designer suits, and the flashy briefcase I carried on public transportation while I rushed to a big meeting I was running. I wanted a career.

"Then do it."

"I will." I paused, feeling a weight being lifted off my chest. Then I looked at my friend, missing her for the millionth time since she left. "Thanks." I didn't know what else to say, but I thought she'd pick up on it.

"Anytime."

We talked a little bit about her and Berneli. Violet was struggling a little with the idea of him teaching, because that was how they met. He insisted she was being ridiculous, and she insisted the fears weren't going away.

"Violet, Berneli cares about you. He's not just going to throw that away for some lay. You're too good in bed for that," I reminded her, pleased to see it made her smile.

"Valid point. I just…"

"Stop worrying about problems that aren't there. Berneli is in your bed every night, and he's given you no reason to doubt him, right?"

"Well, true but…"

"Then you need to find a way to trust him or come home. You didn't fly over there because you wanted sex on the regular. There are plenty of guys here who would be more than happy to take care of that for you. You went there because you love him. So love and trust him."

"Ugh, you're right. I'll try to calm down some and give him some slack."

"You better or I'm going to send him a message to change all his passwords on his phone and computer. You shouldn't be snooping."

"I never said I was snooping!" Violet insisted, but after a stern look from me, she was singing a different tune. "Okay, I only snoop sometimes, but…"

"Stop snooping!"

"You are no fun, my friend."

"Love you too." We hung up as Annabelle walked over to me.

"Violet still snooping?" she asked without missing a beat.

"Yeah," I said, laughing a little.

We were on our way to the cafeteria when my phone rang. Taking a deep breath, I answered and waited for the worst.

"Hi, Mom."

"Christie, where did you go? I had a surprise for you but you weren't in your bed." She sounded out of breath and a little confused.

"Mom, I left you a note on the fridge. I'm with Annabelle again."

"Good, I have a surprise for you. I'll pick you up at school and we can all go together. You're saving us a call, so we don't have to get in touch with Annabelle."

"Wait, who is this 'us' you speak of?" Did Rob fly home or something?

"I'm not telling. I'll be in lot three in about ten minutes, so be ready." Then she hung up the phone before I could get another word in. The people in my life really needed to learn to say goodbye or something before clicking off.

"I have no idea what's going on, but I think I need a sticky bun," I told Annabelle and we rushed to the cafeteria.

***

Mom pulled up with her Range Rover and I was about to open the door, when someone came bursting out of the car. She was five seven, about one hundred and twenty pounds, and most of that was in her chestnut hair.

"Mindy, what are you doing here?" She was my best friend, but she's been away at school in New York.

"Your mom insisted I come down today to be a part of the big surprise. So..." She pulled a sleep mask out of her pocket and placed it over my eyes.

"Wait," I said, as panic struck me. I wasn't the biggest fan of surprises. "How about we put the blindfold on when I'm in the car?"

"Good call," Mindy responded, winking her hazel eyes at me. "We wouldn't want you hurting yourself. It would completely ruin the afternoon."

I slid the mask back off my head and climbed into the passenger seat. Then, trying not to roll my eyes, I put the mask back on and I heard Mindy climb into the car.

"Come on, Annabelle. You're invited too, Sugar," my mom called to her.

I asked a million questions, but they wouldn't tell me where we were going, who we would see, or why we were going there. I had nightmares about a situation like this, but in my dreams, strangers did this. Nonetheless, I was still scared shitless.

Finally, Mom stopped the car and I heard car doors open. Mindy guided me out of the car, insisting I couldn't take the mask off yet.

"Guys, I'm not sure this is the best idea right now," I heard Annabelle comment quickly, but they brushed her off and ushered me into the building.

Past my mother's perfume, I couldn't smell anything, but I heard cheesy music playing in the background. The floor was soft, probably carpeted, since I didn't hear any high heel noises. When I tried to reach my hands out to touch something, Mindy swatted it away.

My mom left my side and I heard her say that we were ready for my appointment. Were we at a new salon or something? Maybe they'd decided to get me to see a psychologist because of my doubts with Rob. Well, I could mitigate that straight away since we were broken up...or at least I considered us broken up.

After a few more minutes of standing still, I felt another hand take mine. It must have been Annabelle, because I smelled her token vanilla perfume. It did calm me a little, knowing she was there. True, she may have said this was a bad idea, but she could help contain the crazy train my mother and Mindy were on.

"All right, darling, take the mask off," my mother cheered.

I slid it off my head and fought the urge not to pass out when I saw where we were.

Chapter 7

Mom and Mindy were both holding up long white dresses covered in jewels, tulle, and lace. Hundreds of other gowns were on racks all over the store, and from the back room, I heard someone saying yes to her dress.

We were in a bridal salon.

"Surprise," my mother cooed, grinning from ear to ear. "Aren't you happy? We're gonna find you a dress so we have plenty of time to get it altered. If I can get the designer to make you a whole new one, I will. I only want the best for you."

I pasted a fake smile on my face and turned to look at Annabelle. "Did you know about this?"

"No, I found out when we pulled up.'

Before I could say another word, a consultant was in front of me, taking measurements.

"I need you to take off that bulky sweater, honey," the consultant said as she tried to wrap the tape measure around my waist.

Automatically, I took the sweater off, and stood in the middle of the bridal salon in my tank top and leggings.

"Stripper Barbie," Annabelle whispered. "I think they want you to go into the dressing room before you start making the other girls feel crappy about their love handles."

I grabbed her wrist. "Fine, but you're coming with me." I turned to my mom and Mindy, who were so caught up in looking at dresses, that they didn't notice how upset I was. "Guys," I called, and they finally turned to look at me. "I'm gonna have Annabelle come in the dressing room with me. Why don't you pick out some dresses?"

"Good idea, Chris. I know exactly what you like," Mindy assured me and went back to the rack. Mom seemed to take what Mindy said as a bit of a challenge and attacked a different set of gowns.

The consultant followed us into the dressing room and continued her measurements. When she left, I crumpled to the floor.

Annabelle knelt beside me. "So, do you want me to go out and tell them that this isn't going to happen? I can say you broke up with Rob last night, or that you're on your period and don't want to do this today. Should I say I hate all the dresses to cause controversy so we have to come back another day? Just tell me what to say and I'll say it."

"I want you to call Jason and have him pick us up. I can't do this now. Once I'm in the dress, I feel like it'll snowball. Mom will pay for it, or alterations, or order a new dress. Something will happen and she won't get her money back for whatever it is she does. I don't want her to do that."

Annabelle took her phone out of her bag and

called Jason. He answered almost instantly and she hung up right after giving him the address.

"Okay, so he'll be here in ten minutes. Should I stall until then?"

"No, let's just stay in the fitting room. Hopefully it will take them forever to pick a dress."

As if. Mom came rushing into the fitting room about two minutes later and thrust a gown into my arms. "Darlin', I found the perfect dress." She turned to look at Annabelle and beamed like she won the lottery. "Annabelle, come sit outside with me while the consultant gets Christie into this dress." She linked her arm with Annabelle's and practically pulled her out of the room.

The consultant came in next and ordered my clothes off. I was wearing a leopard bra, which made me laugh a little, as it would be all wrong for the dress. The consultant noticed it too and ran back out of the room. She came back holding a white bra, surprisingly enough my size, and a white slip.

"Put these on and then I'll tie you into this dress." She left the room and I quickly did as she said, hoping I could get in and out of the dress before Jason got here.

The consultant came back as I was stepping into the slip and then spread the pile of tulle my mother had called a dress out on the floor.

"Okay, step into the middle and I'll pull it up and over."

I did as I was told again and sucked in a deep breath. As the consultant pulled the dress up, I let out that breath with a sigh of relief. I would never, under any circumstances, wear this dress. It was about as wide as it was tall, the bottom was lace on top of tulle, on top of even more tulle, and the bodice had a giant flower on the side, and the short sleeves cut me funny.

The dress looked awful, but I could see my mother loving every inch of it. True, I did look pretty in the dress, but I felt a bit more like the flower girl than the grown up bride.

I walked out of the fitting room and I instantly made eye contact with Annabelle. Her eyes grew big and she coughed, clearly trying to cover up a laugh. Then I looked at Mindy, happy to see a look of disgust on her face. But next to her, sat my mother, bawling her eyes out as if I were going off to a convent and this wedding was her last chance to get a grandchild.

"Mom, this isn't my dress," I managed to say, hoping she'd get the hint to calm down.

"Well, of course it isn't. I don't know why you didn't try one of my picks first. This is just so juvenile," Mindy insisted, turning to my mother.

"I *am* juvenile, Mindy. I'm standing in a wedding dress at nineteen," I reminded them.

"Why don't I help you get out of that dress," Annabelle offered, waving her phone in the air a little.

"Yes, that's a good idea." I almost ran back to the fitting room.

I stood there, waiting for Annabelle to undo all the little buttons, but I'd made the mistake of looking in the mirror. What the hell was I doing? I didn't even look grown up in the mirror. I was too young to be getting married, and Rob was the wrong guy to be married to. I started breathing a little too heavily. The dress was too tight. *Too tight*. I needed out of the dress.

"Annabelle, get the dress off. I can't breathe." I reached around to try and rip the buttons off if I could. Screw the money. I felt the walls around me going a little fuzzy and I fought the urge to pass out.

All of a sudden, Annabelle wrapped her arms around me tight and squeezed me within an inch of my life. "Just breathe," she reiterated over and over again.

Copying her slow and steady breathing, I closed my eyes and let my basic instincts take over. After several deep breaths, I opened my eyes and the world wasn't fuzzy anymore.

"Better?"

"Yes, but I still need the dress off." She nodded her head and worked on the rest of the buttons. "And, Annabelle, when I do get married, I want a dress that zips."

"Got it," she replied, as she helped me step out of the dress.

I had managed to put my bra back on and I was almost in my leggings when the consultant walked back in with at least five dresses threatening to drown her. I was about to scream at her when Annabelle stepped in.

"Listen, we don't want to waste your time, but Christie's mom brought her here before she got engaged, and this is all a little too overwhelming. She's not going to try on any other dresses, and I'm going to take her home. But her mom isn't going to just let us walk out…is there any way you can distract her for about five minutes so we can leave?" Annabelle spoke in such a business, no nonsense tone. I was impressed.

The consultant smiled sweetly at us. "Don't worry. You'd be surprised how often this happens. I'll go show them some veils in the back, and you can sneak out."

We thanked her and I grabbed my sweater, throwing it on like a safety blanket. The consultant was about to walk out when she reconsidered and turned back to me.

"Don't get married until you're ready. It doesn't matter what your mother or your friends say. If it's meant to be, you'll feel it in your heart." She patted my shoulder and then walked out.

Annabelle snuck a peek outside the curtain, and I grabbed my things, ready to make the mad dash.

"Let's go," she called and we rushed out of the store.

Jason's car was sitting, double parked and running. As soon as we jumped in, he stepped on the gas and tore out of the parking lot. It reminded me a little of the way Shane drove and I couldn't help but smile.

In his infinite wisdom, Jason drove us to a breakfast place down the street from the bridal salon. I told them to go in ahead of me and I stayed in the car to send Rob the text.

Christie: I tried to tell u last night. I can't do this relationship anymore. We're done. I don't want to get married, and I don't want to try to work it out. Please don't try to change my mind.

It's made up.

It was a long text, but I felt like it couldn't get any more final than that. Then, it was my mother's turn. She, I was afraid to call.

Christie: Rob and I broke up. I don't want to talk about it, but I ended it. I'm w/ Annabelle, so don't worry. I'll be home by 10.

Then, I did what I almost never do. I turned my phone off and headed into the restaurant to eat my sorrows away with toast, hash browns, and whatever else I could shove into my mouth.

Annabelle and Jason were a big help. They didn't talk about weddings, or dating, or anything. Instead, we talked about the comedian coming in a few weeks, and the plans they had for Homecoming. It was a great distraction, and I wasn't even worried about the fact that I wouldn't have a date for the Homecoming dance. Especially when Annabelle told me that Violet was planning to come home for a long weekend. It would be nice to see her and we could go together. It'd be a chick date.

Jason dropped us off at the movies, and we spent the rest of the day doing what I had wanted to initially. We watched two movies, back to back, and ate even more terrible food. By the time the second movie was over, I felt thoroughly disgusting, but my mood had dramatically improved. I had also added a couple things to my not settling down list. I'd never officially added the dance thing, so now seemed like a good time.

6. *Go to a club and dance all night*
a. *Probably should learn to dance first*
7. *Do something illegal*
8. *Try something new, like maybe cliff diving*

Since I was able to cross off the double movie day, it seemed only fair to add a few more. Besides, I think Shane could help me cross off a few more, and that thought excited me enough to risk going home a little early.

***

When I pulled into my driveway, I saw my mother peeking out the front window. She had heard my car and knew I was there. No point trying to sneak in now. I walked in the front door and she pointed to one of the plush chairs sitting in our living room.

"Sit down, young lady."

I nodded and sat down, noticing Mindy sitting on the couch across from me. She looked like she had been crying.

"Listen to me. I have never been so embarrassed as I was today when I found out you left us. Do you know I'll never be able to step foot in that shop again? I've spent *weeks* establishing relationships with those women so that everything would be perfect for this day, and then you treat me like this?"

"Mom, I didn't want to be there. Rob and I broke up."

"What?" Both Mom and Mindy spoke in unison.

"I don't want to do this. I don't want to marry Rob in a few months and drop out of school. I like school. I have friends there and I don't want to—"

"What about me?" Mindy asked in tears. "I hopped the train early this morning to spend the day with my best friend and you run off with some girl you've known for a couple months. We've known each other forever."

"I know, Mindy. But you surprised me. I just broke up with Rob last night, and I didn't want to talk about it yet. If I knew you were coming down, I would have warned you. Both of you are furious with me, but what about you? Surprising me with a trip to the salon before I'm even engaged!" I felt the fury start to build up inside of me. I wouldn't allow them to turn this around on me.

"Rob told me he got the ring. It's always been the plan for you two to get married in June. I don't know why you are acting like this is a big surprise," my mom shouted.

"You're right. I should have been honest with you guys. But I did text you, Mom," I conceded. That part was my fault. "I should have said that I was unhappy a long time ago, and we could have avoided this. But I'm not going to marry him. I'm not even going to be with him anymore." I remembered Annabelle's advice and I tried to be as

79

clear as I possibly could.

"It's just cold feet," Mindy said, shaking her head at me.

"No, it isn't," I assured her. "I want different things now."

"Like what, another man? Are you cheating on Rob? Because he deserves better than that," Mindy insisted.

"I know he does. We've been on a break for the past few weeks. I told him I needed some time to figure out what I wanted, and maybe experience new things but…"

"I'm sorry. I will not sit in this room and listen to you saying you cheated on Rob. That man would do anything for you," she shouted, walking up to me and pointing her finger in my face. "He's one of my best friends too."

I stood up as I saw red. "You're not listening to me! I said that we were on a break."

"I noticed that, I also noticed you haven't confirmed that you aren't seeing another man," she stated, and then grabbed her purse and stormed out of the house.

My mother sat down on the couch next to the chair and looked at me. "Are you seeing someone else, Christie?"

"No, I've been spending some time with a boy I met at school, but we aren't together, and we aren't having sex." No, that would be next weekend, but she didn't need to know that part.

"I can appreciate that you want some time to figure things out. Marriage is a big commitment. But I don't think you're going to figure anything out if you're seeing other boys. I think it would be best if you just went to school and came home. If you want, some of your friends can come here."

"I'm sorry, are you grounding me? I'm nineteen." I was completely shocked.

"No, I am simply giving you a suggestion. As you said, you're nineteen and can make your own decisions." With that, she got up and walked to her room, closing the door behind her.

I sat there for a little longer until I heard my dad moving around in his office. Trying to avoid a fight with my father, I went into my room and closed the door, hoping to get a little homework done. I had a test coming up in my statistics class and I wanted to go over my notes. Annabelle and Violet hated this class, so I was initially a little nervous about it. But it didn't seem too bad so far. Then again, the class just started.

About halfway through my notes, I took a break and turned my phone on. There were about twenty text messages from my mom and Mindy. Frankly, I was a little surprised. I had expected a whole lot more. But once I was done deleting those, I noticed that I hadn't gotten anything from Rob. Maybe he hadn't seen it yet, or just maybe he was respecting my wishes and leaving me be.

I sent Annabelle a text telling her that everything was fine and was about to toss my phone on my bed when I realized I missed a text.

Shane: What's goin' on? Did u dream bout Friday yet?

81

He had sent it three hours ago. That was long enough to wait.

Christie: Nope. Too busy with hw.

I waited a few minutes to see if he'd respond and he did, almost immediately.

Shane: Good call. Get it done with so we have longer to spend 2gther.

Christie: U only won 1 night.

Shane: Yes, but u didn't specify wat 1 night means. I see it as 5 pm until 5 am.

Christie: That seems like a long time.

And it did. How much sex could you possibly manage in twelve hours? I wasn't going to be able to walk the next day…or for the next week.

Shane: That was ur fault. U gotta specify the terms b4 u agree. Didn't ur bf teach you that?

I rolled my eyes, frustrated with this conversation. I never should have mentioned Rob to Emma, especially now that we were broken up for good.

Christie: I don't have a bf. We're done.

He didn't respond for a few minutes and I stared at my phone. I hated waiting for messages. We both know you are looking at your phone, thinking about what you're going to say. Just get on with it.

Shane: Works for me. I guess I'll teach you a thing or 2 now.

Christie: Oh, so ur my boyfriend now?

My heart raced as I sent that to him. Is that even what I wanted? Did I want to jump from one relationship to another? Wasn't the whole point of this for me to experience new things? I bit my lip, waiting for some kind of response from him.

Shane: Not yet. But after fri, I'll ruin u 4 any other man.

I smiled, glad he wasn't jumping into the relationship.

Christie: That sounds like big talk. Hope you don't disappoint.

Shane: I never do. Sleep tight while u can.

I tossed the phone on my bed and turned back to my homework, trying to contain the grin on my face and the butterflies in my stomach. Before Shane came around, I couldn't remember the last time I felt like this. With Rob, everything was predictable and normal. We went to dinner and a movie, kissed in the car a little, and then he dropped me off at home. If my parents weren't home, he'd come in and we'd fool around. But there was no excitement.

With Shane, I didn't know what to expect whenever we were together, and I liked it that way.

***

Monday was a pretty busy day for me. I had statistics first thing in the morning, accounting, and then an ethics class. I carried all my books with me and tended to work on the homework in the library in between classes. But today, we'd be doing a lot of quiz review in stats.

After about fifteen minutes, I was bored. I had studied this last night, and I felt pretty confident that I knew it. At least, in theory, I knew it. So I took my list out and crossed off the movies and doing something illegal. I was going to count going to the street race as illegal. Plus, I figured I'd probably go to another one, so I'd be doing two illegal things. Look at me, quite the overachiever.

Still, the list felt a little empty. No one wanted a bucket list with eight things. Ten seemed more appropriate. I needed to come up with three more things to do. Now that I didn't have the deadline of getting engaged in November, I decided to make the deadline the end of December. This way I could start the year a little more experienced and unique. I thought about it for a little while before settling on my last three.

9. *Find a hobby besides shopping*
10. *Find a marketing internship or job*

11. Meet some new people

Happy with my list, I looked it over and started thinking about ways to accomplish it. Maybe I'd look to see if the school had any Zumba classes, maybe I could learn to dance, or at least try to get some rhythm, and work out at the same time. I also probably should go see the career center about the internships. I'm sure they could point me in the right direction to start looking.

I made a note in my planner to talk to the career center and drag Annabelle with me to Zumba. If I was going to look foolish, I wanted someone to laugh with. My professor was introducing the final topic for the quiz, so I put the sheet away and returned my attention to the board.

The rest of the day went pretty smooth, and I met up with Annabelle and Jason for dinner. There I broached the Zumba class.

"So it's every Thursday night. I think we should go."

"Maybe not. I don't dance, like, at all," she insisted, looking a little horrified.

"That's why we should go together. I can't dance either. We can stand in the back and look like idiots together, and maybe we can learn a couple moves for Homecoming. Violet will come back and won't recognize us at the dance."

"But Violet can dance. She probably won't notice."

"Good, then maybe she won't make fun of our regular dance moves," I suggested, smiling big. "Please, I want to check it out, but I don't want to go alone."

"Fine, I'll give it a try. But no promises for next week."

"I'll take it," I said, thrilled that I had convinced her. The rest of the conversation went over Homecoming. It was in two weeks and we still didn't have a theme. The executive board just couldn't agree, and Annabelle was getting a little anxious. Her type A personality desperately wanted to plan.

"What about 'Fall in Paris'? Paris has really recognizable landmarks and it's beautiful. We can hang fake leaves from the ceiling like the mirrors you guys did last year, and we can set up a big photo op with the Eiffel Tower. Then you can serve croissants with chocolate and coffee in cheap china. We can also hang some white Christmas lights from the ceiling to pose as stars," I suggested.

Annabelle's face lit up. "Have I told you lately that I love you?" She took her phone out and started texting madly. I looked at Jason, who watched her lovingly.

"I guess she likes the idea," I said to him.

"Yeah, good call. But if I were you, and the e-board agrees with this idea, I'd try to get her butt to at least five Zumba classes."

I nodded at him. "I like the way you think, mister." We talked more about different ways we could decorate as Annabelle made the decision that this had to work because it was too good of an idea.

Chapter 8

Tuesday was my chill day. I only had one class and then the EET meeting. The class went fine and then I headed to EET. We voted on the Fall in Paris idea and it won almost unanimously. So now we just had to decorate. I sat with Annabelle as she helped to set up groups to take over different aspects of the dance. Once the groups were set, we got into decorations pretty hardcore, and it was up to us to work on painting the Eiffel Tower.

Like my mom, I had some painting talent. It wasn't as impressive as hers, but it did help to calm me. I sketched out the different bars along the legs of the tower and found myself experiencing a bit of peace. Maybe this was something I should look into doing. Or, maybe it was something I should talk to my mom about doing together. It might help with all the animosity building in my house. I stopped painting and made a note in my planner to look up some beginner classes for us to consider.

Wednesday came pretty quickly and I was pumped for my quiz. Well, pumped was a weird word. I was ready for it, and ready for it to be over at the same time. I finished the quiz within twenty minutes and then put my head on my desk to relax a little. My professor didn't like people leaving early, because it distracted the other test takers. However, this time, our professor called my name and asked me to bring my test up to her.

I stood up on nervous legs and walked to the front of the class. Did she think I was cheating or something? Professor McMann took my quiz and quickly graded it while I stood there and watched. As she flipped through the pages, I saw a whole lot of checks and a smile broke out on my face. It was nice to see I did know what I was doing.

She wrote 98 on the top and showed it to me, before putting it in her bag.

"I'd like you to stay after class so I can discuss an opportunity with you." She smiled and dismissed me to go back to my seat.

My mind raced with possibilities. Maybe she'd want me to TA next semester, or tutor. I wasn't the biggest fan of other people, but then my list popped in my head. It would be a good way to meet others. So I resigned myself to give whatever opportunity she presented a chance. As the class filed out, I stayed in my desk, waiting for the room to empty. Finally, the last student turned their test in, and Professor McMann came up to me.

"Miss Peters, I've been watching you fiddle around in class, do other work, and text these past few weeks. However, when you turn your work in, it's almost all correct. I was eager to see your quiz because I had a theory about you."

"I didn't cheat, if that's what you mean, Professor," I insisted, suddenly deeply offended.

"Oh, I know. I watched you finish your test with impressive speed. Your head stayed down, your hands on your desk, and your eyes didn't wander. No, you just seem to have a knack for this class and numbers. What are you studying?"

"Business with a specialization in marketing."

"Perfect. The firm I work for offers an internship every year to one of my students who I feel shows promise in the field. We focus on marketing and how well different types of marketing plans are doing profit-wise for our clients. It seems to fit in your wheelhouse."

"Actually, that sounds great. Thank you for the opportunity," I babbled, shocked she was considering me.

"I will make a decision after your projects are turned in two weeks from now, and after your next quiz. Keep up the strong work and I can honestly say you're one of my leading candidates. However, don't take this as a chance to slack off. Just because you do well on one quiz doesn't mean you have the position," she warned, giving me a firm look behind her red glasses.

"No, I understand. I'll definitely work hard on this," I assured her, nodding like a bobblehead.

"Great, I'd recommend researching product marketing plans and ways they can be monitored for success."

I agreed and thanked her again before running out of the class. I had plenty of time before the project was due, but I felt the need to get a jump start. We had been let out of class early because the quiz hadn't taken the whole period, and even with our little talk, I still had a lot of time before my next class.

So instead of the library, I went to my car and grabbed a blanket. Annabelle liked to study outside, and I was in the mood to do the same. It was a nice day and I was dressed to sit outside comfortably. I was wearing black jeans with rips in the knees, a purple loose tank top blouse with a cream oversized sweater on top, and brown ankle boots.

I picked a spot under a tree and took my computer out to get some research done. Luckily, the school's Wi-Fi reached this far, so I was ready to go.

After about an hour, I seemed to be really cooking, and had several sheets of paper filled with notes. I lifted my arms in the air and stretched a little as someone fell down next to me and slid under my arm.

"Hey, beautiful," Shane greeted, wrapping his arm around my waist.

"Hey, what's up?" I asked as he leaned in and gave me a kiss.

"You looked hard at work. I wanted to make sure you took a little break."

"Aw, so considerate. What do you want?" I asked as he broke out into a big grin.

"Nothing, I just saw you and wanted to see what you were up to. Is that a crime?" He picked up my notebook and started looking it over. "Okay, looks like a good start. I could give you a hand if you'd like."

"You know about statistics?"

"Yeah, I'm not just a metal head. I'm here for mechanical engineering. Math is a big part of that. I'm good with more than just engines."

"And here I was thinking you were only good with your hands," I muttered, grabbing his fingers that were slowly sliding up my thigh.

"Well, that too." He squeezed my leg and grabbed my laptop.

There we sat for another hour, going over different possibilities, different equations, and several different marketing methods. Other than the occasional hand slip, Shane was a big help. He started rattling off facts, formulas, and suggestions almost too fast for me to write them down. It was strange. Earlier, at the street race, I thought I'd seen him in his element. But here he was, talking to me about math as if it was his other passion. Watching him fiddle with his car, it's easy to forget his dad is literally a brain surgeon. There were two sides to this guy and it was almost endearing that I got to see them. I wondered how many other girls he brought into both of his worlds.

"So, just a question," I began as I was packing my notes up to head to my meeting. "If you love cars so much, why are you here for engineering? Why not go to a trade school to be a mechanic or something like that?"

"I'm Asian. My parents gave me two options, doctor or engineer. Frankly, it was nice of them to give me the choice. Not all my friends got that chance. I figured, if I was doing mechanical engineering, then there would be a crossover with cars and engines."

"So at the end of the day, you found a way to make your parents happy and to keep yourself happy."

"Well, yeah, I guess you could say that."

I stood up, nodding, and slid my bag over my shoulder, seriously considering this. I needed to find something like this compromise at home. Mom was barely speaking to me and Dad was on her side, so he only spoke when it was necessary. It was driving me crazy.

"See, I'm having an ethical dilemma right now," Shane explained to me, breaking me out of my thoughts.

"Oh yeah, what's that? Are you thinking of changing your major to something more related to cars?"

"No, I'm going to graduate with an engineering degree and get a job at some impressive firm and race my car on the weekend. When I have some money saved away, I'll open my own garage."

"So what's the dilemma then?"

"I feel like I should carry your books to class or something, but that is a really girly bag," he told me, pointing at my floral tote.

"Are you not secure enough in your manliness to walk with a girl to class and carry her bag?"

He stood up a little taller and grinned at me. "No, I'm secure. I just know that people will think the bag looks better on me than you."

I rolled my eyes and slammed the bag into his gut. He grabbed it and slid it up over his shoulder.

"Violence is not the answer. I thought you were

a flower child."

"Sometimes you're infuriating," I told him as he slung his arm around my shoulder and we began walking back to the castle.

"True, but at least I'm not boring."

Shane gave me a quick peck on the cheek and handed me my bag as we got to my next class. Just before he walked away though, he leaned in and whispered in my ear.

"Remember to wear your sexy panties on Friday." He raised his eyebrows and smiled at me.

I grabbed his shirt before he could walk away, and leaned in. "I don't wear panties," I whispered. Then I turned and entered the room before he had a chance to respond.

As I sat down, I felt my phone vibrate.

Shane: Down girl, don't make me take you to the bathroom and force you to prove that.

Christie: I do what I want.

Shane: I no, its wat I like bout u.

I went home from class that night in a better mood, but that was quickly crushed as I came in the front door. Mom was sitting in the living room reading a book. I tried to greet her, but nothing. No response. When I tried to talk to her again, she got up and left the room. I sent her a text message, but she didn't respond.

I went to go and find my dad.

"Listen, she just needs time to get over the

shock."

"But she can't keep taking it out on me."

"I know. But you have to understand, you made this big decision without her. You didn't confide in her, and she was embarrassed in front of her friends. She feels like you made her look like a bad mother. Did you know two of the women from the bridal shop are on the board of one of the charities your mother runs? Now she feels like they won't take her seriously."

"What was I supposed to do?"

"You were supposed to come talk to us."

"And what would you have said? Would you have just said it was cold feet?"

"Christie," Dad started, and then stopped to rub his face. He looked up at me seconds later and I couldn't help but notice the lines around his eyes. He looked tired. Mom probably wasn't letting him get much sleep. "Yes, and I still think it's cold feet. That man is the best man you'll ever find. He isn't just some bum on the street. He loves you fiercely and he wants to take care of you. What more could a father ask for?"

"How about what I want? I'm your daughter."

"You are. And for several months, you said this was what you wanted. Now all of a sudden you change your mind?"

"Yes, because I wasn't happy."

"Well, you're not happy now either." With that, he got up and walked out of his office, leaving me standing across from his desk. He was wrong. I was happy. Maybe if I could explain that to them, they'd see that it never would have worked with Rob.

I didn't want to tell them about Shane just yet. Frankly, I wasn't even sure what to tell them. But there was one person I could tell. She was probably still pissed at me, but it was probably time for me to talk to Mindy.

"If you're going to yell at me, then I'm hanging up," she said instead of saying hello.

"No, I owe you a big apology and an explanation. Over the summer, I was struggling with the idea of getting married so young."

"But why? We've been talking about getting married young, having babies, raising them together, and then looking like beautiful MILFS forever." We made this plan when we were sixteen, and at the time, there was nothing more that I wanted. It was the life we both knew.

"I know, but then when I was facing the prospect, it scared me. I tried to talk to Rob about it, but he didn't want to hear it, so we took a break. While I was on the break, I met this guy named Shane. He makes me feel alive in a way that I never felt with Rob. So, I realized that if someone else made me feel this way, then I couldn't be with Rob. It wasn't fair to him."

"So you're just jumping into this relationship with this new guy, like, a week after ending things with Rob?"

"No, things with Rob and I have been done for a while now. I just didn't want to face it."

"Are you in love with this new guy?" she asked me in an accusatory tone.

"Mindy, it isn't about Shane. It's about me. I want to finish school and experience life. With

Shane, I get the chance to do that. If next week we never see each other again, my feelings for Rob aren't going to change. I want different things now. There's this internship that…"

"But how do you know? You and Rob were together for four years. That time and those feelings don't just go away," she insisted.

"What I wanted changed. I'm trying to tell you that those feelings, as strong as they were, just don't mean what they used to. I've grown, but he isn't growing with me. "

"Okay. I just don't want you to regret anything."

"I won't. That's why I did this."

***

I spent Thursday morning in class, but for the afternoon, I had a plan. Unfortunately, I would be back to do Zumba with Annabelle tonight. She had reluctantly agreed and we were both filled with a mix of excitement and fear. But first, I had to deal with my mother.

I headed straight home after class and I walked into the kitchen, where my mother was cleaning the stove, and grabbed her phone off the charging doc.

"I am taking your phone hostage. Follow me to the car now or I will take it with me to my outing." I turned around and walked to the car, hoping she was behind me. Her heel clicks confirmed she was there, but she wasn't talking just yet. I had to remind myself that small victories would help me win the battle.

We drove in silence. I turned on our favorite

Broadway musical soundtrack after a few minutes. I couldn't stand the quiet, and I hoped it would help loosen her up. After the second song played, I could hear her humming along. I didn't want to just bust out in song, but I didn't want not to acknowledge it. I started humming too, and together, we slowly started singing a little louder. I looked straight ahead for fear if I looked over at her, it would break the magic. Ten minutes later, we pulled into the parking lot and I handed her a bag.

"You may want to change into this. It would be a shame to ruin those designer pants." I handed it to her and grabbed my own bag that I had stored in the back. "There is a bathroom inside, so you don't have to strip in the car."

She looked at the bag and then at me. Her lips were pressed together in a thin line. The same line when she wanted to argue with my dad but chose against it. I held my breath, waiting to see if she'd decide to fight me, or just do what I ask.

"Where is inside?" she finally asked. There was some attitude in her voice, but I thought her eyes looked a little curious.

"I thought you might like to take a painting class with me. I was looking into getting a hobby and I thought that you'd like to come."

She rubbed her hands together and her fingers kind of waved. It was like she was itching to get ahold of a brush.

"Well, I could use the chance to brush up on my skills." She climbed out of the car and almost ran to the front door.

Laughing, I followed her inside.

It was my first professional painting class, so I spent a lot of the class trying to pay attention to what the instructor was saying. However, my mom turned into the teaching assistant. She was giving out pointers and suggesting techniques left and right. I had never see her in this element and it was overwhelming and heartwarming at the same time.

We walked out of the class an hour later and my mom pulled me into a big hug.

"Oh darlin', I needed that. It's been so long since I worked my creative muscles in a way that was completely selfish. I wasn't planning for the house or some party. It was just raw painting and I loved it."

"Mom, this is how I feel now. There is this big internship at school and I'm in the running. It's for a calendar year, starting in January. I'm not ready to settle down just yet, and I hope you can respect that. I think this is my new dream."

"Listen, I just want what's best for you, and I really thought you wanted this. I still think he is what's best for you. But I want you to be happy. I think Rob will wait for you if you want him to."

"I tried to bring up waiting and he shut it down. Besides, I'm not sure if he's what I want anymore. I just feel like I'm going through the motions with him."

"Okay, but promise me you will think about it? Not just for the night, or the week. But really give it some thought. I'd hate to think you threw away your chance at love because you were being hasty."

"I will," I promised and we headed back to the house. I wanted to say I had thought about it. I was sure of the decision I'd made, but I didn't want to fight. I'd do what she asked and think about it some more. It probably wouldn't change my decision, but maybe it would change her reaction to it.

I also thought about telling her more about Shane, but I didn't want to say anything just yet. I don't think she would like our night of pleasure very much. Her strict Catholic values would probably cause even more problems for us.

Tomorrow would be interesting. It could mean a lot more than just a good time, it could be some of the best sex ever that leads to feelings and completely ruin everything, or it could be just a physical thing. The point was, I was thrilled that the options were out there—but a little less thrilled that I had to go back to school for Zumba with Annabelle.

"Are you sure we have to do this?" she asked as we stood in the back of the school's gymnasium.

"Yes. We're trying to do something new. I can't dance to save my life, but I am a boss at aerobics. Maybe the two will be similar and I can learn some moves before I make an ass out of myself at Homecoming."

"Ugh. Fine. But don't judge me too harshly. This is probably going to be a disaster."

"But it will be a fun disaster."

Chapter 9

I woke up early on Friday and hopped in the shower. I needed to shave...*everything*. There was a lot to prepare for when you had sex for the first time with a guy. Movies these days confuse girls about that. You can't just happen upon a guy and bang him within hours of meeting him. If someone is able to do that, then they spend an awful lot of time on personal upkeep and I commend them. Me, on the other hand, I needed to take the time to get ready. Maybe it was because I was self-conscious, or maybe I just didn't want to be remembered as the girl who had prickly legs. Shane was definitely the kind of guy to bring that up over and over again.

Then, I did my make-up and then put the powder, eye shadow, eyeliner, and blush in my bag so I could reapply all of it. Last minute, I tossed in my favorite red lipstick. I liked to think of it as good luck, but it also would be funny to leave a mark on his cheek.

Classes dragged on and I felt like they would never end. But then again, I hadn't heard from

Shane yet. I didn't actually know when he was expecting me, if he was expecting me, if he was picking me up, or anything else. It was making me a little anxious. Part of me wondered if he was backing out. I'd been looking forward to this night for almost a week now. If he backed out, I'd be unbelievably frustrated in more ways than one. Plus, I actually liked spending time with him. But I wouldn't beg. If he didn't get in touch with me, then I'd go home and maybe have my mom teach me a thing or two about painting. We could have our own little class. It'd be nice. Not exactly the Friday night I was looking forward to, but at least I'd be working on something from my list.

At six, when my last class ended, Shane hadn't texted me, and I wasn't about to text him first. So, instead of heading to a sex cave, I went to my car. As I got closer though, I noticed that there was a single red rose sitting on the hood of my car. Attached to the stem was a note.

No, you didn't get off easy. I'm still coming for you. Meet me at the mall asap. Park across from the burger place.

Confused, I opened my door and sitting in the passenger seat was the rest of the bouquet. There was a note attached to them too.

I'm not that cheap. I did buy you the whole thing- S

I laughed and turned the car on to head to the mall. I felt jitters flow through my whole body. It seemed like I was on uppers or something. I tried to keep my breathing calm before I passed out and caused a giant accident. It would completely wreck everything if I ended up spending the night in the hospital and his father had to check on me. But before I realized it, I was speeding down the road, letting the adrenaline get the best of me.

When I pulled into a spot next to Shane's bright blue Subaru, I looked around. He was nowhere to be found. I got out and stood by the car for a second, waiting for him to appear. He didn't, so I walked inside the burger restaurant.

Shane was sitting at a booth with a wrapped present on top of a table.

"What's this?" I asked, taking in his button down shirt and dark jeans. He looked nice, but it wasn't his normal uniform. I kinda liked the leather jacket.

"Well, the thing about women is that you don't actually get them in the bedroom. They enjoy sex better when you've gone all out for them. So, that's my plan."

"But we're at a fast food burger restaurant. This isn't exactly all out," I said, looking around to see if a waiter was going to start serenading me.

"Oh, I planned accordingly. We need protein to have a long night, and your favorite food is french fries. It's the best of both worlds," he added, grinning at me. "So, what's your order?"

"Um, fries, a second order of fries. And a junior cheeseburger with all the fixings."

"Got it." He got up and walked away, but then

rushed back. "Don't open the box."

"Wait, what? You're just going to leave me staring at this box and I can't open it. That's rude." I reached out and stroked the ribbon.

"No, you can't open it," he insisted and walked away to the cash register.

I shook my head and checked that he was really gone. When his back was turned, I lifted the box off the present. There was a card sitting there, so I quickly grabbed it and pulled it out.

Christie, put the lid back on the box and don't open it until you're told- S

I stared at the card open mouthed, and couldn't decide whether I was annoyed, shocked, or amused. Shane called my name and I turned to look at him. He gave me a little wave and smiled like the smug little asshole he was. I gave him the finger and put the card back in the box, crossing my arms over my chest to pout a little.

"I told you not to open the box," Shane chastised me as he sat down across from me with the food.

"Obviously you knew I was going to open it. You're playing games," I insisted, grabbing a handful of fries.

"I did, but you'll like what's inside. It'll be worth the wait." He unwrapped a burger and dug in.

***

"Are you sure you're done with the fries?" I asked him as I inhaled the last couple.

"Well, it's too late now if I wasn't. Remind me to buy you even more fries next time."

"It's like a sickness. I will continue to eat fries until they're all gone."

"Well, now that we've discussed one of your sicknesses, let's talk about this box." He walked to take the tray to the trash and then placed the present on the table. "Okay, you can open it now."

I ripped the box off the present and dug into the tissue paper. After taking everything out of the box, there was nothing but the card telling me not to open it.

"What gives? There's nothing in here." I looked up at him in time to see him laughing hysterically.

"Oh, that's right. I haven't bought anything for you yet."

"So what's supposed to be in the box?"

"Follow me." He grabbed my hand and the present as he slid out of the booth.

Shane dragged me through the mall, walking fast, until he stopped in front of the lingerie store.

"Seriously? I'm not trying on lingerie for you," I informed him, not impressed. "Is that your sickness?"

"Don't worry, I like the surprise of taking a woman's clothes off and seeing the sexy things underneath. You said you don't wear panties, so why deprive myself of that kind of joy? Nah, I'd rather buy you a set that I liked. Then, the next time you saw them in your drawer, you'd think of banging me."

"That sounds a little controlling."

"Don't be jealous that you didn't think of it first.

Now," he looked me in the eyes, "let's shop."

I followed him in and watched Shane flipping through the racks. He would look at a set and then look at me. At first, I felt a little objectified. Then I shoved that part aside and decided to enjoy it. If he was going to buy me a new panty and bra set, then I was going to make sure it was expensive and that I'd wear it again…with or without Shane.

"Okay, I'm not actually picking you out a set," he told me after we walked through the whole store. "I set you up an appointment with one of the consultants so that you ladies could pick out something you liked and I can still be impressed." He handed his credit card to the woman who walked up to us. "Make sure she buys something sexy and the most expensive thing in the store. This girl deserves the best."

Shane waltzed out and I turned to look at the consultant. "So, your boyfriend seems nice."

"Oh, he's not…well, yes, thanks." I thought about correcting her, but then I decided not to bother with it. I'd just enjoy the moment.

"Well, my name is Charlene, and I'll help you find something for you to feel pretty and attract him." She took me to a dressing room and did a quick measurement. Apparently, I was wearing the wrong size, but I kind of thought she said that because she wanted me to buy more bras from her.

I sat in the fitting room and just started laughing. This was definitely a lot different than the wedding dress fitting I was dealing with last weekend. No anxiety threatened to paralyze me and I was actually excited to wear what the consultant brought in. Plus,

I'd be wearing it for a completely different reason and a completely different guy.

She returned and handed me some of the prettiest bras I'd ever seen. The first was a midnight blue with little diamonds on it. When I tried that on, I felt a little bit like Stripper Barbie. I actually took a picture of it and sent it to Annabelle. This was a little less bra and a little more performance outfit.

The next was a pale pink bra that was almost all see through lace with elaborate flower details that kept my nipples from being too obvious. I slipped it on and felt sexy. It was like the magical jeans from that book series. I felt something flowing through me and I knew this was the bra for tonight. The panties that went with it were also lacy, but they had no lining. I slipped those on and spun around in the mirror. I needed this set.

"How do you like that one?"

"It's amazing. It feels like a second skin and a boob job at the same time."

"Great, try this set just to be sure, but I'll put this in a box for you." Charlene handed me a silver bra and panty set. It was satin, and when I placed it on, it was the softest thing I'd ever felt on my body. The cup of the bra fit perfectly and the band had a thin layer of lace over it, making the bra pretty, but not taking away from the fabric.

"This one is amazing too," I said to Charlene when she checked on me again.

"Well, Mr. Choi told me to charge whatever you wanted, so get them both."

"Works for me, but I think I'm going to put the pink set back on, if that's okay."

"I figured you'd want to wear one out. Take the tag off and I'll ring it up for you."

I put the set on and then put my clothes back on. As I was standing at the register, I texted Shane and told him we were done. I was ready for the next phase in the adventure.

Shane met me outside and took the lingerie bag from me and handed me another bag.

"You know, I'm feeling a little guilty, I haven't gotten you anything."

"Make it up to me later," he told me and wrapped his arm around my waist, grabbing my ass at the same time. "Open the bag."

Inside of it was a box of rich looking milk chocolate. I grabbed a piece of chocolate and offered it to him.

"You have the first bite."

He opened his mouth and took the whole piece, his lips lingering on my fingertips. I felt a sensation flow through me as I thought about what those lips would be doing to me later. His eyes never left mine and it was all becoming too intense.

I looked down and grabbed my own piece, walking in silence as Shane talked about his race tomorrow.

"Wait, what?" I asked in the middle of his sentence.

"I said you're going to be there, right? I won the race by a landslide, we discussed this. I'm way too superstitious for you not to come."

Nodding my head, I gave him a big smile. "Did you call out a newbie so you'd be sure to win, basically ensuring that I'd have to come to all of your races? Did you set me up?" The more I thought about it, the more I figured that he probably did. This was why he didn't accept Chuck's call out.

"You're giving me too much credit. I'm not that smart." He slid his hand down to my hip and pulled me closer to him.

I looked over at him and there was a smug smile on his face. I actually did think he was that smart. It felt good that he seemed to be going through a lot of trouble to spend time with me.

When we got to the cars, Shane walked me over to my driver's side door.

"Follow me." He opened the car door for me and stuck his head inside. "Those flowers are really nice."

"Yeah, some creepy guy broke into my car and left them there."

"One person says creepy, another says romantic."

"Well, I think the police would call it stalking," I told him, trying to keep the smile off my face.

"Did you like them?"

I nodded my head, avoiding his eyes.

"That's the difference, and that's all I care about." He leaned in and gave me a kiss, wrapping his arms around my back. Shane gently pulled away and opened his eyes. "Let's go."

I climbed in the car and we drove off, heading to…well, I didn't know where I was going.

But Shane seemed to be having too much fun. He was swerving, speeding, and driving a little erratically. I gave him a call.

"Hey, don't be a jerk. I'm not a street racer," I yelled at him when he picked up.

"I'm just trying to see how bad you want it." He hung up and slowed down.

I shook my head and continued to follow the best I could. Shane finally pulled into an apartment complex and parked. I pulled into the spot next to him.

"Where are we?" I asked when he opened my door for me.

"My apartment."

Chapter 10

Shane led me into an old fashioned stone building and into the lobby. The concierge smiled and greeted Shane from behind a dark mahogany desk. It was elaborate and had gold claw feet. It looked like it belonged in a museum. Actually, the whole place looked a bit like a museum. There was elaborate metal work hanging on the wall and plush red couches and chairs scattered around the room.

We walked over to gold elevators and Shane hit the up button.

"This is really nice." I continued to stare, stopping at a giant bouquet of white roses on one of the tables near the elevators. The vase holding them was painted with a scene of heavenly angels. I gently stroked the side and felt the design. It was something my mom would go crazy for and spend way too much money on. This place was definitely not some cheap apartment a normal college kid would have.

"Thanks, my parents wanted me to be able to focus on school, so they bought me the apartment."

We walked into the elevator.

"Seriously, that's amazing."

"It is. I'm lucky they're so traditional." He smiled at me, and then walked me to the door of his apartment on the ninth floor. "The inside though, is even nicer than the lobby." Shane opened the door for me and I walked in.

I was prepared to be taken to another time with old fashioned, but heavy, furniture and richly colored walls. But that wasn't what I saw. Instead, the lights were dimmed for that romantic lighting every movie depicted, candles were lit all over the white countertops and tables. Rose petals covered the floor, directing us to the bedroom.

"Too cheesy?" he asked, looking at me, trying to read my face. His eyes were wide and his hand covered his mouth while he waited for me to respond. He actually looked nervous.

"No, this is perfect. I've always wanted to walk into a room like this. What did you do, run here while I was shopping?" This was amazing. How could he have done all of this? I mean, it was just supposed to be sex. Just sex. I looked over at Shane, a confident smile on his face.

"No, let's just say I owe one badass bitch a favor." He pulled me into a sweet kiss and then smiled big at me. "I told you I'd give you a night you'd never forget, so let's get to the good part." Shane took the lingerie bag and placed it on the kitchen table, then he picked me up, wrapped my legs around his waist, and walked me into the bedroom.

He laid me down on the bed and pulled his shirt

off before climbing on top of me. I wrapped my arms around his neck and we kissed deeply, and passionately. His smooth chest felt amazing as I slid my hands up him, running my fingers over his ripped muscles.

But I wanted skin to skin contact. I reached for the hem of my shirt, but Shane's hands stopped me. "Excuse me, don't you remember me saying that one of my favorite parts of this was unwrapping the present?"

"Fine." I pouted and moved out from underneath him. I crawled off the bed and stood in front of Shane. Taking his hand, I pulled him to the edge of the bed. I stood in front of him, just out of reach. Then I slowly reached for the bottom of my shirt and lifted it, pausing every so often to build up the tension a little bit.

As I pulled it over my head, I turned around, showing Shane the back of the bra first.

"What I like about this is the clasp. It's secure and doesn't feel like it's pulling or anything," I told him, still facing away from him.

"What are you doing?"

"I'm making sure you appreciate the bra you paid for." Then I turned to the side, hand over the cup, showing him the band. "The design goes all the way across the band. Isn't it pretty?"

"Yup, very pretty," he whispered in response.

I turned all the way around, covering my breasts with my arms. I gradually lowered them, revealing the lace flowers, and most importantly, the rest of my chest.

"Yup, very pretty," he repeated as I gently

stroked the curve of my breast.

"It feels even better," I promised him. He leaned forward to try and touch, but I swatted his hand. "The thing about this bra, is that it came as a set." I reached for my leggings and slid them off my legs, making sure to bend over and stick my ass out. "Isn't it nice that they match?"

"Yup, very pretty."

I walked over to him, standing in between his legs, and placed my hands on his shoulder. "Can I feel the merchandise that I spent good money on, or are you continuing the show? I wouldn't mind a dance."

"I don't dance."

"Good, I don't think I could keep my hands off you any longer." He wrapped his arms around my back, pulling me into him. Then he flipped me around so he was on top of me. With a hand, he reached up to grasp my chest, gently massaging as he grabbed my ass hard with his other.

My head fell back as a soft moan escaped my lips and Shane began kissing my neck. With his teeth, he nipped at the skin around my collarbone, causing me to cry out and grind against him at the same time. He continued kissing and nipping a trail down my chest until he settled over the pretty bra he paid for. With a swipe of his tongue, he licked the swell of my breast showing above the lace.

I shoved my fingers in his hair, desperate to grab something as pressure began building up inside me. I shut my eyes tight, refusing to give way to my feelings just yet. It was too soon. He hadn't even slid inside me and I was practically purring in his hands. Ugh, his hands.

With a finger, he slipped inside the band of my panties and ran along my thigh and center. But he kept stopping short of actually penetrating me. I tugged on his hair harder and heard him snicker.

"You're always in such a rush. We have all night. Just stop thinking and let all those emotions overtake you," he growled before covering my lips with a kiss again. This time though, when his finger slid past my core, he stopped. Gingerly, he entered me, exploring, but not really taking a deep look around.

I wiggled my hips under him, trying to get the kind of release I needed, but it wouldn't come. Reaching down, I tried to take my panties off, but he swatted me away.

"I paid good money for those. Leave them on for now. When I think you're ready, I'll take them off."

I cursed under my breath as he chuckled. With his other hand, he reached for my right breast and began licking through the lace, focusing almost entirely on my nipple. Every now and then, he'd blow a little, sending a cold sensation to my breast, causing me to shake uncontrollably. Then he switched to the other one, all while carefully flexing his finger inside me. Then he focused on my g-spot, that shallow spot most guys ignored, and I felt myself start to come undone. My body started to ache for him as I shifted under him.

"Excuse me, stop moving. You'll enjoy it more if you let me do my thing."

I groaned loudly, but it quickly turned into a moan as his pace increased.

Finally, he finished with my other nipple and kissed a line down my stomach, settling between my legs. He reached for the panties and took them off. "See? Patience is a virtue."

I rolled my eyes at him, and went to respond, but an animalistic sound erupted from me as his tongue replaced his finger. Rob had always been really bad at this, so we never did it. Shane was most definitely not bad at this. He licked me, circling it gently, but not lapping at it like a dog, and I cried out his name as the first shock of orgasm overtook me. My toes curled, my back arched, and my hips shook violently as he made sure to stay with me through the whole thing.

Shane stood up, a smug look on his face, and undid his belt buckle then his pants. As his jeans fell to the floor, I stared at his boxer briefs. They said Calvin Klein across the top and were a deep black, though the color hid nothing. My fingers started to itch, as I wanted nothing more than to feel what he was hiding. But the asshole didn't take the boxers off.

He climbed on top of me and ground against me for a second, sliding my bra straps down with his teeth. He kissed my shoulder, down to my breast, and then slid his arms underneath me. I felt the clasp come off and he helped me out of the bra.

Chest to chest, I pulled him against me, enjoying the way his skin felt against my tender nipples. Shane tossed the bra on the floor and pulled me on top of him, grabbing onto my breasts with both hands. I leaned into him, grinding against the soft fabric of his boxers, feeling my excitement building again. He felt big and I needed to see it. Curiosity was killing me.

I slid off his hips and reached for his waistband, dragging it down his legs and throwing the boxers onto the floor. As I looked up at him, I giggled a little in excitement. What I felt was even better. I reached for it, feeling him grow even harder with my touch. I slid up and down his shaft, as Shane shut his eyes tight and ran his fingers through his messy hair.

"Fuck this," he screamed and reached for the drawer next to his bed, producing a condom. He had it out of the wrapper and on him in record time. I watched as he climbed off the bed and pulled my feet to him so that my legs were hanging off the side and I was laying down on it. He lifted them in the air and slid inside of me, leaning on top of me as he took me deep. Like really deep. Like he found my spot with the second pump deep. I yelled as he pushed into me, each time feeling my body light up more and more until I couldn't take it anymore. The second orgasm hit me harder than the first and I swore like a sailor as the aftershocks shook me all over. I felt it from the tips of my toes all the way to my hairline, but that wasn't even the best part.

Watching Shane follow me over the edge, holding nothing back, but taking what he wanted all the same, overwhelmed me. It wasn't just something to do. He wasn't going through the motions. And he wasn't just trying to get in, get out, and get over it. Shane made sure I was good and then took what he wanted. It was a two way street for him.

I looked at him as he took the condom off and tossed it in the trash next to his bed. Sweat gleamed on his forehead as he collapsed on me, breathing heavily and sighing with satisfaction.

"That was insane," he murmured in my ear.

"Yeah," I responded breathlessly.

"So round one is done. Give it a second to sink in."

Chapter 11

That second turned into hours as we both laid there, not quite sleeping, just relaxing in each other's arms. I wasn't sure what he was thinking, but I was a little terrified to move. It was all ridiculous. Shane had gone above and beyond what I had expected, and I wanted to do it again, several more times actually, but I didn't want this to be it. If I said that, would I scare him off? He wouldn't have done all of this for just anyone, right?

I thought about what Annabelle and Violet would say to me. Annabelle would say sleeping with Shane was a rebound from Rob, and I should get up and leave before it messes with my head any more. It was great sex, but was it worth the trouble it was going to cause? But Violet would say I should enjoy my time with him and go again. She'd remind me I'd already caused the trouble, so I might as well do it again.

Shane pulled me closer and kissed my shoulder gently. "Listen," he said softly in my ear. "I was hoping to soften you up with the food, lingerie, and the sex, so that when I asked you this, you'd be willing to talk about it."

"Well, that sounds ominous." I stiffened up. What if he asked me to leave? Okay, we had sex, now can you head out? I'd feel like an absolute idiot.

"Okay, what's going on with that boyfriend, ex-boyfriend, or whoever that guy is?"

I sighed. Definitely didn't see that question coming, but my pulse started racing. He was asking about my ex. Guys only asked about your ex for one reason, they were interested. Shane was interested in more than just one night. I relaxed into him a bit more and slipped my fingers through his and pulled his hand to my chest so I was cuddling it.

"We were together for four years, and I realized I probably haven't loved him for at least six months. He'll graduate from his military college in May, and in June we were supposed to get married. I think he was planning on proposing around Thanksgiving. He'd be going active duty right after the wedding. The military gives you all these benefits if you're married, and Rob wanted to take advantage of them. Our families have been friends for years, and it seemed to make sense. It's basically the perfect arrangement."

"But...?" he prompted.

"But I'm not ready for it," I responded, sitting up and looking at him. "I don't want to get married and settle down yet. I want that internship, and a million other opportunities. I want to go to Italy and drink my way through wine country while staring at old world architecture. I want to really experience life

119

before I'm saddled with a husband and kids. I even have this stupid list of things I want to do before settling down."

"Show me the list," he requested softly.

I don't know what made me do it, or even what he'd think about it, however I went to my purse and pulled the list out of my planner. I handed it to Shane and held my breath.

He looked it over, laughed a little, and then smiled up at me. "Well, you just had sex with someone you shouldn't. But we did it in the bedroom, so I don't think we can cross that off just yet." Shane rolled over and grabbed his phone. He took a picture of the list and then handed it back to me. "We're gonna do all of it."

"Well, I did the stupid movie thing, so…"

"That's fine. I do love movies though, so maybe we'll just do it again." He stared at the list a little longer. "Does it count if I give you an exotic cooking lesson? My mom has this book of old school recipes from Korea. I'll grab one and get some tips from her."

"That could be fun, but no dog."

"Agreed. Now, about this skinny dipping thing…"

"Yeah, I was thinking we could start with the motorcycle thing. It's too cold for the swimming thing."

"Oh, don't be such a wimp."

"Okay, let's go skinny dipping. How sexy do you think it will be when you walk into the cold water and your little friend gets even smaller when it shrivels up from the cold?"

"Ouch, you're hitting below the belt. Well, I guess we'll just have to think about some of these other things another time. But I'll teach you to drive the bike tomorrow. Just promise me you'll be nice to her."

"I promise," I said and leaned down to give him a kiss.

He pulled away for a second, and smiled. "Now, time to be nice to me."

***

I was sitting on top of Shane's motorcycle with a heavy helmet on my head, and the new leather pants Shane snuck out this morning to buy me. I felt like a badass, but then again, my feet were still firmly on the ground.

"All right, let's go over this again," Shane repeated for the third time.

I groaned and rolled my eyes. "I know all of this."

"Well then, it won't matter if you say it again."

"Fine, the hand clutch is on the left and I'm supposed to use it to when shifting gears. But the shifter is by my left foot. On the right handlebar is the accelerator and the front tire brake. The rear brake is by my right foot. So left is gears while the right is stop and go."

"Fine, but last thing, you don't drive a motorcycle, you just ride it."

"That makes no sense."

"Sorry, I don't make the rules." He climbed on the back of the bike and grabbed my waist. It helped settle me a little knowing he was there. At least if we crashed, I wouldn't die alone.

"All right, let's give it a little and try to go really slowly."

I did as he said, and after a few kicks on the clutch, I felt the resistance give way, with a hit to the accelerator, we were off. Sure, we were off in the parking lot of a nearby elementary school and there were no other cars around, but I was doing it.

We went around in circles for a few minutes, and as I navigated the turns, I felt Shane's grip start to loosen a bit. I was getting it, so I upshifted, speeding up a little and then a little more. It wasn't long before I felt the adrenaline pumping through my system and I upshifted again.

"Okay, we're just in a parking lot. Slow down a bit," he yelled at me.

I downshifted and slowed down, hitting the brakes. My feet hit the ground again and I let out a yell. I'd actually done it. Shane slapped my thighs and cheered too.

"Right, now I want to hit the highway," I told him.

"Um, maybe let's just hit some back roads first. I built this bike from the ground up and your lead foot is making me nervous."

"Said the race car driver."

Shane laughed and I started the bike up again.

We made it around the block a few times with minimal issues, but it wasn't enough. Ignoring Shane's yelling, I pulled onto the highway and really let the bike loose. We were flying. Luckily, it was still early on Saturday morning, so there weren't a lot of other cars on the highway. I watched the speed limit come and go on the bike's display screen and I pushed her harder as the adrenaline from earlier was back, stronger than ever.

My mind emptied and I just had to focus on Shane and the road. It was the most peace I think I'd ever experienced in my life. After another hour, my fingers were starting to freeze and I made a mental note to invest in some riding gloves. Reluctantly, I headed back to Shane's apartment and parked the bike.

"I told you not to go on the highway. What if we'd crashed? Are you crazy?" Shane yelled at me as we climbed off the bike and took our helmets off.

I smiled at him and grabbed his jacket, pulling him to me. "I trusted you." Then I kissed him, wrapping my arms around his neck, pressing myself against him, urging him to take advantage. With only a second of hesitation, Shane grabbed my ass and gave me the response I'd been looking for. A make out session hot enough to set a house on fire.

Shane stopped the kiss, and looked at me for a few seconds, not saying anything. Then he gave me that wicked smile. "Watching you ride that bike was quite possibly the hottest thing I've ever seen, once I got over the fear you were gonna kill us. That was crazy dangerous."

"I'll make it up to you," I said, my voice a little raspy. I pulled Shane into the apartment and then up into his bed.

***

After another round together that quickly moved into the shower, we were both famished. I walked into the kitchen, wearing only Shane's t-shirt, and started making us lunch. Apparently, Shane's mother was consistently afraid he would go hungry, so she kept his kitchen stocked with food. He even knew how to cook some of it. But now, it was my turn to do something for him. Well, another something. What happened earlier in the shower didn't count.

I was browning some ground beef when he strolled into the kitchen, basketball shorts hanging loosely on his hips. His abs took my breath away and I quickly looked down at the food before I jumped his bones again.

He wrapped his arm around my waist and gave my neck a little kiss. "Mhmmm, what're you making?"

"Tacos."

"Sounds good. Afterwards, I need to go see one of my boys about a couple repairs on my car before the race. You're welcome to stay here though. I can pick you up before I head over."

"No, I need to get home. Take a shower, change clothes, assure my parents that I'm not dead in a ditch, that kind of thing."

"They worry about you, that sounds familiar."

"Oh yeah, your parents are controlling too?" I asked him as Shane handed me the skillet to brown the meat.

"You have to have heard about Asian parents, right? My parents feel like all of their accomplishments mean nothing if I'm not even more successful than they are. But they define success as being a top notch doctor, or engineer. They might even be happy if I wanted to go into business and I got my MBA. My life has been planned out for years."

"Sounds familiar," I repeated, a little dejected that we both had to deal with the same kind of pressure.

"Yeah, I guess it does. But you got out of yours. I'm still dealing with mine."

"It sounds like you're kinda making it your own."

"Well, there are some benefits to it all. Like this apartment, my parents bought it for themselves almost more than me. It's a big deal that they were able to buy it for me. They are so successful that they were able to buy me this fancy place and still vacation to the islands every year. It's a great story for them to tell at hospital fundraisers and cocktail parties."

"At least they let you live on your own. My parents shut down the idea of me even applying for colleges that were more than fifty miles away from our front door. Forget living on campus. Did you know that rapists and murderers troll college campuses every night?"

"Oh, shit, guess I've got to be more careful." He laughed and sat down at the breakfast bar while I finished cooking.

I gave him a plate and we started in. "So, how did you get out last night if your parents are so strict?"

"Homecoming is next weekend. I'm in the club

that sponsors it, so I told my mom I was working on the decorations with my friend Annabelle. She's met my mom, so I'm allowed to crash at her place as long as I promise not to go out past ten." I was trying to eat my taco without making a giant mess, but I'd stuffed it too full. So much for looking like a lady.

"Seriously?" Shane asked as he shoved more taco in his mouth, looking as classy as I did.

"Oh, yes. Some people say nothing good happens after midnight, but my mom strongly believes you should be home at ten. Don't even risk being out around eleven."

"Well, I guess it's good she doesn't know what we were doing at like one in the morning."

"Yeah, definitely for the best. Anyway, I'm going to head home, change, and tell my mom that we aren't done and I'm spending the rest of the weekend getting ready."

"So you just assumed that you'd be staying here?"

"I can think of a thing or two that might convince you to stay," I suggested, raising my eyebrows at him.

"Down, woman! I gotta get the car in shape." He gave me a kiss on the forehead and we finished eating.

"All right, I need to get ready to leave this apartment or I'm going to lose the race tonight and it will be completely your fault." He grabbed my plate, putting it in the sink. "I'll handle the dishes later, but I gotta get dressed and head out."

"I can do them. I'm in no rush," I said and

walked over to the sink.

"Be careful, woman, keep doing things like this and I may just have to wife you up before you finish that list."

"Haha, you're so funny." I rolled my eyes and continued washing the dishes.

Shane headed out and gave me a key. "Lock up before you leave. Head back here when you're done and I'll pick you up. Thanks again." He kissed me on the cheek and then headed out.

I stared at the door after he walked out, a little shocked about the key. Then I placed it in my purse, refusing to think too deeply about it. He needed me to lock the door. Guys don't get too intense with things like this. I needed to turn the girl brain off. So, naturally, I finished the dishes, cleaned the stove, and made the bed before heading out. I grabbed my purse, locked up, and attached the ring to my keys with the intention of giving it back to him tonight. I'm sure that's what he wanted anyway.

Chapter 12

Mom didn't question me about Homecoming, in fact, she was really excited about it. Dances and things like that excited her. She'd chaperone if she could. Plus, Annabelle sent me some pictures of decorations she was working on as long as I promised to stop by on Sunday and help out. When I showed the shots to Mom, she practically screamed and ran from the room.

"Mom," I called after her. She had run to the ladder that led to the attic.

I waited for her at the bottom and she climbed down with a giant Eiffel Tower in her hands. It was the size of her torso, had light bulbs in it, and was made of what looked like hard metal. She quickly plugged it into an outlet in the hallway and it lit up.

"I wanted to redo our bedroom with a Paris theme, but your father hated it. I have tons of stuff you all could use for the dance. Let me get it all down and you can take it with you back to Annabelle's. Oh, I'm so glad this stuff has a use," she squealed and headed back up in the attic.

"Do you want some help?" I called to her.

"No, darlin', I don't want you up here. It's all beams and you could hurt yourself. Anything I can't lift or get down, I'll have your father grab it."

Sighing, I went to take a shower and get ready to see another race.

I was putting on my make-up when my mom came in. "Also, I think I have the perfect dress for you."

"What? The perfect dress? How do you have a dress for this?"

"Well," she began and headed out of my room and into hers. "I bought this dress years ago. Your dad wanted to take me to Paris for Valentine's Day and I wanted to look nice. But we found out I was pregnant with you a month before we left, so we decided to cancel the trip and I decided to save the dress until I went to Paris."

"But you've been to Paris. Multiple times," I reminded her, sitting down on the chaise in her huge walk in closet.

"Darlin', it was never the same nor was my figure," she said, flipping to the very back of her closet.

"Mom, you look great."

She stopped and smiled at me. "I know I do. You'll understand one day when you have your babies. Things just change."

I was going to respond, mostly because I felt guilty, but I couldn't find the words as Mom was holding a dress out for me. It was quite possibly the most beautiful dress I'd ever seen. It was a green velvet wrap dress with spaghetti straps and an open back.

"Try it on," she said, smiling at me.

Forgoing my modesty, I stripped down and eagerly grabbed the dress. It felt like heaven as the soft fabric caressed my body, falling just about at mid-thigh. This dress, although in my mom's closet, was made for me. My narrow hips looked curvy, my breasts pushed against the fabric seductively, and my waist looked tiny. I turned around and took a look at my open back. The fabric started again right about where my jeans would rest, and for what was probably the first time in my life, my ass looked perky and full.

"Wow," I breathed, awestruck, and I turned to look at my mother. She had tears in her eyes. But unlike at the bridal salon, her face looked pure. There was no motive behind this, and it was nice to share it with her. I reached out to take her hand, and gave her a bright smile. "I love it, Mom."

"I know that you will probably want to get ready with your friends, but maybe you could send me a few pictures when you're ready?"

"I think I'll ask them if they want to get ready here. There's more space."

"That sounds nice. I can make some getting ready snacks too," she suggested, wiping her tears with the back of her hand.

"I'd like that." It was like the prom I didn't get to have.

A few days before my own prom, Rob's brother had died in Iraq. No one was in the mood to go, even though Rob had told me I could just go with my friends. We spent the night curled up together, watching family videos with his parents. I closed my eyes, trying to keep the tears away. Jimmy was a good man and had always been nice to me. But I think this was the start of my downfall with Rob. He became determined to start our lives immediately. Even though he was eager to become closer, he closed himself off. No matter how hard I tried, he wouldn't open back up. Sometimes I think I stayed with him so long after I knew it was over because I felt bad about Jimmy and not because I wanted to.

"Oh yeah, darlin'. Who are you going to the dance with? That new boy?"

My head shot up. I didn't know if Shane went to dances, or even if he would consider it. "Um, I don't know yet. I think we may just be going as a group. Violet will be back from study abroad and it will be nice to see her."

"Maybe Rob will be able to come up. I know he'd love to be able to escort you to the dance," she suggested softly.

My face fell and just like that, the moment was gone. "Mom, that's over. I don't want that life anymore. Rob isn't willing to compromise on it, and I'm not willing to either. Please, just don't bring him up again." I bit my lip a little, hoping she'd accept this answer, hoping we could just go back to having the nice mother/daughter moment in her closet. But her face looked too disappointed. It was like she was watching me crash and burn and couldn't do anything.

"Okay, I just wanted to make sure. I'll leave you to get dressed, but don't get any ideas about taking anything else from my closet." She tapped my chin and headed out.

I sat on the chaise and looked around. She may have said not to take anything from her closet, but to me, it sounded like an invitation to go shopping. I looked around to find something I could possibly wear tonight. It was mostly just her standard dressy outfits, so I walked to the back, where she'd found my dress, and flipped through the clothes there. I found a short, a line burgundy skirt with buttons from the top all the way to the bottom. It was cute and I loved it.

I tried to sneak out of the closet, but Mom was sitting at her vanity and noticed me trying to hide the skirt. "I guess you can keep that. It's no longer my style, but stay out of my closet, Christie."

"Whatever you say, Mom," I assured her and headed back to my room.

I paired the skirt with a short sleeve black t-shirt, and black ankle boots. Leaving the outfit displayed on my bed, I went to the kitchen to help Mom finish dinner and then clean-up. Plus, I had some homework I needed to take a look over.

At around nine, I got dressed, touched up my make-up and hair, then headed to the car to go meet up with Shane. Mom was so excited about the dance, she didn't question me when I walked out the door. I pushed the guilt aside. Lying to her had become such a necessity over the years but I hated doing it every time.

I pulled into Shane's parking lot and grabbed the leather jacket he had lent me earlier. Slipping my arms in it, I climbed out of the car and looked around. Shane's car wasn't in the parking lot, so I went inside and up to his apartment.

With a shaking hand, I pulled his key out of my black Chanel bag and opened the door. It felt weird and right at the same time. When I opened the door, there was a giant bouquet of pink roses with a card.

Hey,

I need to get to the race early. Emma's coming to get you. Be downstairs at 9:45. See you soon.

S

P.S. I know I could have texted you this, but I like the idea of you walking around my apartment.

I smiled and smelled the flowers. They were as fresh as they were beautiful. "Very smooth," I whispered to myself as I took my phone out to text him that I got the message and I'd wait for Emma.

My phone said it was 9:40, so I headed downstairs to wait. Once I got out of the elevator, I got an alert that a text had come in. It was Shane.

Shane: What, no thank u.

I smiled, imagining him feigning wounded and hurt.

Christie: I figured I'd thank u l8r.

I looked up and saw Emma's Corvette. She

skidded to a stop in front of me and I slipped my phone back into my purse.

"Hey girl, ready for a new race?" Emma asked when I climbed into the car.

"Yeah, I'm excited. Are you racing today?" I was wondering why she didn't need to be at the race early.

"No, I had a class project so I wasn't able to get my car ready in time," she said and pulled out of the lot.

"Where do you go?"

"Same as you and Shane. Elton Hall."

"Oh, sorry. I haven't seen you there." I quickly thought back, scouring my brain to think of a time I might have seen her, but I came up empty.

"I mostly go at night. I have to work during the week to pay for tuition."

"What are you studying?"

"Law. I'm going to be a kickass lawyer one day."

"I believe it." And I did. She had that confident and formidable air that screamed lawyer. "Is that why you race? For some extra cash."

"At first. But it became my release. I work in a law firm as a secretary. My grandmother knew someone and helped me get the job. I'm there forty hours a week, and then in class four days a week right after it. It's hard, and sometimes I just need a break from it all. Nothing beats the rush you feel when you race. Now, I race for enough money to race next week and get my fix."

"I like that. Shane let me ride his bike today and I felt the same thing. Well, something like it."

"It's even better when you drive."

"Oh, I was driving."

Emma turned and looked at me, mouth agape and eyes slowly blinking. "He let you drive? Have you been on a bike before?"

"Well, I've ridden with Shane, but it was my first time taking control."

"That's a really big deal."

"It was just for, like, an hour or so. It's not like he gave me the bike," I told her, confused why she was making a big deal about this.

"I think the fact that you don't get it explains just how big of a deal it is. Bikes aren't like a car. You don't just let anyone ride. There has to be like a stupid amount of trust for Shane to put his life on the line and let you drive. An inexperienced rider could be really dangerous."

"I never thought about it that way," I said and stared out the window. I guess he *did* trust me. I was just walking around his apartment with a key. But then again, I trusted him. I'm not even sure why. We haven't known each other for that long, but something deep in my gut said that Shane was worth it. This thing between us, was worth it.

I decided not to explain that to Emma. It wouldn't come out right, especially after I had just mentioned my ex to her. Besides, she may tell Shane before I had the chance to and that seemed wrong.

We were quiet for the rest of the way and Emma pulled into a makeshift spot near the line of other spectators. Shane was leaning under the hood of his car, his glorious ass high in the air. I smiled. He was the sexiest when he wasn't trying to show off. But he was the cutest when he did.

Emma started to walk away, but I quickly followed after her. "Wait, are you planning to go to Homecoming next week? I know it's a Saturday, so you may be here, but my friend Annabelle and I are going to get ready at my house, and I thought it'd be fun if you came too."

She smiled at me and looked down at her feet. "Um, actually, I've never been to a dance, so I don't think it's for me."

"Oh, come on! I didn't get to go to prom either, and I missed last year's Homecoming because my boyfriend couldn't make it back in time. So it's my first dance too. It's gonna be a lot of fun, and if it sucks, you can just leave. I'm gonna ask Shane to go with me, so you'll know us. There are no rules about who you can bring, so pick a date and come."

She kicked the dirt with her boots and looked around. "Deal, but I don't think I'm gonna bring a date. I'd much rather come and dance with everyone else's."

We laughed and exchanged numbers.

I walked over to Shane and grabbed a handful of ass, surprising him.

"I hope that's Christie, because if it's Max, it might be bad for the other racers to see me offering you sexual favors."

"Well, I guess it's good that it's me."

He slid out from under the hood and looked me over. "You look beautiful. Much better than last week."

"I don't know," I said as he gave me a kiss on

the cheek. "The sweatpants were really comfortable."

"You looked good in them too. Did you guys get here all right? Did Emma's car break down again?"

"No, we were fine. Just talking about some things."

"That can't be good," he said, and ran his hands through his hair.

"It's not a big deal. We were talking about Homecoming. It's next Saturday, so I'm not gonna be able to come to the race. Well, I probably can, but I may be a little late."

"Oh yeah."

"Yeah, and I was hoping you might be able to talk to Max about racing later in the night because I'd like you to come with me, if that's okay."

"Will this count as dancing all night in a club?" he asked, reciting one of the things off my list.

"Since I don't have a fake ID yet, and all the clubs in this area are for people over 21, then, yeah, I say it counts."

"I promised you I'd make your list happen, so I guess I gotta go." He gave me a chaste kiss on the lips and winked as he pulled away.

"Great, Emma is gonna come too, but like not in a threesome kind of way, just in a tag along kind of way."

"That's a shame," he said, and I hit his arm.

"Shut up." I gave him another hit for good measure and then continued. "I thought she'd bring Frank, but she said she wanted to go solo."

"Yeah, I heard things were a little rocky with Frank," Shane told me as he draped his arm around my shoulder and steered me over to Max's van.

"Did he do something? What happened?"

"Oh, that's right. You don't know Emma. She doesn't really date long term. It's mostly they hook up for a few weeks and then she moves on. Frank was just her latest victim."

"Well, at least she has fun."

Shane and Max talked for a bit while I looked around at all the racers. Chuck and Heather seemed to be fighting again, and Newbie Troy was talking smack with a couple other drivers I didn't know. Then, I heard it. It was the unmistakable sound of a slap. Heather was on the ground and I rushed over to her.

"Leave her the fuck alone," I yelled at Chuck as I dropped to the ground to check on Heather's rapidly swelling eye.

"Stay out of this, bitch. You don't know what you're dealing with." He raised his hand at me and I closed my eyes, bracing myself for the impact, but it never came.

I opened my eyes and looked up to see Shane standing over Chuck, who was holding his bleeding nose. "You okay?" he asked, holding his hand out to help me up.

"Yeah, I'm fine." I then supported a dazed Heather, helping her to her feet beside me.

"Good. Chuck, I think you should probably head home for a while," Shane ordered. "How about we get to racing?" Shane looked around at everyone, then glared at Chuck still on the ground.

Frank and Max walked over to Chuck with nasty looks, hopefully signaling that he wasn't welcome.

He took my hand and hurried me away. "Are you crazy? What the hell were you doing jumping in the middle of that? He could have done something to you too. This isn't his first time acting out against his girl."

"And what, you guys all stand there? Big tough men, you are." I glared at him, furious at the wimp he'd proven to be. I thought he was better than that. Hell, I *wanted* him to be better than that.

Shane grabbed my arm, pulling me close. "Do you know why I was there to block that prick from hitting you? I was coming to help her too. Don't insult me, thinking I'd be okay with a man treating a woman like that."

I exhaled a sigh of relief. "You're right, I'm sorry." I rearranged my face so it wasn't so irate and then looked over at Heather. She was with Emma, crying on her shoulder, and the rage came back. "But why does he keep coming back then? You guys let him do this and then race?"

"Look, it's not that simple. I don't make the rules in this world. Max only sees dollar signs, and Chuck bets big, and usually loses even bigger. The world isn't perfect. What do you want me to do?"

I looked at the pain in his eyes, and then at my feet. I shouldn't have assumed that Shane would let something like this slide. He had a good heart. But this asshole needed a lesson. "Go tell Max you're gonna race him tonight. If he loses, he can't come back."

Shane smiled big and gave me a kiss. "You always surprise me. For a bet like that, he's gonna want some big cash. Let me see if I can borrow some from a couple guys. I definitely didn't bring enough."

I grabbed my purse and pulled out a wad of a thousand dollars. "I wanted to do some betting, so I went to the bank. Race with that."

"That's very sweet, but I'm not taking your money." He turned around and started to walk toward Max. I grabbed his arm and stopped him.

"I want him gone. He's gonna hit a woman, I'm gonna take something he loves away." I stood firm, the money in my hand, and my eyes burning a hole through Shane. It felt important for me to be a part of this. I wanted to show Heather I stood up for her. People were willing to fight for her.

Shane took the money wad out of my hand and kissed me again. "Don't worry, I'll be handing this, and a lot more, back to you after I kick his ass."

"You'd better. I want to keep betting."

Chapter 13

Shane and Chuck were going to race first while everyone was still hyped up on the drama. I gave Shane a kiss and then a thought hit my mind.

"Why didn't you want to race Chuck last week when he called you out?" Shane had rejected the call out and raced Newbie Troy instead. I thought it was to impress me, but now I wasn't sure. A bad feeling crept through me and I wasn't used to ignoring those.

"Chuck tends to race a little dirty. I didn't want things to get out of hand with you watching me," he said and then stroked my cheek gently.

"What do you mean, he races dirty? Are you trying to tell me I just put you in danger?" I asked and shoved him hard.

"You're not allowed to cross the centerline and Chuck has done it twice in close races, claiming he lost control of the wheel. Both times he was losing by about a fender. He just gets mad and reacts. One of the drivers ended up in the hospital. Chuck clipped the back of his car."

141

"Why the hell wouldn't you tell me this?" I hit him again, feeling dread flow through me. I'd majorly screwed up. By trying to protect Heather, I'd just put Shane in a lot of danger. He never even questioned it. I asked him to do something, and he said yes. I was officially the second worst person here tonight. I covered my face with my hands, afraid to even look at him.

"The other driver was fine, and the guy made it out of the hospital a few days later." He pulled my hands off my face and kissed my knuckles. "See, my plan is just to be so far ahead of Chuck that this isn't even an issue." He smiled and pulled me into a kiss. "It's cute that you're worried."

I growled and backed away from him a little. "See how cute I am if you end up in the hospital," I warned. "

"Will you be wearing a sexy nurse outfit while I heal?"

"No, I'm going to call your mother."

The smile on his face faded instantly. "That's not funny."

"Then don't lose," I told him and I walked off so he could get ready for the race.

***

Shane drove up to the starting line and I held my breath. Max reiterated that if Chuck lost, he'd have to find himself a new place to race. If he won, he'd win three thousand in cash and be the number one on the list. Shane and Chuck agreed, and the flashlight was blinked. The guys took off with a roar of thunder and flames.

My heart pounded as Shane pulled ahead, but he didn't have the lead he was hoping for. Chuck was mere inches behind him and I felt a rush of sheer terror overwhelm me. I could barely watch the rest of it when Emma took my hand. I squeezed hard as we watched Shane cross the finish line first, but just as he did, Chuck clipped the back of his car. My eyes grew wide and I felt pain. Just pain everywhere. It was almost like I was in the accident too.

Shane went spinning out of control with a light pole coming dangerously close to him. I screamed, or at least I think I did, as I couldn't hear anything other than my heart beating rapidly in my ears. I tried to run to the scene, but Emma grabbed me and held me down.

"Don't go. The nitrous in his car could cause a fire or an explosion. The guys will get him," Emma shouted as I fought to get her off me. This only confirmed that I needed to be there.

I elbowed Emma in the face and she let go of me on instinct to grab her nose. I rushed over to where Shane was, but stopped short. He was climbing out of the car through the passenger side. I let out a sigh of relief that he was all right, and then picked up speed to be by his side when his feet hit the ground.

Frank was with him when I caught up. He was standing, but nursing a deep cut on his arm. I opened my purse and grabbed some tissues, pressing them against his forearm.

"Ow, Christie, that hurts," he hissed, cringing.

"Then you shouldn't have crashed!" I replied,

wiping at the tears of relief falling down my cheeks.

"At least I don't have to go to the hospital," he told me, smiling up at me.

"The hell you don't. What if this needs stitches or you have a concussion?"

"Well, we have a sort of doctor here who can stitch up my arm, and I was wearing a helmet, so I should be fine. But if you're concerned, they say that a concussion patient needs to be kept awake for the night. I can think of one or two things we can do during that time."

I laughed and kissed him. "Not even close. I said I wouldn't be your nurse."

Frank cleared his throat. "How about we get this cleaned up for the next race, and you guys finish this later? Besides, Ollie should take a look at that cut. It's pretty gross."

"Agreed," I said and we both helped Shane get up.

Chuck didn't even stop. He just kept driving as if he hadn't caused the accident.

***

Ollie was in medical school and came to race for the same reason as Emma, he was constantly stressed and needed a relief. The racers used him as a doctor, so no one had to explain to an emergency room what happened. If it was mild enough, he took care of it. If not, he usually called a friend at the hospital nearby. Luckily, he wasn't needed most nights.

He was a nice guy and stitched Shane's arm up

pretty quickly. After that, we watched the rest of the races from on top of the hood of one of his friend's cars.

"So, what's going to happen to your car?" I asked him after one of the races.

"One of the guys will tow it to the shop we use and we'll work on it. I probably won't be able to race next week, so we can enjoy the dance."

"Way to look on the bright side," I said, giving him a gentle kiss. "Are you sure you feel all right?"

"If you ask me that again, I'm gonna start lying and tell you I'm dying. I just have some bumps and bruises that will be fine in no time."

"I feel guilty. Maybe I shouldn't have asked you to race."

"Someone shoulda done it a long time ago. You were right, that asshole lost the only thing he loved tonight. It feels good that I got to take it away."

"It's damn sexy too."

"Oh yeah? We could go over to the field. No one will miss us."

"You just got out of a bad car crash and you want sex?"

"At no point will I ever look at you and not want sex. Just assume that if I'm staring in your direction, I'm picturing you naked. It's pretty much a guarantee that if I even so much as glance at you, I'm thinking of all the dirty things I'd like to do to you. And if I dare to gaze at you from afar, I'm remembering all the things you did to me the last time I had you."

"Holy shit." I grabbed his hand and we climbed off the car. "I guess since you got in a car accident,

I'll be doing all the work."

"It'd be a nice change."

"Shut up."

***

Shane and I spent Sunday on the couch watching television. He didn't want to admit it, but he I knew he was sore all over. He kept covering his groans with laughter and jokes, but he couldn't hide it from his eyes.

I made us food, and helped him take a shower without getting his stitches wet. I did everything but what I really wanted to do. He kept insisting he felt fine and we could mess around, he even tried to start something once, but I ended that when I noticed how fast his breathing was coming. Shane finally admitted that it hurt to breathe.

I tried to stay over Sunday, but Shane insisted he would be fine. "Listen, we both know your mom would freak out if you stayed out another night. Just go home and I'll get some sleep. If I need you, I'll call."

"But what if something happens while I'm gone?"

"Like what? I'm just sore. Nothing is going to change, and if it does, I'll just call Emma. She lives two blocks over and can get here fast."

"I'm going to text her to make sure she knows that she's gonna be on call, since I know you won't tell her. Then I'll stop by in the morning before class."

"See? You *are* nursing me back to health. I knew

you were full of shit."

"Don't make me call your mother to check on you."

"I'll be fine. Don't worry so much about it. I will call Emma if I need to and I'll see you in the morning." He gave me a kiss and reluctantly walked me to the door.

"Wait, your key," I said and extended it to him.

"Nah, you keep it. I might need you to come in and take care of me again. It'll help if I end up bedridden after all of this."

I rolled my eyes and headed out, nervous I had to explain to Annabelle why I bailed on decorations. That actually might be more dangerous than getting home after ten.

***

The week went by pretty quickly. Shane skipped two days of classes while he was recovering from the accident, so I only saw him when I stopped by in the morning and the afternoon. When he was back up and running, I didn't have a spare second to stop by his place. Annabelle had me on strict decorating duty, especially on Thursday and Friday. As I missed last weekend, I was happy to help.

She loved the decorations my mom found in the attic, but that didn't mean she was anywhere near ready. I was working on elaborate centerpieces Friday when we heard a familiar voice.

"What's up, sluts?" Violet called as she walked into the EET classroom where we were working on decorations.

"Hey!" Annabelle and I screamed, running over to hug her.

Violet was in town for a long weekend. She and Annabelle were crashing at my house tonight and then she was heading to see her parents after Homecoming.

"How was your flight?" Annabelle asked when we were done hugging.

"It was good, but walking away from David at the airport was rough."

"Oh, you won't miss him. We'll keep you plenty distracted today and tomorrow. Besides, the carnival is supposed to be amazing," I assured her.

"Yeah, I'm glad to have a lot to do. I missed you guys," she said and pulled Annabelle and I into another hug.

"What about me? Am I chopped liver?" Jason asked from outside the circle of hugs.

Violet let go of us and jumped into his arms. "I missed you too!"

"Nice to see you back, Vi."

"So, let's get back to the decorations," Annabelle ordered once the hugging had finally stopped.

"What do you want me to do?" Violet asked Annabelle.

Annabelle's eyes went a little wide and she looked around at all of her beautiful things. "Why don't you relax? You've had a long flight."

"Is that code for 'don't touch anything because I'm afraid you'll mess it up'?" Violet accused her.

"Yes, but I say it with love. Christie is working on the centerpieces, you can help her. You don't need to be able to cut in a straight line to do that."

Violet looked at me and smiled, walking over to the table where I was trying to arrange orange and gold flowers with brown leaves.

"Christie, is it me, or is she being a little bitchy?"

"A little bit, she's been snapping at people all day. I think Jason is gonna get PTSD or something before the day is out. She's probably stressed out or PMSing."

"Hopefully it stops before the sleepover. So, tell me about Shane."

I started to explain to Violet when Annabelle walked over to us. "Wait, who is Shane?"

I'd never told her about him. I started to explain everything at the beginning, but her face grew more and more grave.

"Why haven't you mentioned any of this to me? You just said you needed to get out of the house and you wanted some decoration pictures. You should have told me about Shane." Tears started to trickle down Annabelle's face and she rushed to the bathroom.

"Was she crying?" Violet asked, looking at me seriously. "She doesn't cry." Then she looked around and stalked up to Jason. "Excuse me, step away." The three of us walked away from the other volunteers and Violet looked at him expectantly. "What the hell is up with Annabelle? She just started crying because Christie didn't mention a piece of gossip."

"I don't know. She's been crying at the drop of a hat lately. I told her she looked pretty this morning and she started crying. I've just been chalking it all up to stress."

Violet and I looked at each other and instantly knew it wasn't stress. We ran full speed to the bathroom and found her bawling on the floor of one of the stalls.

"Oh, honey," I said, crawling under the stall and pulling her into a hug. "I just didn't know how to tell you. I knew you'd be a little judgmental about the fact that I was starting something with a guy and like jumping into bed with him quickly."

"I would have judged you a bit, but I would be happy that you've moved on," she managed to say in between sobs. "Why are you keeping things from me?"

"I won't. I'll tell you everything about Shane, but I think there's something else we need to talk about first." I unlocked the stall door and Violet stood at the opening. We dragged Annabelle out and she leaned against the sink, trying to get her breathing under control.

"When was the last time you got your period?" Violet asked her gently.

"I'm late," she confessed hesitantly. "One weeks late."

Violet and I looked at each other and nodded. It was what we suspected.

I handed her some toilet paper and brushed some of her hair out of her face. "Have you taken a test yet?"

"No, I've been afraid of what it would say. What if I'm pregnant?"

"Then we'll worry about it then. You need to take a test and then we'll figure out what you want to do."

"I'm Catholic, there is only one option. I have to drop out of school, hope my mother doesn't kill me, and raise the baby."

"Hold on. There are other options. You could put the baby up for adoption, you can take classes at night, and work during the day. A baby doesn't mean your world is over," I insisted.

"And what about Jason? You need to talk to him," Violet reminded her gently.

"I don't want to. What if he leaves me? Or worse, what if he proposes because it's 'the right thing to do'?" she said with air quotes.

"Okay, I think we all need to take a step back. I'm gonna go get a test, because we all know I can't help with the decorations, and you can take it tonight at Christie's house. It will help to have some peace of mind before tomorrow."

Annabelle nodded her head slowly and Violet pulled her into another hug.

"When this is dealt with and you're fine, because that's how I think it will turn out, we're putting your ass on birth control," I told her and we headed back to the classroom while Violet went to the convenience store.

Jason questioned us a couple of times but we brushed him off for now. The poor guy looked heartbroken and helpless. It was almost painful to see how much he cared for her and how much this was eating him up.

I told Annabelle and Violet, when she got back, all about Shane. Violet was excited, while Annabelle stayed quiet. She insisted that she was happy for me, but I knew she truly wouldn't be until she found out if she were pregnant. We finished the decorations about an hour later and said goodbye to Jason. I promised him we'd take care of Annabelle and see him at the carnival tomorrow. Reluctantly, he agreed and headed out. Then everyone piled into my car and we headed to my house.

It was after nine, but Mom was a force to be reckoned with, as usual. She had made us an array of snacks, had facial treatments arranged on the coffee table, and foot massagers in front of the kitchen table chairs.

"Welcome to the Homecoming spa!" she cheered when we walked in the door.

I forced a smile on my face, reminding myself she didn't know about our little dilemma.

"Mom, this looks great. We're just going to drop off our stuff in my room, and we'll be down in a few minutes."

"Great, I'll get the footbaths ready for you." She scurried off and I brought the girls to my room.

"So, my friend Emma is coming over tomorrow to get ready. I invited her tonight, but she couldn't come," I said, stalling because my mother had like a bionic ear or something and could hear whatever I said in my bedroom as long as the door was open. We all made it inside and I quickly closed the door. "Okay, she can't hear us now."

Violet handed Annabelle the bag with the test in it and I opened the door to my private bathroom.

"Don't just stand out here and listen to me pee. Turn the TV on or listen to some music."

We agreed, and I turned some music on my phone.

"So, is Shane okay after the accident?" Violet asked, trying to keep the subject off Annabelle.

"Yeah, I checked on him today, but he wasn't in his apartment. I found him at his friend's garage underneath his car. He promised me he'd be ready to go to the dance tomorrow and ready to race next week."

"Well, that's good. I'm excited to meet him."

"Me too, and a little nervous. He's kind of an asshole at first. I just hope you guys give him a chance before you write him off for a jerk."

"No, he sounds like he treats you well. That's all I care about. Well, that and I hope he's good in bed."

"Girlllll, he is!" We laughed until the bathroom door opened. Annabelle was standing there, holding the stick. "Don't throw that around. It has pee on it," I told her, trying to lighten the mood.

She walked back into the bathroom and placed it upside down on the sink. We followed her in there and Violet set a timer on her phone. "No matter what this says," Violet told Annabelle, "you need to take the second test tomorrow. That's why they sell them in a two pack."

The alarm sounded, telling us it was time to check the stick. Annabelle reached out to grab it with a shaky hand and then quickly pulled her arm back.

"Someone else check, I can't look."

I reached out quickly and flipped it over. The electronic reading said "not pregnant."

Annabelle fell to the floor in a fit of laughter and tears. I tossed the stick into the trash, making sure to cover it with some tissues. I made a mental note to take the trash out to the dumpster tonight in case my mom decided to take the trash out.

"Now, you have to stop being overly emotional. Your excuse just went out the window," I told her.

"Done, I'm going to be a freakin' ray of sunshine from now on."

"Uh, guys? Annabelle you need to take the test in the morning too. Pregnancy hormones are more dominant in the morning. We may not be out of the woods just yet," Violet stated.

"Yes, I know. But I feel like it almost doesn't matter. It says 'not pregnant.' The one tomorrow is basically just confirming what we already know. I'll take it for you, but I'm feeling pretty confident."

Not wanting to burst her bubble, I agreed that she should be fine, but that we should take the test again just to be sure. Then we headed out to begin our spa treatment, all in a much better mood.

Chapter 14

We woke up early the next day and forced Annabelle into the bathroom to take the test. This time, she didn't drag us in after her, and came out a couple minutes later with a big smile on her face. We're all good.

We got ready and then rushed back to the school for the carnival. There was no drama. Everything was on time and everyone appeared to be having a lot of fun. We rode all of the spinning rides and chowed down on cotton candy and popcorn. It was a good time, but we only got to enjoy about half of it. About two hours into the carnival, Annabelle dragged us all to the gymnasium to set up the decorations that we've been working tirelessly on.

I set up all of my mom's trinkets, including the Eiffel Tower lamp, a few picture frames, and the dramatic curtains as part of a backdrop for pictures. The centerpieces all looked amazing, and I was glad that Violet only tried to help with one of the extras we had made. Annabelle might not have been all that bitchy when she told Violet not to touch the decorations. She was not crafty in the slightest but she always meant well.

Once we were all done, the gym looked amazing, and I quickly snapped some photos to show my mom. She'd be pleased to know that she had helped create this beautiful world.

We hopped back in my car and headed to my house to get ready. At least I thought we were headed to my house. When we walked in, it looked more like a beauty parlor.

"Surprise!" my mom screamed when the three of us walked in. There were two people Mom introduced as hairstylists, two manicurists, and one make-up artist. "I wanted to treat you girls. I know how hard you have all been working on the dance and I wanted you to look beautiful."

I smiled and gave her a quick hug. She always went over the top, but it always came from a good place. Judging from the look of awe on my friends' faces, I could tell they were impressed, and I was thrilled. This was going to be perfect, and Shane would be shocked when he saw just how good I looked.

We walked over to the hairstylists and started discussing looks. I was about to sit at the table and start my hair when Emma texted me. She was here.

"Mom, my other friend is here. I'm gonna go get her."

I headed outside and waved at Emma as she climbed out of her Corvette. Instead of fuchsia hair, she was rocking bright red hair.

"Hey, girl!" she called, opening her passenger side door to get her dress. She held it up to me. It was a short dress with a sweetheart neckline and a puffy tulle skirt. The red bodice had black studs and rhinestones all over it and the skirt was a layer of black tulle over a layer of red. It was vampy, sexy, and I loved it.

"That dress is amazing."

"Just call me 'Miss Steal Your Man,'" she teased as she walked up the front steps.

"Eh, you can take Shane."

"Not a chance in hell. That pretty boy can't handle me. Looks like you'll just have to find a way to please him."

"I'm sure I can manage something." Before we walked inside, I stopped Emma. She had no idea what kind of crazy she was about to walk into. "Okay, a word of warning. My mom likes to go above and beyond. She hired people to do our nails, hair, and make-up. I hope my prissy world doesn't freak you out."

"No, I'm excited. I've never had any of that stuff done professionally. As long as I don't look like a Disney Princess, I'm down."

We walked into the house and the primping began full force.

Mom walked around with virgin margaritas, topping everyone off when they were getting close to done. I followed behind her with a flask of tequila and dropped some in everyone's cup…well, not Annabelle's. She'd insisted she was done drinking anything I mixed her after the snow day last semester. I'm pretty sure Mom was aware of what I was doing, but she didn't say anything.

When my hair was done, half pulled up in a

messy knot on my head and the rest in big beautiful curls, I went to my bathroom before I had to sit any longer. While I was in there, the pregnancy test in the trash caught my eye. I don't know what possessed me to do it, but I just had to know. Annabelle almost never drank anyway, but I thought a drop or two of tequila would loosen her up. After all, she had drank with us before. Now, she had rejected even the smallest drop.

I grabbed some toilet paper and lifted it up. This test said 'pregnant.'

My heart fell in my chest and I panicked a little. What if going on all those rides had damaged the baby? What if all the walking around and stress from the decorations had put too much pressure on Annabelle? What if the test from yesterday was the mistake? I needed to talk to Violet.

I walked back outside and saw Violet. I waved at her a couple of times before she finally looked up at me. I motioned for her to follow me and she quickly made an excuse, blowing on her fingernails as she headed over.

"What's wrong?" she asked as I pulled her into my room.

"Annabelle's test from this morning said pregnant."

"Shit."

"She needs to see a doctor. Obviously, one of these is wrong," I groaned and chucked the test back in the trash. "Why wouldn't she tell us?"

"You know Annabelle. She's been working on Homecoming for, like, three months straight. She probably didn't want to ruin the day."

"That makes sense. Well, you know her a little better than me. What do you say we do?"

"Let's let her have tonight. She deserves it, and we can call her out tomorrow before I head to my parents'. I can stay an extra day here if I have to."

"No, you must miss your parents. I'll take care of whatever it is after she goes to see someone tomorrow. One of the urgent care centers can probably help her out."

"All right, but I'm only three hours away if she has a break down or something."

"Thanks, babe. All right, let's finish getting ready. If she is pregnant, this is probably our last big night out together."

Violet agreed and we pushed the pregnancy from our minds, trying to just enjoy our time together.

I'd told Shane that I'd meet him at the dance. I claimed it was because we were having a girls' day, but I didn't know how my family would react. It didn't bother me, but Shane was Korean, and my parents had always imagined me with a white guy. Not to mention, growing up in the south had made my mom a little, well, she wasn't always the most open when it came to considering other races. I didn't want them ruining our night. I probably wasn't giving them enough credit, but I didn't want to take a chance. Shane was a good guy, but he was also a badass street racer. Actually, now that I thought about it, that was probably the bigger problem.

We appeased my mother and smiled for a couple dozen pictures. Emma with her sleek straight hair and smoky make-up, Annabelle with her simple but sweet updo and natural make-up, Violet with her elaborate side bun and bright make-up, and me with my classic curls and expertly contoured make-up. We all looked good.

Mom ushered us all outside to take some pictures by her perfect flower garden when a limo pulled up.

"Mom, you didn't have to get us a limo. The car would've been fine," I insisted.

"It wasn't me, darlin', but I'm a little embarrassed I didn't think about it."

"It was me," Emma piped up. "You were all so nice to have me over that I wanted to do something in return."

"Well, aren't you just the sweetest thing," Mom cooed at her. "Don't waste time, go stand by the limo so I can get some pictures.

"Mom, we need to go."

"Christie, smilin' for a few photos isn't going to make you late. But arguing with me about it will." She shooed us the limo and we smiled as she took more photos with her cell phone. "Okay, you all have a good time tonight. Christie, please be home around eleven."

"Oh, Mom, I'm staying with Annabelle tonight."

"I don't think so. Annabelle needs some time with her boyfriend. You just come on home after the dance."

"Well, is it okay if she stays at my house?" Emma asked. "I feel like I missed out on some girl time last night."

My mom looked at her with a softened expression and agreed. I had brought my bag outside and left it by the door, so I rushed in my high neutral colored heels to grab it and dropped it off in Emma's car.

Everyone else had already climbed in the limo, so it was just me. Mom gave me a quick air kiss so as not to mess up my make-up and I opened the door. It took everything within me not to scream and alert her. Sitting in the limo was Shane.

I smiled at him and slid onto the seat, quickly closing the door behind me.

"What are you doing here?" I asked him, taking in his black suit and emerald tie. He was breathtakingly handsome and I was overwhelmed just looking at him. Then he leaned in and gave me a soft kiss on my neck, again so as not to mess with my make-up. He really was perfect.

"I don't get a thank you for renting this limo for you? I have a good mind to go tell your mother that she raised you without manners." He made a go to open the door and I shouted for the driver to go.

"I didn't expect you to be here. Emma said she got the limo."

"Yeah, Shane told me he was doing this in advance. I was prepared," Emma piped in. "You're also not staying at my house, either."

"Okay, well, that part I figured out." I turned to Shane and make-up be damned, I gave him a big kiss. As I pulled away, I wiped the lipstick off him and leaned into him, inhaling his new cologne. He smelled like springtime. I didn't know how else to describe it. It was nice, but at the same time, there was something about the leather, car, grease, and fumes smell I'd grown accustomed to. I mean, I guess this was his other side.

"You look amazing," he whispered in my ear as everyone else talked.

"So do you. I'm very impressed with the suit."

"Well, I contemplated my leather jacket and jeans, but I figured I didn't want to make all the other guys jealous, so I had to put the suit on."

I rolled my eyes and looked over at Violet and Annabelle, who were chomping at the bit. For a second, I forgot there were other people in the limo.

"Shane, this is Violet. She's the one that's been in England, and this is Annabelle."

"Hello, ladies."

"Thanks for the limo. It's the first time I've ever been in one," Violet told him. She started pushing buttons all over, raising the partition between us and the driver over and over again.

"Right, and Christie, I love that dress," Annabelle offered. "You look like Paris Barbie."

I smiled at her, until I felt Shane trying to hold in some laughter.

"Paris Barbie?" he asked in my ear.

"Annabelle thinks that I have an outfit for everything, kind of like Barbie."

"Does that make me Ken?"

"Nah, Ken didn't have a penis," I purred under my breath and squeezed his leg.

"Then I guess I'm a G.I. Joe." We smiled at each other but then the music started blaring.

Apparently, Violet found the radio button. Some pop song was now blasting around us so loudly we couldn't hear each other complaining about it. At first it was a shock, but then everyone started dancing. Well, everyone else did. I sort of bobbed

162

my head, hoping I was kind of in time with the music.

We finally pulled up to the school and the driver got out to open the limo door for us. Shane tipped him and we headed into the dance.

"You really didn't have to do that," I whispered to Shane as we walked into the gym.

"Just accept that I like doing these things. All you're doing is ruining my fun by questioning it."

"Well, I wouldn't want to ruin your fun."

"Exactly, now let's get this dance thing over with."

"Wait," I called, grabbing his arm as he started walking to a table. "I want to get some pictures."

"So you want to remember our night together?" He raised his eyebrows at me and smiled.

"I look good. I need to remember that." I started to walk over to the backdrop but Shane grabbed my arm and spun me around into him. Surprisingly, I didn't fall over.

"Trust me, I definitely cannot forget how good you look in that dress." He looked deep in my eyes and we stood there for a second longer. "All right, where do we take the pictures?"

I dragged Shane over to the backdrop and we started posing, but every time I looked at Shane he made a face. I slapped him on the arm and glared at him. "If you don't smile or look the slightest bit happy, I can promise you that I will find a different guy to go home with."

A flash of something in his eyes caught my attention but he quickly masked it with a painted on smile.

"You've got ten seconds of genuine smiles before my face cracks...ready, go." Shane looked at the camera and smiled. For a moment, it took my breath away and I forgot to smile back. God, he was sexy in a suit.

Then I turned to the camera and smiled big, happy to finally get my cheesy prom picture.

"Are you happy now?" Shane asked me as we headed to the table my friends had commandeered.

"Yes, I am." I kissed him on the lips and settled down.

We had some of the snacks that Annabelle had spent hours deciding over, and then everyone insisted it was time to dance. Emma almost ran to the dance floor and started gyrating with enough enthusiasm and skill to make me, and any other girl looking, feel inferior. Violet ran after her, finding her friend Kyle, and then Annabelle and Jason moseyed on over to the dance floor, doing their own subdued version of dancing. Then, there were two.

"Didn't your list say you needed to dance? Why are you still sitting there?" He stood and extended his hand to me.

"I'm really not a good dancer," I muttered, taking his hand cautiously.

"Who cares? Is there someone here you're trying to impress? Another guy you're looking to take home, maybe?"

"No, I just, I don't want to look ridiculous."

"Well, you probably are going to look ridiculous, but everyone here is so focused on how they look dancing, that they aren't going to care how you look. And if they do care, it's just that they're jealous of how amazing you look."

"Just don't let me fall," I told him and we walked onto the dance floor near my friends.

Shane pulled my hips close to him and settled his hands there, as I leaned my back against his chest, still a little afraid to move. He picked up on it and started to force my hips in a little circle. Gradually, the circle increased and I started to let loose a little. We danced liked that, awkwardly circling with each other before Shane walked away. He held up a finger, signaling one minute, and I stood there for a few seconds, not moving, not dancing, and definitely not okay.

Emma came to my rescue. She grabbed my hands and started to lift them up to the beat of the music.

"Spread your legs a little and move your hips," she shouted over the music.

I listened and closed my eyes, trying to find some kind of rhythm. But it was not really working. I opened my eyes again and I saw a fun smile on Emma's face. If I was going to act crazy, it might as well be with her. Tossing my head back, I flipped my hair back and forth, trying hard to get into it. After a few more seconds, it started to come a bit more naturally and I actually began to enjoy myself.

Shane walked back to me as the song ended, and I looked at him, confused. Then, I heard the beginning of a familiar song. He smiled big and whispered in my ear, "Come on, Prom Barbie, let's dance." The "Barbie Girl" song by Aqua blared through the speakers and Shane spun me around.

"You requested this?"

"Yeah, I had to drop a couple dollars. Apparently this isn't a normal dance song. Now get going, you have no other choice. It's your song," he told me and started to spin me more.

I pushed all sense of doubt away and quickly fell into what I considered to be my best moves. I shook my hips, bobbed my head, flipped my hair, and spun whenever Shane reached for my hand. When the song ended and some rap song I'd never heard started, I didn't revert to the self-conscious girl that I was before. Instead, I continued dancing, relishing being in Shane's arms.

But all good things must come to an end, and the ladies' bathroom called the four of us. I left Shane, who quickly headed to our table, and followed my friends to the bathroom. We were laughing until, all of a sudden, Violet was on the floor.

"What the hell?" I wondered if she'd been sneaking drinks or something. It would be quite rude if she didn't even try to share.

She reached down to her ankle and I saw what happened. Her heel had broken off. "Well," she groaned. "I guess I can go barefoot the rest of the night. Half the girls in there have already taken their shoes off."

"Ew, don't be so dramatic," Annabelle chastised. "I have super glue upstairs in the EET office. Let's just run up there and fix the shoe. You'll be fine."

"Nice," Violet responded, and we all started to go upstairs. "You all don't have to come up," she told Emma and me.

"It's all right," I replied, a little too happy to be away from the dance.

166

"Yeah, I need to cool off," Emma added.

"Considering you've gone through, like, five different dance partners, I don't blame you," I teased, lightly elbowing her.

"Hey, it's time for me to find a new man. I gotta keep my options open."

We talked for a little longer and Annabelle fixed Violet's shoe. Then we all ran to the bathroom, realizing we shouldn't have skipped that step to reattach the heel. By the time we were heading back to the dance, we'd been gone for a while. Shane was probably getting antsy, so I started rushing, well, moving fast, but not fast enough to sweat. Okay, maybe I glistened a little bit.

I was about to walk into the gym when I heard my name called.

"Christie?"

I whipped around and saw a sex on a stick man staring at me. His blond hair was cropped short and his brown eyes shown bright. But it was his suit that took my breath away. His shoulders were broad and filled out the jacket, his long legs were muscular, and the hem was perfectly tailored. This guy came from money and probably lived in the same world that Mindy and I came from.

"Uh, yeah?" I replied.

"Jeff," he offered. "You're in Professor McMann's statistics class, right?" he asked me, strutting to my side.

"Yeah, you sit toward the back, right?" It dawned on me as I stopped looking at his taut chest and actually looked at his face.

"Right." He smiled at me. "Anyway, McMann

told me about the internship and mentioned that you were up for it too. I just wanted to say good luck." He extended his hand to me so I shook it, smiling up at him. "Can I escort you back to the dance?"

"Sure, but I have a date in there."

"All the pretty girls are always taken. No worries, we can still walk together." We headed back into the gym together, talking about the project and our plans for it. There probably should have been some competition, but it was actually nice to get into it with him. Besides, we had picked two completely different topics.

He said goodbye and walked off. I started toward our table and saw Shane sitting there with some girl. She was Asian, beautiful, and skinnier than me. Naturally, I hated her. I stopped walking and watched as they stood, her short dress falling way too high on her thighs, and Shane definitely noticed as he watched her ass swish back and forth while she glided over to the dance floor. He grabbed her hips and ground against her like he had done with me. She leaned her head back and rested it on his shoulder, pushing her boobs out further than the push up bra she was clearly wearing. She looked way too comfortable in his arms.

My jaw clenched and I fought the urge to rip her hair out. Then I shook my head, trying to get a grip. It wasn't her fault that Shane's hands were all over her. No, that asshat was holding her on his own. My rage shifted to him and my eyes felt like they were going to bulge out of my head.

"What's up? Why aren't you dancing?" Emma asked me. I didn't even hear her walk up to me.

"Oh, not much, just trying to decide what's the best way to kill Shane." I pointed at him dancing and she followed my finger.

"Ah, that's the ex I was telling you about at the race."

"And, what? I was just the rebound chick until she was ready?" My voice was raising in octaves and I was getting more upset with each beat of the music they shimmied to.

"I think we need to take a step back, here. They're just dancing. Let's just relax a second." Emma grabbed my hand and pulled me to the table. "Wait for the song to end and see what happens. Maybe they wanted to have a dance for old times."

"You know that flask you have strapped to your thigh that you've been subtly adding to your drink all night, thinking no one would notice? I'd like some." Like I thought earlier, it was rude not to share.

Emma laughed and shook her head. "Yeah, alcohol is not gonna make this better. Just relax a second." She said 'relax,' but I saw her leg shaking and her fingers drummed on the table.

I sat there for another couple of seconds and then decided to screw it all. I walked over to where Jeff was sitting with his friends. Emma tried to grab my arm, but I kept moving with a purpose. "Wanna dance?" I asked him quickly, before I could lose my nerve.

He smiled up at me and stood quickly. "Sounds good." Jeff grabbed my hand and we went over to the dance floor.

I tried to quickly find the rhythm again, but it

wasn't as easy as it had been earlier. Jeff seemed to be fighting with my hips, trying to force them to grind on him as opposed to dancing with the music. It was quite possibly the furthest thing from sexy I'd ever felt, but I kept trying, determined not to look over at Shane.

The song shifted to a slower number and Jeff spun my hips around so I was facing him. He pulled me close to him and draped his hands a little low on my back. I shifted a bit, and they raised a tad, but then quickly returned to my very lower back. My bare lower back. As I placed my arms on his shoulder, I felt his hands ripped off me.

Shane was standing there, fury in his eyes, and practically foaming at the mouth. I tried not to let his hyper masculine side arouse me, but it was no good. Then, I saw his ex standing behind him, and I remembered I was mad at him.

"Get your hands off her ass!" Shane shouted at Jeff.

"Dude, back off," Jeff insisted, trying to pull me behind him.

"That's my girl you're groping."

"If she was your girl, then why'd she ask me to dance?"

"Because you were dancing with your ex-girlfriend!" I screamed, interrupting the guys.

"Because you were gone for over half an hour with this guy," Shane yelled, pointing at Jeff.

"What? We have a class together. We were just talking about the internship."

"Talking, is that what they call it these days?"

"All right," Jeff interrupted us. "Clearly, you two

have some shit to work out. I'm just gonna go and let you all deal with this. But bro to bro, we were just talking until she asked me to dance." Jeff walked off and left Shane and I glaring at each other.

He didn't say anything and I felt heat rising up my cheeks and all over my body. Lots of people were staring. I didn't need to make an ass of myself when I was dancing. I managed to do it just talking.

Shame fell into the pit of my stomach and I stormed out of the gym, ignoring the different people shouting my name as I went by. I kept running, not really sure where I was going but positive my heels weren't going to push me much further. Finally, my legs almost gave out and I collapsed onto a bench outside, heaving and gasping for air.

"Are you done running?"

I turned around and looked at Shane, standing there, barely breathing hard, and it made me even more frustrated. I was dying and he was sexy as ever.

I reached down, taking my heels off, and began walking away fast. My car was still at home and I had no way of getting there, since my purse was in the gym and my cell phone was in it. There was nothing to do but keep walking. Maybe he'd go back to that slut and I could turn around and head back in the dance without having to deal with him.

"Seriously, you're walking around in that beautiful dress and bare feet. Come on, just talk to me, Barbie."

I whipped around and charged him, sticking my

finger in his chest. "No, you don't get to call me that. My friend, Annabelle, calls me that. You are clearly *not* my friend."

"No, I thought I was something more."

"Based on what? The fact that we've slept together? Spent the last couple weeks attached at the hip? I thought that too, and you placed your grubby hands all over the girl who left you. What, does she want you back now? Was I just the girl that kept her spot in your bed warm?"

"Yeah," he screamed. "She does want me back, and instead of bangin' her in the library like she suggested, I'm standing out here arguing with you."

"Well, by all means. Go back and get it on with the love of your life. Don't feel like you have to bring me home just because you brought me here." I was furious, hurt, and embarrassed. I knew the key didn't mean anything deeper than convenience, but here I was, tearing up over some guy. Maybe I should have stayed with Rob. Then at least I knew what I had. "Why were you dancing with her in the first place?"

"I told you, you disappeared and came back with the perfect Ken doll. I thought that…"

"Thought what? I was in the library with him? Didn't you notice that Emma, Annabelle, and Violet were gone too?"

"Yeah, but they came back and you didn't."

"So instead of asking me about it, you just walk off with your ex?"

"She sat down and I was just catching up with her. It was nothing else until I saw your friends come back without you. Then I glance at the door, and you've got pretty boy drooling all over you."

"We were just talking about our project. Then, when I saw you dancing with her, yeah, I grabbed him to make you jealous. It's not like we ever said we were exclusive or anything. I thought maybe you were taking advantage of that."

Shane ran his fingers through his hair and then placed his hands on his hips, looking down at the ground. "Listen, woman, do you want me to walk up to you and hand you a note asking you to check 'yes' or 'no' if you wanted to be my girlfriend? I don't know what else you want from me. You have a key to my apartment, I came to this stupid dance, I spend almost every spare minute I have with you. Actions speak louder than words, but I'm out of actions. Please, be my girlfriend. I want to be exclusive." He dropped down onto his knees and took my hands. "Look at this, I am down on my fucking knees, ruining this expensive suit for you. Don't touch another man, don't even look at another man, just be mine and we can avoid this crap in the future."

I nodded, smiling down at him.

"Happy now?" he asked, standing up and then giving me a kiss.

"Yes. I hated seeing you with that girl. I felt myself getting physically ill and several violent actions flashed through my mind."

"Anything good? How were you going to kill me?"

"I was going to put a dent in your car and watch you shrivel up and die of sadness."

"Ugh," he groaned, wrinkling his face up in

devastation. "You're a cold woman. Let's go back inside." He wrapped an arm around me and started steering me back to the dance. "We can go back to teaching your severely uncoordinated ass how to dance.

"No, I just want to grab my purse and leave. I made such an idiot of myself in there."

"All right," Shane agreed and slipped his jacket off, placing it on my shoulders. "I'll go get your bag and tell everyone that we're heading out to have makeup sex." He winked at me and then began walking to the dance.

"Wait, Emma's car is at my house and my bag is in her car. How's she going to get back? How are *we* getting back?"

"The limo picked me up here, so my car is in the lot. I'm sure Emma will find some guy to give her a ride. If not, maybe Violet can drive her. I'll set it up. Just sit there and don't run off with another guy."

"Yeah, yeah, yeah," I muttered as he kissed my cheek and walked away.

Chapter 15

Shane pulled up to the street near where I was sitting. "Let's go, Barbie," he called.

I stood up and walked over to the car and let myself in. "So are you going to be calling me that from now on?"

"Possibly, I kinda like it."

"Why?"

"Think about it, Barbie can do anything. Yeah, she's pretty and may have an outfit for everything, but she can also do whatever she wants. I believe that about you."

I stared at Shane, shocked and a little in awe. It was a beautiful statement, but the thoughts behind it were even more profound. I leaned in and kissed him, pulling his shirt toward me, unbuttoning it so I could feel the smooth muscles of his chest underneath.

Shane pulled the seat release and pushed it back all the way. I climbed on top of him, straddling him, ducking my head to keep it from hitting the roof of the car. He slid his hands up my skirt, stroking my

175

legs.

"These windows are tinted, right?" I asked, pulling away from Shane for a second.

"Yes…"

"Good." I pulled my straps down, exposing my breasts for him. Shane reached up for them and started to caress my nipples. I moaned loudly and leaned down to kiss him again. Breaking away again for one second, I asked, "You have a condom, right?"

"I'm a race car driver. Car sex is always on my mind." He sat up a bit, reaching for the center console. There was an unopened box sitting there.

"Good to know that even though it's on your mind, you haven't gotten any before now," I teased and kissed him again, running my fingers through his hair, pulling it until Shane let out a groan.

I slid down Shane's body a little and pulled off his belt, frantically undoing the button and zipper. But his boxers were still in the way. Shane lifted his hips, pushing me up in the process, and slid his boxers and pants off. I laughed and grasped ahold of him, feeling how hard he was, enjoying the effect I had on him.

He reached up under my skirt and tried to slip my panties off, but I was in the wrong position for this. I couldn't get them off and I was a little embarrassed.

"See, this is why I normally don't wear them. They get in the way."

Shane kissed me again and then pulled away to reach into the center console again. His hand came out with a knife.

"Shane…" I started to say, a little nervous and maybe more excited than I should be.

"Relax," he insisted and slid my dress up, revealing the lacy tan thong I was wearing. He pulled the band away from my skin and quickly cut it with two different swipes. The panties fell down and I quickly ripped into the condom box, covering Shane as fast as I could. He closed the knife and tossed it back in the center console.

We haven't had sex since the time in the field, and I was craving it like a drug. As he slid inside me, I felt a release flow through my system that was quickly followed by a flowing sensation as my muscles tensed with pleasure. I started riding Shane, holding his arms down so he could do nothing but watch as I ground against him, tilting my hips forward to reach my deepest spot.

Gasps began to force their way out of my mouth as I felt him pulsing inside me, getting ready to find his release. Shane quickly swallowed my moans as he fought my hold and grabbed my head, pulling to a fierce and passionate kiss. But I couldn't hold on. I broke away as the climax hit me hard, feeling Shane following me over the edge. He screamed, a lot louder than me, as we both enjoyed the aftereffects bursting through us.

We sat there for a second, just looking in each other's eyes, almost too caught up to move.

"Did that live up to your expectations?" I asked Shane, biting my lip a little.

"Yes, but I think we need to practice some more. I'm not sure it was our best."

I rolled my eyes and crawled off of him. "Let's

go get my bag before someone comments on the car shaking."

"If you insist."

***

We pulled onto my street and stopped by Emma's car so I could quickly grab my things. She must have been thinking of me because it was unlocked.

"Should I lock her car?" I asked Shane after I grabbed my bag from her backseat.

"Yeah, go ahead. Emma can pick a lock, so if she didn't bring her keys, then she'll be fine."

I smiled and climbed back into his car. "All right, let's go."

Shane took me back to his apartment and we spent the night making up…again. We were sitting at the breakfast bar, enjoying some pancakes, when I got a call from Violet.

"Sorry to interrupt you guys, but I have to go soon and we need to deal with Annabelle."

"Oh, crap. I got really distracted," I said as Shane pulled me onto his lap.

"I would be too. That's one sexy man you've got there."

"Thank you!" Shane screamed.

I shoved him and agreed to come over.

"Do I really need to drive you to see your friends? Can't you stay with me?" he asked, nuzzling my neck before giving it a little nip.

"Yeah, we have to deal with something," I told him, extending my neck to give him more access.

"Is everything all right?" Suddenly his voice was serious and he wasn't teasing me anymore.

"Um, we're not sure yet. Annabelle is having a little problem and Violet is leaving to see her parents, so she needs me."

"Fine, I'll let you do your girl thing and I'll do my guy thing with my baby."

"I hope you mean your car?" I asked him suggestively.

"Obviously." He kissed me on the forehead and he went to get dressed.

I watched him walk away, admiring the way his strong back muscles rippled with each step.

I texted Violet when Shane dropped me off and waited outside. She met me quickly.

"Did you say anything to her?" I asked.

"Not yet, I figured we could tag team this. Annabelle's on her way back from Jason's apartment. She was nice enough to let me crash in her dorm while she stayed the night at his."

Annabelle, as if her ears were ringing, showed up then and we all went into her room.

"So, did you guys have fun last night?" she asked us and we all sat down on her bed.

"Oh, no, we're not playing nice anymore," Violet told Annabelle.

She whipped around and stared at us. "What are you talking about?"

"Annabelle, I saw your other pregnancy test in the bathroom. It said pregnant. We need to get to the doctor, like, right now." I hoped I wasn't being to firm with her, but I was afraid she'd continue pretending everything was fine.

The smile on her face faded quickly and she looked at us with shame on her face.

"I'm not going to the doctor. It's not true. I've had no nausea or morning sickness. The test was wrong and I'm *not* pregnant," she insisted as she started to pace around her little dorm.

"You can't play this game," Violet warned her. "Denial is only going to get you in even more trouble."

"Just…enough. I don't want to get into this. Last night was perfect and Jason was so sweet and gentle. We've been struggling a little lately," she murmured, staring down at the ground. A little tear glistened in the corner of her eye but she brushed it away.

My heart broke for her. Here was someone who had a backup plan for her back up plan. Yet, when chaos hit, she was completely lost. I walked over to her and placed my hands on her shoulders, stopping the pacing so she couldn't avoid my stare or my words.

"Is that because you've been super hormonal?" I asked her softly.

"No, I've just been stressed. That's why my period is late. It's the stress of it all." She jerked away from me and moved to go to the bed. But as if the bed was too far, she just sat down on the floor and hung her head, rubbing her temples. "What if I am pregnant?" She looked up at us, tears welling up in her eyes. These she let fall.

"Then we'll help you," I promised her. "I love baby sitting and…"

"And I'll be back from England, so I can take

over to make sure Christie doesn't turn your daughter into a beauty pageant queen."

"Hey," I whined, hitting Violet. "Some of those pageants have really big cash prizes."

We all laughed superficially, and quickly stopped.

Violet and I just stared at Annabelle, waiting to see which way she'd go. It wasn't long before our friend was back. She wiped her tears, adjusted her shirt, and grabbed her bag.

"Let's go to the campus doctor," Annabelle conceded quietly. "I don't want this bill on my mom's health insurance."

We headed to the school's urgent care, but on the way, we ran into Jason.

"Hi Vi, Christie," he said and then kissed Annabelle on the cheek. "You left your phone."

"Oh, thanks," she whispered, her hand shaking a little as she took the phone from him.

"Is everything all right?" He looked concerned and confused at the same time. Jason took her hand and left a light kiss on her knuckles, but as he let go, I noticed he was shaking too. His face was pale and his eyes wide as he stared at her, waiting for her answer.

Violet and I stayed quiet, and waited for Annabelle to take the reins. Her lip quivered and she looked at Violet, begging for help. She shook her head and gave her a little push toward Jason.

"Yeah, I'm just feeling a little sick," Annabelle finally managed to say. "I don't want you to worry. The girls are just taking me to the doctor."

Violet coughed and gave Annabelle's shoulder a

little shove.

She turned around and glared at her. "Well, it's true," Annabelle insisted.

Jason looked from Violet to Annabelle with a furrowed brow. He may not have known what was going on, but he definitely knew something was up. "I can take you," Jason offered. "Vi needs to get to her parents', and I'm sure Christie doesn't want to spend her Sunday sitting in a doctor's office." Jason wrapped his arm around her and tried to walk toward the center.

"Yes," I piped up, before they got too far away. He needed to know why they were going to the doctor. I was afraid if he didn't, Annabelle would talk her way out of it. "Jason, you should take Annabelle to the doctor, but there is something you're going to need to hear first."

He looked over at me, and then back at Annabelle, and then at Violet. "What the hell is going on?" Jason dropped his arm from her shoulder. "The three of you are up to something and it's bullshit. Someone just tell me already."

"Jason," Annabelle started, her voice shaking hard. "I'm late."

"Well, let's go. The doctor will probably wait for you. What time was your appointment?"

"No, my period."

Jason fell to the bench beside where he was standing and just looked up at her.

"I'm so sorry," she managed to say.

"No," he said, staring at her. "We should have been more careful. It's not just your fault." He stood up and pulled Annabelle into a big hug. "Come on, honey, let's go see the doctor and get this figured out. We may be worrying for nothing."

"But it could be something huge," she cried into his shoulder.

"Then Violet and Christie are going to fight over the role of godmother." He let go of her and wiped her tears away gently.

"But—" she started to say but he quickly cut her off.

"It will work out one way or the other. Let's just, uh, let's just get to the doctor and then we can worry about the result."

"Okay, so we're going to let you guys deal with this," Violet said and slowly began backing up.

"Wait," Annabelle called. She pulled Violet into a huge hug, holding her tight. "Thanks for being a pushy bitch. I needed it."

"Anytime. I'll call you before I get on the plane," she promised. "I'll miss you."

"Make sure Berneli takes good care of you."

"He always does, especially in the mornings."

"And the sweet part of the conversation is now over," Annabelle said, laughing.

"I don't do sweet for too long," Violet reminded her.

Then Annabelle turned to me and gave me an equally tight hug. "And thanks for being nosey. I appreciate it."

"Of course, I gotta get my gossip fix somehow."

"I'll text you both when we find out," she assured us and then they walked off, hand in hand.

"Well, that was a lot easier than I pictured. I honestly thought I'd have to tell him myself."

Violet ran her fingers through her hair and sat down on the bench.

"She had to do it."

"I know." She nodded her head slowly and just stared off in the distance.

"Poor thing. She's a frazzled mess. Do you think there is a chance she's pregnant?"

"I don't know. Annabelle has a crazy strong stomach, so the lack of morning sickness doesn't surprise me. But at the same time, she worked so hard to make Homecoming great for everyone, she really could just be stressed out."

I sat down next to her. "Yeah, I hope she's all right. Makes me glad I'm on birth control, that's for damn sure."

We both snickered a little and then sat in silence for a few minutes, pondering the implications.

"I think she'll make a great mom. Maybe she'll hover a little, but if anyone can make school and a baby work, it's Annabelle," Violet said confidently. It was true, I could picture her crazy schedule set up perfectly so she could make everything work. Her organizational skills and motivation would really be her saving grace.

"And just think, Jason as a dad. He would be the sweetest dad on the planet."

Violet nodded at me and we returned to silence.

"I hope it isn't true," I said after a few more painful minutes.

"Me too."

They'd make the best of it, but it still wasn't ideal. I didn't know what to say. It seemed weird to bring up Shane and how everything calmed down. I almost felt like I shouldn't be happy while my friend was in crisis. So instead, the silence continued. I don't know how long we both sat there, silently hoping Annabelle would come running out of urgent care with a big smile on her face. I wasn't sure if they could do their tests immediately, but I had a feeling they needed to send out a sample. We probably wouldn't know today and since it was the weekend, we probably wouldn't know tomorrow, either.

"How did your night go?" Violet asked me suddenly. "Did you guys make up?"

I turned to her and sheepishly smiled. "Yeah, things are better."

"How much better?" she asked with a sneaky grin on her face.

Well, Violet seemed to want to lighten the mood so I figured it was a good time to take her up on that. "We talked it out and had some good makeup sex."

"Always the answer," she said, laughing. "Did you admit that you have feelings for him yet?"

"We're official now. I guess Shane didn't feel like he needed to say we were a thing, because he thought it was obvious, and I needed him to confirm it, but I wasn't going to ask."

"Typical. But have you thought about this guy being your rebound for Rob? Or at least have you considered that Shane might be thinking that?"

I looked at her and just shook my head. I didn't really know how to explain this. From the outside looking in, it obviously looked like a rebound. But when I was with Shane, it was anything but. I sat for a second, thinking about that. "I don't think so," I finally stated. "I finally feel alive again. With Shane, I don't know what's gonna happen, what he'll say, or even how I'll react. He surprises me and looks at me with this…I don't know…this pure joy in his eyes. After Rob's brother died in the Army, everything changed. It was like our entire relationship was on a schedule and we couldn't deviate. We'd go to the movies on Saturday, his parents' for dinner on Wednesdays, and brunch on Sundays at my house. It was like we were an old married couple. I tried to mix it up, but Rob became cold and standoffish. I mean, fuck, we even planned sex. Then when the wedding stuff happened, I tried to stop it, but it was like he stopped listening to my complaints and continued forward, insisting it would be fine."

"Did he see someone, like a therapist?"

"No, he refused."

"I did too for a while. After I was attacked, I had a real big problem sleeping. Annabelle kept suggesting I see someone and finally I listened. I still get night terrors every now and then, but they've lessened. Maybe you can suggest it again. I think it would really help."

"I haven't spoken to him since I ended it. I asked him not to talk to me."

"I know, but whether or not you guys are together, I'm sure you care about it. If he listens, you could be saving his life."

She had a point. I wanted the best for Rob. He was a sweet man, and one day, he'd make an amazing husband and provider for someone who wanted to be taken care of. "I think I'll shoot him a text. His future wife may need to thank me one day."

"That's the spirit." She nudged me with her shoulder and gave me a smile.

"I know we dealt with the Finn thing, but how are you doing about it?"

"Coming back to this school was a little intimidating, but my therapist says I need to face my fears. This is just a building. Trent is graduating this semester and he won't be here to bother me. Finn can in no way contact me, but if he did, so what? Berneli is in England. He can't do anything. I don't want to hide anymore. This is my school."

"I'm proud of you." I looked over at her, amazed at how strong she was. I didn't know how I'd react in the same situation, though there was a good chance my dad would have hunted Finn down with several of his cop buddies, so it was a good thing it didn't happen to me.

"Thanks, and you know what? I didn't have a terror last night. It took me a little bit to fall asleep, and I may have put a Disney movie on, but I did it."

"Look at you! Badass chick over here, everyone watch out," I yelled to the five other people in the courtyard.

We talked for a little bit about Violet's classes and the amazing time she was having in England. She admitted it was weird being the one with the accent now, but she loved it there. Berneli was working hard, but he cooked her dinner almost every night, probably for the best, and he was almost finished with his second textbook. So far, they were still happy together. She admitted that they fought a little bit about the fact that Violet still hasn't told her parents about them. She was afraid they'd drag her home if they knew she was dating her professor.

"I'm just not sure how long I can keep it from them. Luckily, they aren't on my social media accounts, so they don't see pictures."

"I think you should tell them. You're a grown woman and can make your own decisions. When they visit you for Thanksgiving, I think you should introduce them."

"What if they cut me off, emotionally and financially?"

"Then you finish your semester, come back home, and get a job. Or, take out some student loans to support yourself. There are plenty of ways. It's not like you need an apartment to stay in. The rest of your bills should be pretty low."

"Yeah, I don't know about that."

"Violet," I said sternly, standing up and looking down at her. "You just made a big deal about Annabelle not being honest with Jason, and now you won't do it yourself. Put your big girl panties on and talk to them. I can understand if you don't want to ruin this trip, but you do need to tell them."

She looked at me a little wide eyed, and then stood up too. Violet nodded her head and clenched her jaw. "I'm a hypocrite."

"Yes, and what's worse, you're going to ruin your relationship because of it. Are you ready to lose Berneli because you won't talk to your parents?"

"No, no, I'm not." She nodded her head again, but this time she looked determined.

"Good, now can you take me to my parents' house before heading to yours? Shane brought me here."

"Yeah, no problem."

***

The rest of my Sunday was pretty mellow. I worked on my project and avoided some other homework that I'd get to eventually. Before I fell asleep, I fiddled with my phone. I did need to text Rob, but I couldn't figure out what to say. I didn't want him to think I was being nasty or trying to rekindle things. Several drafts later, I decided to send him a message on his social media. I had too much to say.

Rob, one of my friends went through a trauma, kinda like when you lost your brother. She went to a therapist and it really helped her. I think you should give it a try. I know you've always rejected the idea before, claiming it wasn't necessary, but I think it is. You've never dealt with your grief and it shows every day. I want what's best for you and your future. Please consider this.- Christie

I quickly sent the message before I could change my mind. Then I fell asleep.

Chapter 16

I met up with Annabelle the next day for lunch. She was anxiously awaiting her results, no longer in denial, but actually facing her issues…well, facing them in her own way. The urgent care doctor had forced her to go to the hospital because she needed to get an internal sonogram. She kicked her feet but Jason got her to go finally. He'd done some sweet talking to the nurse and they managed to get the bill sent to school.

"This is my plan. If I'm pregnant, the baby will be due in July."

"Wait, how the hell do you know that? You don't even know if you're pregnant."

"Okay fine, I'm guessing. But it will probably be June or July. But anyway, it would be great, because I have two months to adjust before school. Jason's classes, at least for the next year, can all be taken online, so he's going to work during the day. I'll watch the baby and take classes at night. To help out, I'll get a weekend job and work, like, twelve hour days."

191

"Sounds like you have it all figured out."

"Yeah, it would be a shame that I'd have to quit EET, but we could make it work. And obviously, that is if our parents won't help us. I'm sure my parents will be furious, but I can't imagine them writing me off."

"Then you're lucky. I'm glad you figured this out, but let's not make any hasty decisions."

"No, I know. I just feel calmer when I plan."

I was going to respond, but I got a call from Shane. He'd never called me before. "Hello?" I answered, concerned.

"Hi, it's just easy to call about this. So, feel free to say no, but um, all right, so my ex called my parents and told them about you. They called me and asked who you were. I told them that you're my new girlfriend and they invited you to dinner," he responded very quickly.

"No, I can do that. Parents usually love me."

"That's because you haven't met Asian parents."

"Thank you for putting me at ease."

"Anytime, Barbie. What are you up to on Thursday? Around seven?"

"I can make it happen."

"Good, and by the way, make sure you wear underwear, I think my mom has x-ray vision."

"That is quite possibly the scariest thing I've ever heard."

"I'll pick you up around six-thirty."

I hung up the phone and Annabelle had a bright smile on her face. "You're meeting his parents?"

"Yeah, I guess so."

"Scared?"

"Hell yes. I'll just be on my best behavior and wear a pleated skirt with a high neck blouse. They'll never know I spend my nights bangin' their son and recklessly encouraging his street racing."

"What parent wouldn't love you?" Annabelle teased.

The next few days went by slowly. I was nervous about dinner, nervous about my upcoming statistics exam, nervous about my accounting paper, and nervous about Rob. He never responded to my message, but it showed that he'd read it. I didn't know what I expected. I wanted him to assure me he was going to see someone, but then again, I didn't want to risk falling into our old cycle. He had to do this on his own.

I was in my room, getting ready to see Shane's parents, when my mom walked into the room.

"Don't you look pretty," she told me, looking over my skirt and blouse selection. "What are you planning tonight?"

I took a deep breath, and turned to face her. I couldn't tell Violet to talk to her parents if I was still afraid to do it myself.

"Remember that boy I was telling you about?"

She nodded her head, encouraging me to continue.

"Well, he and I decided to become a couple at the Homecoming dance. He invited me over to meet his parents tonight."

"Oh, that's exciting, but when is he coming here? Can I see a picture of the two of you?"

I grabbed my phone and pulled up one of the pictures that we took at the dance. I handed her the phone and the smile on her face fell for a second. But then her Southern attitude kicked in and the smile was right back. It just didn't reach her eyes, and I didn't think the Botox was the reason.

"His name is Shane," I told her.

"And is he Chinese?"

"South Korean. He's studying to be a mechanical engineer," I said, hoping she'd be impressed with his major.

"That's so ambitious. Um, good for him then." She got up quickly and started to walk out of the room.

"Mom," I called and she quickly turned around, putting the fake smile right back on her face.

"What is it, darlin'?"

"He's the one who ordered the limo because he wanted to treat me. Shane is a good man, and I really like him."

"That's great, but you all just met, so let's just not move too quickly, okay?'

"I know we did. We're still getting to know each other."

"Good, good. I'm happy to hear he's a good man." Then she walked out of the room without looking back.

I pushed her words behind me. She was probably just shocked. My parents had never forced racial boundaries on me, or anyone I'd ever dated. But the truth was, he was the first guy who wasn't white Irish Catholic.

My phone went off. Shane had texted me, saying he was outside. I looked in the mirror, fluffed my hair a little, and adjusted my lipstick. Then I got my purse and ran out to the car, pretending I didn't see my mother putting some vodka in her coffee cup.

I climbed into the car, but my mother came running out our front door. She pounded on the door and I rolled down the window to talk to her.

"Christie Margaret, you get your butt back in that house right *now*."

"Excuse me?"

"And *you*!" she yelled, pointing at Shane. "My daughter deserves respect, and sitting outside on that cell phone isn't showing respect. If you expect to pick her up ever, you will walk to the door, come in for a drink—maybe an iced tea—and then you may go. None of this drive by thing." She reached for the door and yanked it open.

I looked over at Shane and beckoned him inside. He smirked at me, amused by this show, and followed us inside.

Mom offered him a seat on the couch and I sat down next to him. She sat on the arm chair across from us.

"So, tell me about yourself, Shane."

"I study mechanical engineering at school and I hope to get in a job helping to build defensive weapons for the government. Or I may sell out and work for some corporate hack and make millions. Depends on how I feel when I graduate next semester."

"Mechanical engineering…wow, that seems hard. I guess you're older than Christie is?"

"Uh, yeah, two years, I think. I don't actually know her birthday," Shane admitted, looking at me a little embarrassed.

"It's in December," I told him and Shane nodded.

We all sat there for a few minutes of silence and I looked over at Mom, begging for her to say something.

Shane cut in, though. He took my hand and smiled politely at my mom. "I'm really sorry, but we need to go to my parents' now. My mom made dinner and I'd hate to be late. Maybe I can take you and Mr. Peters for dinner some other time and we can get to know each other."

Mom jumped up. "Hold on," she said and then rushed to the kitchen. She came back a few minutes later, holding a container of cookies. "Christie, first you walk out to meet some boy in his car, and then you plan to show up at someone's house empty handed. This is not the daughter I raised," she chastised.

"No, we were going to stop by the store to get flowers. I was afraid if I made anything, she'd think it was an insult to her cooking," I stated, defending myself.

"Well, I don't think Shane's mother is going to be insulted by a couple cookies. If she is, then you just come straight home because that's ridiculous," she told me and gave Shane a nasty look.

"I think my mom will love the cookies. She usually makes pie, since that's my dad's favorite. The cookies will probably be a good addition," Shane insisted, accepting the container of cookies from my mom.

"See, Shane likes cookies. Now go before you're late to that woman's dinner. I'm sure she's been working hard." Then she turned to Shane and took a big sip from that coffee cup. "I'll talk to my husband about your dinner invitation and get back to you." She smiled big, but again, it didn't reach her eyes. At least she was trying, though.

Mom shuffled us out of the house and stood waving from the front door.

"Oh, and Shane?" she said before closing the front door behind us. "Don't think you got off easy. If there is a next time you're here, we're going to have a much longer visit."

I climbed in the car and hoped he hadn't heard the "if."

Shane started the car and drove off, probably a little faster than Mom would have liked. He took the corners hard and the tires screeched. Now that we were on a straight road, he floored the gas.

I gripped the handle on the door, as we were going way too fast for daylight. "I didn't realize we were going to be that late."

"Why did she say *if* there is a next time? Why wouldn't there be a next time?"

"Because my mom is rude."

"No, actually, she seemed really nice other than that. She just seemed to want to be included," he insisted, pressing on the gas harder to run a red light.

"What do you want me to say? You're just new to her and she…"

"She doesn't like that I'm not Rob," he interrupted me.

"Well, that's true. She's known Rob since he was, like, thirteen," I explained. "She just isn't used to change."

"That must be why she still has pictures of the two of you together on the mantel. Or maybe it's because she's still hoping the two of you will get back together."

I squeezed my eyes shut and silently cursed my mother. Why were those pictures still up? "She probably is," I told him. "Just because she's in denial about my past relationship, doesn't mean that I am. I'm in your car, heading to your parents' house."

"Then why didn't you take the pictures down? Are you just dating the bad boy to get it out of your system? What happens when you've sowed your wild oats? Do you call that guy back up and leave me in your dust? Or worse, do you just find yourself a rich country club boy, leaving us both with our hearts in your palm? Maybe we should call you 'Christie, Destroyer of Souls.'"

"Stop the damn car," I replied softly.

Shane cut across three lanes and pulled over to the side. When he did, I immediately opened the door and got out with my purse.

"Christie, get back in the car."

I kept walking, without looking back. He must have gotten out after me because I heard another car door slam.

"Christie, it's cold. Come back in the car."

"And what?" I called back to him, still not looking back. "Listen to you doubt my character?" I was livid. Just the other night we were talking about all our feelings, and I even told him about Rob. Yet, here he was, doubting me. Those pictures were a part of my past. What was I supposed to do, erase those four years of my life? Never look back at the good times I had with Rob and my other friends? No, I was allowed to have a past, and I'd damn well enjoy the fun we'd had.

"What do you want me to think? Your house is still a fucking shrine to that kid."

I whipped around and glared at him. "Listen to me, you giant, jealous, thick-headed ass. I just broke up with that kid a few weeks ago, but my family is still close with his. They will remain close to his, and I will run into him over the years. If you aren't secure enough in your manhood to deal with that, then tell me now so I can find someone who isn't so macho. I'm not perfect. I come with a past, and that past has a guy in it. Deal with it." I raised my eyebrows at him and crossed my arms. I was done with this jealous crap. It was nowhere near as sexy as books and movies made it out to be.

Shane held my eye contact for a minute, a fierce look in his eyes at first. But then the frustration faded and he looked at me softly before shifting his gaze down. "You're right."

"I know I'm right. And you're hardly one to talk. Your ex is the one who tattled on us to your parents. Why does *she* still talk to them?"

"I don't know. She was close with my parents too. They thought that, eventually, we'd get married."

"Do I have something to be worried about with her?"

He looked back up at me and held my gaze, as if promising me something. "You're the one I want to

199

be with. There's nothing to worry about."

"Then why are you questioning me?"

"Because…" He stopped talking and paced a little.

"Because why?"

"I just don't like him. His smug face irritates me."

"Well, that's ridiculous."

"Whatever, let's just get back in the car and head to dinner. It's going to be a long night if we're late."

"No, I need to know why you're questioning me." I had to resist the urge to stomp my foot like a child.

"This is not the time to have this conversation. It's cold and we're on the side of the road."

"It's not like I asked for this fight. Tell me."

Shane stuffed his hands in his pockets and started kicking some of the rocks. His shoulders dropped and he wouldn't look at me. But he took a deep breath and finally started talking. "I know it's been a few weeks, and some people may think it's too soon, and I'm not sure if I've ever even felt this way before, but I think there is a chance I could be falling in love with you." He looked up at me, his lip quivering slightly, but his eyes grew wide and soft. He looked so hopeful.

I smiled and rushed over to him, sliding my arms around his waist. I felt a huge weight lifting off my chest as his body warmth filled me up. "I think I may be falling in love with you too."

Shane grabbed my face and pulled me toward him, kissing me with such force that I had to grip tighter to him to keep from falling over, but I didn't care. Standing on the side of the road, grasping onto this man, I'd never felt more at peace.

"Are you happy now? I had this big, beautiful moment planned when I'd tell you, but you just couldn't wait."

"I don't like waiting." I kissed him softy, almost afraid to let go. He knew the real me and he loved me. Shane saw through all my bullshit and still thought I was worth it.

"That's for damn sure."

"But I need this jealous thing to stop. I can't keep this up. I'm not with Rob, I'm not with that guy from my statistics class. I'm not with anyone else, and that's my choice."

"You sure?"

"Positive."

"Well then, let's get in the car and head to dinner. If I run every red light, we just might make it on time."

"So you'll drive like you normally do."

He opened the car door for me.

Chapter 17

We pulled up to a beautiful stone building with the most immaculate yard that I've ever seen. The front of the house had two beautiful bay windows on either side of the front door. On one side was a gorgeous glass sunroom and the other side was a giant garage with four parking spaces. Shane pulled up to one but didn't drive the car all the way in.

"My mom will kill me if I walk you through the garage. I need to take you to the front door. That's where her elaborate foyer is with the expensive paintings she likes to talk about. My mom is all about impressing people when they come in. Remember when I told you about the apartment, and how they keep it to show their friends how successful they are? Their house is even crazier."

"I will make sure to drop lots of compliments and oohh and ahhh."

"No, don't do that," Shane said a little loudly as he got out of the car. He walked around to my side and opened the door. "Um, she'll know that I told you that. Don't mention the art. Just stare at it a little too long and linger on the vase that's on the table across from the door. Also, if they offer you anything, accept it with both hands. Don't hold out just one."

"Got it." I fixed my skirt and brushed at my hair a little. "Do I look okay?"

Shane smiled down at me. "You're beautiful."

I took a deep breath and we walked up to the double doors with dramatic and elaborate leafed door knobs. Shane knocked and I looked over at him confused.

"Did you just knock to enter your house?"

"It's a sign of respect."

I nodded my head and made a mental note of that.

The door opened, and standing across from me was a beautiful woman. She gave me a somewhat forced smile and welcomed us in. Her black hair fell just above her shoulders, her skin was clear of wrinkles, freckles, and blemishes, and her eyes were hidden behind designer eyeglass frames. Mrs. Choi stood an inch or two shorter than me, but she was wearing high heels. They were a little higher than my black ones, so we were eye to eye. Her frame was small and slender, but when she closed the giant door, I saw some muscle definition in her arms. Legitimately, I was more in awe of her than the amazing Italian painting hanging on the wall.

"It is so nice to meet you Mrs. Choi," I said, snapping out of it. I extended my hand to her and she took it gently, barely holding on.

"You too, Christie."

I made a big to do about turning to look at the

painting. It was a real canvas. Not a copy on a poster or a sheet of paper. After all my mother's comments about art, I finally listened and I appreciated Mrs. Choi more because of the authenticity of it. Go figure.

"Do you like art?" Mrs. Choi asked me, coming to stand at my side.

"Yes, I love art. My mom loves painting, so for my high school graduation, we took a trip to Italy and just stared at art. It was an amazing two weeks."

"That sounds lovely. If I ever had time off from my practice, I'd love to do something similar."

"Oh, you're a doctor too? I'm sorry, I met Mr. Choi when my friend was in a car accident. He looked over her charts."

"Your friend was lucky then. My husband is a very good doctor."

"Yes, I noticed that. What do you practice?"

"I am a pediatrician."

"I love children," I responded, smiling at her, and then I realized that may have sounded wrong. "But obviously I'm not ready for them. I just mean that I want to get my career sorted out first and get married, then have a baby. But not that my career would be more important than a family because, obviously, family is important to me. Not that I would give up my career to be a mom. Well, I might. I actually haven't decided what I would do since I'm nowhere near that point. Not that..."

"Okay, Christie. I'm just going to stop you there. I think we get the point. Why don't you give my mom the cookies?" Shane cut in.

"Yes, here. My mother made some cookies and

we thought you'd like some."

She took the tin and then put the forced smile back on when she thanked me.

"I have something for you too." She turned around and handed me a box with an elaborate bow and immaculate wrappings.

"Thank you." I opened the box and saw a set of slippers. They were grey with little bows on the top and were soft to touch. I looked up at her, offering a smile.

"We don't believe in anyone going barefoot around the house, but shoes track dirt and things in the house, so we usually wear a set of house shoes. If you don't mind, I'd like you to trade the ones you're wearing for these."

"Yeah, no problem. They are lovely and probably more comfortable than my heels." I leaned awkwardly against the wall and took my shoes off. Shane took them and put them on the shoe rack near the door. I put the slippers on and instantly decided I should adopt this tradition to my life. The slippers were crazy comfortable and warm.

"Where's Dad?" Shane asked.

"He is just changing. His shift went a little long at the hospital. Why don't you take Christie to the dining room to have a seat and you can help me bring the food to the dining room." Mrs. Choi then turned around and started walking toward what I assumed was the kitchen.

"Oh, I don't mind helping you, Mrs. Choi."

She whipped around as if I had called her a nasty name. "No, you cannot help me, Christie. You're a guest. Please, just have a seat and we'll be in there in a minute." She then walked out of the room so fast I thought she might have super powers.

"Sorry about that," Shane said softly. "She is a little harsh sometimes, but she'll warm up to you." He gave me a weak smile and then placed a hand on the small of my back to guide me into the dining room.

It actually looked a lot like my mom's. The table could comfortably sit twelve, but some of the chairs had been pulled back against the wall. Now there were only four at the table. Shane pulled one out for me and then helped me scoot it back into the table. It was heavy oak with beautiful red cushions and an elaborate leaf design on the backrest. The table, I assumed, was oak to match, but it was covered with a red tablecloth that had elegant flowers embroidered on top. There were also two elaborate candlesticks that could have been used as heavy weapons, ornate crystal water goblets, and glass bowls awaiting the food that Mrs. Choi was bringing in.

The walls held even more elaborate art. I know there were a lot of people who were fans of modern art, but it seemed like Mrs. Choi and I actually had something in common. We liked the classics. The dramatic paintings depicting people with draped cloths and lavish chalices. I was so busy staring at the art that I realized I never noticed the vase. I cursed under my breath.

"Excuse me, you must be Christie," a voice said from the door of the dining room.

I looked over and saw an older version of Shane. They looked exactly the same. I smiled, and moved to get up, but he shook his head.

"No, it's all right. Stay seated. I'm sure my wife will be here momentarily with the food and we cannot let that get cold." Mr. Choi walked over to me and shook my hand. "It's nice to see you again, Christie. How is your friend doing?"

"She's doing well. I haven't seen her have any problems since she left the hospital."

"Fantastic. I'm glad to hear that." He smiled at me and then looked toward the door.

Sure enough, Shane and his mother entered with more than enough food. There was a bowl with noodles in one of Shane's hands, and in the other was a platter of meat. His mother held a giant bowl of vegetables, and a lazy Susan of condiments. They were placed around the table, and Shane took the seat opposite me, while his mother sat opposite her husband, at the head of the table.

"I hope you like Japchae," Mrs. Choi said with a smile but it sounded more like a challenge.

"I don't actually know what it is, but everything here looks delicious. I'm sure I'll love it."

"This recipe has been passed down my family for generations. The only thing we changed is that sometimes we use this as a side dish, but Shane likes it so much that we like to have it as our main entree. These are sweet potato noodles, so they are good for you," Mrs. Choi insisted and asked for my plate.

I handed it to her and she piled on the food. There was no way I'd be able to eat it all, but there was even less of a chance I'd let her think she won.

After the third slice of beef, Shane spoke up,

thankfully saving me from what would be a food coma. At least there were two doctors here. "Mom, I think Christie has enough food. I'd like to eat some of this too. It's been forever since you've made Japchae."

"Well, if you came home more often, then maybe I'd feel better about making it for you."

"I'm sorry, school is crazy. But I'm keeping up."

"What do you mean 'keeping up'? We have that apartment so that you don't have to worry about anything other than school. Are you playing games with that car again?"

"No, I was just being modest. No problems," Shane tried to assure her, but she opened her mouth to speak again.

"So, Christie," Mr. Choi chimed in, changing the topic. "What are you studying?"

"I'm getting my degree in business, hopefully with a concentration in statistics and marketing."

"That's interesting," he replied.

"Yes, she's up for this big internship with one of the professors. She's been working on it for weeks. I've seen her work, it's brilliant," Shane told them, grinning at me with pride.

"Good luck with that," Mr. Choi said, smiling at me too.

The only one not smiling was Mrs. Choi. She was watching me eat, and I realized I never said anything about the food.

"This is amazing. I really like the seasoning and the sesame seeds. Thank you for making it, Mrs. Choi. I'd love to see the recipe one day." I grabbed another fork full and took a big, but polite, bite.

"I don't just give out this recipe. Maybe I'll give you something for chicken wings."

Shane dropped his fork on his plate and the loud clang made me jump. He immediately started shouting at his mother in Korean. They started arguing back and forth. I looked over at Shane's father, and he gave me a weak smile. Then he jumped into the fight too, but he was louder and more commanding than the other two.

They stopped fighting immediately, and Shane looked over at me. His fury was obvious and my heart hurt a bit for him.

"I love chicken wings. I'm sure the recipe would be good," I said, hoping to ease the tension that was now palpable.

"That's because you aren't Korean," Shane told me. "There is an old custom about a woman making her man chicken wings. They settle in his stomach and then he grows wings and leaves her. So if someone makes her boyfriend or husband chicken wings, she's basically trying to break up with him, or at least try to get him to leave. It's bad luck."

"Oh, got it," I murmured, looking down at my plate, suddenly embarrassed. Maybe I should have looked up some Korean customs or done some more research. I should have learned some of the traditions, and then maybe I wouldn't be making such an ass out of myself.

"Mom said that because she doesn't want us together."

My head shot up and I looked over at her. "Why? Have I done something wrong?" My heart broke a little. If his mother didn't approve, would that affect

Shane? He may have disagreed with her, but it was obvious he respected her.

"There is nothing you can do. There are just some things you can't help," she responded with pity, as if she was apologizing for it.

"Like what? What problems do you have with me already?" My face was beginning to burn as my frustration leaked out. There was no point in being polite anymore. I knew why she didn't like me, and it was the same reason my mother didn't like Shane. "Is it because I'm not Korean?"

"Well, that is part of it. How can we expect our customs to be passed down if you don't know them?"

"I can learn," I told her with as much authority as I could muster. "I respect you and your culture enough to take the time to learn all of these things. Shane can help me, and I'd hope you would too. But we aren't getting married now."

"Then what is the point of dating, if not to try to find the person you want to be with?" she asked me, her voice raising in both volume and octave.

"One day, we might, but I think it's too early to make that decision," I reminded her.

"All right then, but I'm sure you've noticed that we have money. Aren't you the least bit excited about that? I knew that one day we'd have to chase away the gold diggers."

"Mom," Shane growled under his breath.

"No, it's okay. It's a legitimate concern," I said to him, and then turned to her. "I have money too. Not this much, but my family is very comfortable." I raised my head, trying to keep my pride. I wasn't a gold digger and I knew that. She was trying to get under my skin, but I put on my best face. She wasn't going to win this war.

"Right, so you'd want someone from a similar background to keep you in that lifestyle," she commented, folding her hands in front of her.

I fought the instinct to tell her to get her elbows off the table, but I figured that certainly wouldn't help. "And if that was what I wanted, then I'd already have it. My ex-boyfriend offered me that. His family has lots of money, and he is set to be a successful officer in the military. He wanted us to get married in June when he graduated from military school. I left him for that reason. I am in no rush to get married or anything like that, but if that was all I was after, then I'd already have it. Actually, my family is really upset I'm not going through with it. They're all friends, so it was the perfect match. But at the end of the day, I wasn't happy. Your son, your son makes me happy."

"That's brave of you to stand up for yourself," she said quietly, making eye contact with me and holding onto it for a moment. I couldn't tell what she wanted. Maybe she was sizing me up, or maybe she was trying to figure out if I was lying. Whatever she thought, it must have appeased her for now. She gave me a little smile and then she started to eat her food.

I looked over at Shane, and he nodded at me. I didn't know if she liked me yet, but at the very least, she wasn't glaring at me anymore. I took a deep breath, picked my fork up, and continued to eat my food. It really was delicious, but they used way too much salt.

Chapter 18

"All right, you need to call the doctor back." I was holding the phone up with Violet on the video call, while Annabelle sat on her bed, barely moving.

Her doctor called her with the results, but he wouldn't leave a message on the phone.

"Okay," she finally said and picked up her phone.

"Wait," Violet yelled from the phone. "Jason should be here. If you're pregnant, he definitely should be the first one to know."

"Yeah," Annabelle agreed in a bit of a trance. She sent him a text and we all sat there in silence.

"So, Violet, how is Berneli's job search?" I was hoping to end this ridiculous silence and maybe distract us for a while.

"Ugh! I don't even want to talk about it."

"Okay, then," I responded gently.

We were all quiet again for a few seconds until Violet started freaking out.

"All right, I just have to get it off my chest. The college doesn't want David leaving just yet, and

213

he's not sure he wants to leave. On top of that, David can't get a visa until he gets a job. They have to sponsor it. It's a mess."

"So he isn't coming?" Annabelle asked her, taking the phone from me.

"As of now, I'll be coming back in August alone."

"But you are coming back, right?" Annabelle looked at me, almost even more devastated than she was earlier.

I did value my relationship with Annabelle, and I knew she valued me, but she also needed Violet. That girl cared so much about Annabelle and they needed each other. Our friendship worked because the three of us balanced each other out. I'm the brutally honest bitch, Annabelle thought with her head and kept us grounded, and Violet was the one who encouraged us to dream. Take one piece of the puzzle away, and we were incomplete. At least that's how I felt.

"Yeah, I have to come back. I can only stay here for the semester. Student visas are fuckers."

"Does that mean you're breaking up?" I asked her nervously.

"Honestly, I don't know."

The silence continued until Jason came bursting through Annabelle's door. "Do you know? Did you call him? What's going on?"

"Sit down, Jason," I commanded and I got up from the bed. "Uh, Violet and I are going to wait outside while you guys make the call. We'll give you guys some privacy."

I took the phone with me outside Annabelle's

room and sat down on the floor.

"I really hope she's not pregnant," I confessed to Violet.

"I know. Though, it definitely got me to start using condoms again."

"I'm sorry, what?"

"Well, you know. I'm on birth control, and David and I are only sleeping with each other. Plus, it feels way better without them."

"I know what you mean. Rob hated condoms. I'd never really used them before Shane."

"Well, tell now. How is it?"

"You know what they say about Asians and size? Yeah, that's not a thing." I used my hands to demonstrate just how big he actually was…and then I added a little bit for show.

"Damn, girl! I'm glad you're enjoying that."

"*Christie!*" Annabelle shouted from her room. She tore the door open and pretty much jumped on me. "I'm not pregnant!"

Violet and I cheered, both relieved that we weren't going to be Aunties before we were twenty-one.

"That's so great," I congratulated as we stood up.

We all went back into Annabelle's room and said bye to Violet. It was definitely getting late where she was.

"So, what now?" I asked her and Jason.

"Now, I get on birth control."

"Good plan. By the way, so I know this probably not your thing, but Shane and his friends are having this big Halloween party at the track next Saturday. I think it could be fun if you came with me. Emma will be there, but I'd love to have some more friends there."

Annabelle looked at Jason and then smiled at me. "On one condition, we can get out easily if the cops come. I just dodged one bullet with the pregnancy, and I'm not dealing with getting arrested."

"No, they have look outs about a mile away from the track. They walkie people if there is even the slightest sign of cops."

"Then we're down," she told me.

"Honestly, I'm a little surprised you want to come," I said.

"You were there for us during this whole thing, the least we can do is show up at an illegal street race with your new guy in ridiculous matching costumes," Jason teased, tickling Annabelle a little.

"All right, that's enough of the after school special. Let's go get some food," Annabelle said.

***

Shane pretended like he didn't care that my friends had agreed to come. But whenever he talked about the party, he'd bring them up. He wanted to show Jason some basic car stuff ahead of time so Jason didn't make a fool of himself. Then he suggested we all go costume shopping together, you know, to make sure we didn't match.

It warmed my heart that he was so willing to get to know them and bring them into his world. Shane just saw the best in everyone and gave them a chance until he found it. I loved that about him.

We weren't able to go costume shopping as a group though, because Shane had to go to his mom's practice and work for his second internship. But Annabelle and I went, leaving Jason at school so we could have some girl time.

"So, what do you guys want to dress as?" I asked Annabelle as I was flipping through the costumes.

"Um, since we're gonna be in public, I definitely need to be covered."

"Oh, you leave the skimpy stuff for the bedroom?"

"Yeah," she answered, blushing and turning around to look at another rack.

I wasn't letting her get away that easy. "So you've bought more stuff?"

"Jason loved the lingerie. Half the time, we even leave the bra on. I don't know, the lace just like, I don't know, it feels good."

"I bet it does, especially if the lace is unlined."

Annabelle smiled bright and then grabbed a costume. She held it up to me. "I think this is what I'm going to wear. It's fun, right?"

It was a black skater skirt with yellow batman logos all over it. Attached to the hanger was a plain black t-shirt, with one giant yellow batman logo in the middle of it.

"That is definitely one way to get Jason's attention without being overly slutty." Jason was a huge superhero fan. He was going to love this costume. "Are you going to get him a Robin costume? How funny would that be?"

"Oh, god! I'm gonna do it." She flipped through the costume rack, but couldn't find anything for

217

Robin. "So, we need a plan B."

We continued looking through the rack and found an Ironman costume.

"This is perfect," I told her, holding up the Ironman suit.

"Why is that perfect? I don't get it."

"Because Ironman is like the Batman of Marvel. He doesn't actually have powers, but he's rich and builds stuff. It's like a couple's costume, but it's not a traditional couple's thing."

"Holy crap."

"What?"

"You're a nerd. I can't believe I never noticed."

"Shut up," I told her, feeling my cheeks grow hot. When you grew up basically on house arrest like I was, you did a lot of reading. I don't know, somehow I got into comics, and now I had this secret collection you could only look at with gloves. My collection was pretty impressive, and I even had a couple valuable signed comics. No one else knew about this part of me besides my mom and dad. I wondered what Shane would think of it if he knew.

"Wow, now I found your costumes," Annabelle told me, holding up a guy and girl set.

"Amazing." I stopped looking and went straight to the register.

***

Annabelle and I were in my room, getting ready for the Halloween party. My mom thought we were going to an EET event, so she was busy making us a snack, afraid that we'd go hungry.

I slipped my plastic pink dress on and turned to look at Annabelle.

"What do you think?"

"You look exactly like Barbie. It's a little scary."

I adjusted the strap on my pink dress and turned back to look in the mirror. It was too tight, too plastic, and too flawless. I added a pair of pink heels that just happened to match the shade of pink in the dress, fluffed my hair a bit more, and added a swipe of lipstick. I was ready to go.

Annabelle fussed over her skirt for a few more minutes, even though I promised that I couldn't see her ass.

"When's Jason getting here?" I asked as I put my lipstick in my purse.

"He should be here any minute.

"Great, let's head out to the living room. My mom is possibly cooking an entire meal for fifty people."

We walked out, and as if on cue, the doorbell rang. I ran to the door to let Jason in, but stopped dead in my tracks. It wasn't Jason at the door. Hell, it wasn't even Shane.

Staring back at me with a bouquet of flowers, a duffle bag, and a giant garment bag, was Rob. My mouth went dry and I was momentarily speechless.

"Baby, what are you wearing?" Rob asked, walking into my house, giving me a kiss on the cheek.

"A Barbie costume. What are you doing here?" I didn't know what to think, he looked like he wanted to stay a while and I was curious about the garment bag. Did he have his own costume in there or

219

something? But more important than that, why had he ignored my message to leave me be? My shock quickly turned to frustration, which manifested to rage. He'd ignored me. He'd ignored my wishes again. This guy would never change.

Rob dropped his bag on the ground and walked into the kitchen, greeting my mom with a big hug.

"Rob, what a nice surprise. To what do we owe this visit?" My mom fussed over him.

"Joy, I'm here about the military ball. Didn't my mom tell you about it? It's the first week of December. I found this beautiful designer dress, and instead of mailing it, I wanted to see Christie's face when she opened it. I figured it'd be a great early birthday present." He turned and handed the garment bag to me.

As much as I was dying to see what was inside— Rob always had amazing taste—it was hard to ignore a couple things. "Um, why are you here, Rob? We broke up. I asked you to leave me alone." Annabelle came and stood next to me. It was good to feel her presence there. It kept me grounded, which was good, since I wanted to scream like a child. He shouldn't be here and he didn't seem to care.

He waved his hand at me dismissively. "I know the truth, you just got some cold feet about getting married. Well, you don't need to worry. I'm not going anywhere." He tried to kiss me again, but I stuck my hand in his face, stopping his lips before they reached mine.

"No, Rob, I'm actually done. I—"

"Stop, I know that you're just panicking about

this whole thing. Just…enough, okay?"

"Uh, why's the door open?" Shane asked from the entrance. He walked in, smiling at me, and then turned to look at Rob. His smile didn't fade, but I saw a little tick in his jaw.

"Who the hell are you?" Rob asked him, and then he grimaced. "Sorry, Joy, that was rude. I shouldn't be swearing in front of women. The military is affecting me."

"I'm Christie's boyfriend, Shane. I take it you're Rob?"

Rob stepped up to Shane, looked him up and down, and practically growled. "No, I'm Christie's boyfriend. And who the fuck do you think you are? How dare you dress up like a military man. What do you know about sacrificing yourself for your country?"

"Probably the same as you, since you're in college."

"Okay, it's a stupid GI Joe costume. Obviously, he'd never disrespect anyone in the military," I yelled, splitting them up before it got violent. My heart was racing and I was actually scared. I've never seen Rob get in a fight, but his hand was balled up in a fist, and a vein was throbbing in his neck. "Annabelle, why don't you go sit on the couch with Shane so I can talk to Rob."

"Yeah, do what she says, fucking pussy, listen to the woman."

I whipped around to look at him in shock. I've never heard Rob talk like this. Usually it's me with the potty mouth. But Shane didn't sink to Rob's level.

He just turned around and led Annabelle to the couch like a gentleman.

"Why don't we all eat?" Mom suggested, bringing some bowls to the table.

"No, Mom, Rob is leaving."

"I'm not leaving. I just flew up to see you," Rob argued.

"Yeah, and you did that without talking to me and against my wishes. I told you we were done, so will you please just leave?" I was begging him. I didn't want a fight, I didn't want to keep explaining this, and I didn't know what to do. Rob did fly all the way up here, and part of me did feel a little guilty. He was here fighting for me. I should have known things were too good to be true when he didn't respond to my text or my message. "Rob, please. I'm asking you to respect my family and leave before anything goes wrong tonight."

"You mean more wrong than it already has?" Rob shrugged and nodded his head. "Keep the dress. When you're done slumming, you can give me a call. I'll always wait for you." He reached out and tried to stroke my cheek, but I stopped him.

"Rob, please."

He slammed his hand against the doorframe and then walked out the door, grabbing his duffle bag on the way. I put the garment bag in the hall closet and walked over to my mom, pulling her into the kitchen where we might have a bit of privacy.

"Listen, darlin', I'm only going to say this one time. I know you like this new boy, and that's fine, but look at how much Rob cares for you. Are you sure that's not what you want?"

"Mom, he's proving why I don't want to be with him. He didn't call, he just showed up and caused drama after I asked him not to. Mature men don't do that. Shane took a step back and sat down. Rob looked like he was going to hit him."

"Well, Shane *did* antagonize him."

"No, Mom, he didn't. Just...let this go. We'll have some food and then move on."

We all sat down at the table, just in time for Jason to knock on the door. He gave Annabelle a kiss, and then looked over at me.

"Sorry I'm late. What'd I miss?"

Chapter 19

Annabelle and Jason were going to ride in his car. They wanted to have a way to leave in case they got bored, didn't like it, or if the cops were there. Since they weren't racing, I didn't think they could get in too much trouble, but I wasn't sure if you could get arrested just for watching.

Shane was pretty quiet while we "snacked" on all the food my mom made. I knew he was probably looking to talk to me in private, so when we pulled away from my house, I was nervous. He didn't exactly have the best track record when he got jealous, and seeing Rob was definitely not helping.

"Listen, Shane, I didn't ask him to come."

"I know." He rubbed his face a couple times, seemingly at a loss for words. He took a deep breath and then finally looked back at me.

I was scared. I didn't want my mom or Rob to cause a fight with us, but I wasn't sure how to fix it. "Are you upset? I'm sure you heard the things my mom said."

"Yeah, but I'm upset because Rob put you in that

224

situation. I know your mom isn't gonna like me straight off because she still has a hard on for Rob. I'm okay with that. I don't like that this prick just showed up, even though you said it was over. It gives me a bad vibe, and it doesn't give me a fair chance to even try to win your mom over."

"I know. I just don't want you to think that there's anything between us anymore."

"I'm not concerned about that."

"Why not?"

"Because you asked him to leave and now you're here with me. If there was something still between you two, the little fight might have ended differently."

"I'm sorry."

"You have nothing to be sorry about. If anything, I'm sorry you were in that situation." He hugged me tight, gently stroking the back of my head. I closed my eyes, taking in his scent. I'd said it smelled like spring, and I was beginning to pinpoint why. It had the slightest smell of trees with a little mist, like dew in the morning. I took a deep breath, taking it in like an aromatherapy candle. It helped relax me.

"All right, that's enough of this mushy stuff. Let's get your sexy ass out there so I can show you off."

"Aw, that's precious. Will you put it in a Valentine's Day card for me?"

"Only if you open it in hot pink lingerie."

***

Annabelle and Jason pulled in behind us and

Shane got out to show them where to park. I climbed out to a bunch of whistles from the guys.

"Damn, Christie, are you trying to distract everyone?" Max asked, walking over to me.

"Well, you know how much help Shane needs behind the wheel. I figured I'd show a little skin and distract whoever he races."

"Good plan," he said, and he let out a whistle. I blew him a kiss and then looked around.

I saw Emma and waved. As I got closer, I realized that she had the best costume out of anyone. Her hair was half black and half white, her makeup was heavy with bright red lipstick. She was wearing a red leather jacket with black leather pants and a spotted black and white shirt. Emma was Cruella De Vil. It was awesome.

"Girl, I love that outfit," I told her as I walked up to her.

"Oh, didn't you hear? You're supposed to be wearing a costume, not something you got out of your closet, Barbie."

"Haha, I would never wear plastic like this. Please, you should have better expectations for me. I'm a little disappointed."

Annabelle and Jason walked over to us then, in their Batman and Ironman costumes. They were frickin' adorable.

"Are you guys excited?" I asked them as the racers went over to their meeting.

"So, they just race in a straight line?" Annabelle questioned judgmentally.

"Yeah, we just race in a straight line," Emma responded, sounding a little hostile.

"I just don't see the excitement."

"It's a rush," I tried to explain to her. "You're going to have to wait to see it. You'll be hooked in a second. Did you bring some money to gamble on the races?"

"I thought you were kidding about that. I didn't bring any."

"No! That's half the fun. I'll lend you, like, a hundred bucks."

"Not a chance in hell I'm spending that much money."

"I'll take the money," Jason piped in. "It sounds like fun."

"That's a lot of money," Annabelle pointed out.

"Live a little, Annabelle. Maybe if you beg, I'll let you pick a car for me to bet on."

Shane came over, telling me he'd be racing third. We headed over to the crowd of spectators and started placing bets for the first race. Jason was really getting into it, and it was a lot of fun to see how animated he got. Hell, I wanted to spot him more money just to see what he'd do. I saw Shane watching him, and he had a big smile on his face. Then, he headed over and started amping up the other spectators. Soon, he and Jason were the center of attention and they were both thriving off of it. They were a great pair.

The first race went down and Jason's pick won. It was great, and I could tell he was hooked. I would bet the rest of my cash wad that he'd want to come back. Shane couldn't watch the second race, since he was working on his car. I didn't really understand this. Why would you show up to a race and not be positive the car was in good shape? But apparently, this was a pretty common thing.

We were just starting to bet on the second race when I heard my name called. I whipped around, terrified, because I knew that voice. It was Rob.

He stormed up to me with a terrifying look on his face.

"What are you doing here?" I whispered to him, pulling him off to the side. If Shane saw him here, it would create a disaster.

"Christie, what are you doing? You could get in a lot of trouble. Are you trying to ruin our future?" he shouted in my face, leaning forward, wagging his finger like my father used to when I was a little girl.

"No, I'm here supporting my boyfriend. Not you. Rob, I don't know how to make this any clearer. We are *not* a couple. I don't want to get married in June. Please, just leave." I tried to push him away, but he wouldn't budge, and he'd put on at least twenty more pounds of solid muscle to his already peak form.

"Fine, we won't get married in June. We'll wait until whenever you're ready, but let's just move on and go home." He reached out and took my hand, but I quickly jerked it out of his grasp.

"Rob, I—"

"Don't fucking touch her!" Shane ran over to me and pulled me behind him. "Listen, dude, I get you're pissed because losing her must suck ass, but she's made her choice, and has asked you to back off. So do it." Shane's voice seemed to be dipped in venom. It was cold, and if words could kill, Rob would be on the ground with deep wounds all over him.

"Or what? You're gonna get your boys to beat me down?" Rob asked, stepping up to Shane, barely whispering. For some reason, his quiet tone unnerved me more than Shane's attitude. I'd learned long ago it's the quiet that truly warns of danger. Well, I think I heard that on a cop show. Nonetheless, it stood true.

"I don't need to get my boys to do anything. They respect me enough to handle business on my own."

"We'll see about that." Rob cocked back and swung a punch at Shane's face.

He ducked and threw a jab into Rob's stomach. Then he kicked Rob's legs out from under him and he fell to the ground. But Rob had been trained for this. He reached up and grabbed Shane's leg, tripping him up as well.

"Guys, stop!" I screamed as Rob got on top of Shane and started to throw some punches.

Shane brought his arms up so Rob was hitting his forearms instead of his face, but Rob managed to sneak a couple punches around it. I tried to pull them apart, but I was nowhere near strong enough. I looked around and saw Max standing there.

"Max, get the guys. Do something!" I was terrified that Rob was really going to hurt Shane. But Max looked down and no one else moved.

Jason walked over to me and pulled me into a hug. "They need to do this. It's a man thing. If it gets bad, I'll jump in." He let go of me and gently pushed me over to Annabelle.

She linked arms with me and stroked my hand.

"Just don't look. It will be over in a few minutes." She tried to divert my attention, pulling me away, but I wouldn't budge.

"I have to."

"Then have faith in your man." A crowd started to form around the guys and Annabelle and I were eventually kind of pushed into the middle of it. I felt like the referee in the middle of a boxing match.

There was some rolling and Shane ended up on top. He connected a punch with Rob's face and blood started to spurt out. I panicked. What if Shane hurt Rob? He would definitely press charges. Here I was, fucking up Shane's future no matter what I tried to do. I broke away from Annabelle's grasp.

"Okay, that's enough," I said to Annabelle. I ran over to them, and awkwardly hovered until I saw an opening. Shane leaned back a little to dodge a punch and I grabbed his shoulders. "Please stop. Please, he isn't worth it," I shouted several times until it seemed my words made it through Shane's head and he stopped hitting Rob.

Shane nodded his head and tried to stand up, but Rob took that moment to hit him hard across the face. His head twisted to the side gruesomely and I started sobbing loudly.

"Enough, guys," I pleaded. This time, Frank and Jason rushed over, pulling the guys apart. I ran to Shane and hugged him, ignoring the blood dripping down his face. "Are you okay?"

"Yeah, babe. Let me go, I don't want this getting all over you." He tried to shove me off, and after a second, I let him. Then I stalked over to Rob, feeling frustration rushing through me. Frank was

230

helping him stand up, so I looked up at him, and fixed him with my most intimidating stare.

"I'm gonna press charges against that asshole," he told me, pointing at Shane. The blood was still gushing through his fingers, which were clamped over his nose.

"Do it. You threw the first punch, so your case will be thrown out, and then Shane can turn the tables on you," I reminded him.

"Really? You'd take that guy's side over mine? After all we've been through?" he cried, looking down at me incredulously. Rob started shaking his head over and over, like he couldn't believe what was happening.

"Rob, it's not the same. None of it is. I want to finish school, and get a job, and maybe move to the city. I don't know. But that's the point. I want the unknown. Our lives are planned out to a T. It's too much."

"Excuse me for trying to take care of you. There was a time you liked it."

"No, there wasn't," I replied delicately. "I just haven't known how to tell you, especially after your brother."

"Don't you dare mention him." He stepped closer to me, dropping his hands from his nose and standing tall.

I didn't know if he was trying to scare me, but at that moment. I wasn't sure how he was going to react. I never should have mentioned his brother.

"You know better than that shit."

"Rob, I just—"

"No. Christie, you just need to get your act

together. I'll talk to you later."

"Rob," I shouted at him as he walked away. "If you call, I won't answer."

"Whatever you say." He waved at me and then pointed at Shane.

I ran back over to Shane. He was getting seen by the EMT they usually have on call. His nose wasn't broken, and he didn't have a concussion.

"Are you all right, babe?" Shane asked me when I stopped beside him.

"Am *I* all right? *You're* the one with blood all over yourself." I grabbed one of the gauze pads from the EMT's bag and started wiping some of it away.

"I know. I look pretty rugged and handsome right now. I'm sure of one thing, we're gonna have some great sex tonight when you thank me for defending your honor," he said, smiling up at me through the marks all over his face.

"Oh, yeah. It will be straight up medieval." I rolled my eyes and looked at him with concern again. His face was swollen under his left eye, and he had another big welt on his right cheek. I closed my eyes and gently kissed him, trying to will the pain away. It was all my fault he'd been hurt again. But this time, the guilt was even stronger. He said it himself, he was fighting for me. "Are you sure you're doing okay?"

"Absolutely. I'm just gonna steal a shirt from Max, throw my fireproof jacket on, and get ready for my race. I'm lucky that they're even letting me race, since it's been more than the ten minutes since it was supposed to start."

"Um, I'm not sure it's a good idea for you to race. What if something happens, or if you're not really okay?"

"I don't have a concussion or anything. It will be fine, and I need to do something to get my mind off this before I go run that guy over with my car for grabbing your hand."

"Please don't."

"Just give me a moment with the guys to get the car and everything. I'll be fine."

I gave him a kiss, a deep meaningful one with as much passion as I could muster. It wasn't long before we were attracting cat calls from the other guys, but I didn't care. At that moment, Shane was all I wanted, needed, and cared about. As I ended the kiss and looked into his dark eyes, it was my turn to be there for him. He trusted me and I needed to trust his word. If he said he as okay to race, then he was. Shane knew the dangers, if he thought he'd put someone in danger, I didn't think he'd do it. I headed over to Annabelle to wait for him to pull up to the starting line and win his race.

Shane pulled out in front of the other racer almost immediately and he never looked back. I loved watching him race. It was an almost primal experience and it excited me every time. I couldn't wait to make it back to his car and show him just what it does to me when he wins. Not that he needed anymore motivation.

I started to head over to him when my phone started buzzing from my clutch. It was too late for Violet to be calling and my friends, well except for Mindy, were all here. Which meant…

"Hi, Mom."

"Christie Margaret," she shouted on the other end. "You get your little tail into Annabelle's car and come back to this house within two seconds."

"What are you talking about? I'm just at…"

"Don't you dare lie to me. Rob is here and I'm trying to fix this black eye that the hoodlum gave him. I know you're at a street race, and right now, your father is driving around in your Uncle George's police cruiser until he finds you. I don't think you want your friends to get arrested, do you?"

"Mom, that's not what happened! Rob came here and wouldn't leave, so Shane asked him to go because he was causing a scene, and then Rob hit him first."

"Christie, why would Rob lie to me?"

"Why would *I* lie to you?" She was really going to take his word over mine. I was crushed.

"Because you're trying to defend that boyfriend of yours."

"Mom…"

"Christie, we can continue this conversation at home. Now, get in Annabelle's car and come home."

She hung up the phone and I looked around. I needed to get home. Dad and Uncle George would definitely throw everyone in jail because I was being selfish.

I sent my dad and mom a text, telling them I was on my way and to call off the search party. "Annabelle!" I called, grabbing her arm and motioning for Jason to follow us.

I pulled her over to Shane as he got out of his car.

"So, Rob lied to my parents and told them Shane started the fight. Now my dad and his friend are out looking for me, and my dad's brother is a police detective. They said if I go home now, that they'll turn around and no one would get arrested," I told the three of them.

"Let's go," Annabelle insisted, dragging Jason back to her car.

"Annabelle, wait," I called after her. "Can you give me a ride?"

"What the hell? Christie, I'll take you and explain to your parents about what happened," Shane assured me.

I turned to him, placing my hand on his chest. "Right now, I think it's best if I just have Annabelle take me home. I don't want to make them even angrier."

"How will it make it worse?"

"Because Rob is there right now."

"Hold on! You're telling me that you're going to go back to your house with that asshole and I'm not allowed to come with you?"

"What, don't you trust me?"

"Yeah, I trust you. I just don't trust *that* guy." He ran his fingers through his hair and paced in a circle a couple times. "This is my fault. Let me help you fix it," he said, taking my hand.

"I can't right now. I'll call you later." I walked away before he could see the tears escaping down my cheek. "Let's go, Annabelle!" I shouted.

We climbed in the car, and I tried not to let it get

to me, but I couldn't help it. This had been one of the worst nights in my life. I'd managed to infuriate my parents, get my boyfriend beat up, put my friends and all the racers in jeopardy, and cause even more problems with Rob. I felt myself shaking uncontrollably as I went over the night in my head. I thought about the message I'd sent to Rob, and I thought about his fist connecting with Shane's face.

"Do you want to talk about it, Christie?" Annabelle asked as Jason spun off and headed to my house, breaking me out of my trance.

"Nope. Not just yet. I need to talk to my parents and deal with this crap. I just can't believe this. Rob is just not giving up."

"Can you blame him?" Jason asked. "If Annabelle dumped me all of a sudden, I'd be heartbroken. I wouldn't just let it go when she started dating someone else."

"Well, what happened with Janice? Isn't that exactly what went down with her?" I asked a little harsher than I intended. "Sorry, uh, I didn't mean that. I just meant…" I tried to back pedal. I didn't need to take this out on my friends.

"No, it's okay. Yeah, but we weren't in love anymore. Janice wanted to end things too, but she didn't know how. She's dating one of the guys from her Earth Club now."

"I just don't know how I can make it any clearer that I don't want to be with him. And my parents are no help. They have an issue with the fact that Shane's Korean."

"Seriously? Aren't we supposed to be past that kind of thing?" Annabelle commented.

"You'd think. I don't know. I'll just talk to them all at once, and fix this."

We drove the rest of the way in silence. I was mentally rehearsing what I'd say, and steeling myself for the disaster that was sure to come when I walked into the house.

Chapter 20

My dad wasn't home yet when I walked in the door, but Rob was sitting on our couch with an ice pack on his eye, and my mother was fawning over him.

"Sit down, young lady," my mother commanded when I closed the door.

"Mom, you have to let me explain."

"No, darlin', your time to talk is done," she insisted, holding a finger up to me. "That boy got you involved in that horrible life of crime and I won't stand it. On top of that, you were lying to me. What kind of boy encourages you to lie?"

"I'm nineteen and you control my life. Of course I had to lie. You give me no leeway, no time to try and figure things out for myself. What do you want from me?"

"I want what's best for you. And some boy on the wrong side of the tracks dragging you into the underbelly of delinquency is *not* what's best for you."

"Oh, let's just calm down the dramatics. The

underbelly of delinquency? It's just street racing. What do you think happens? They don't deal drugs or run guns!" I started pacing. There was just too much inside me to sit still. I felt like I was almost vibrating with energy.

"It's illegal for a reason. What if someone crashed and you were hurt?"

"I'm nowhere near the cars when they race and Shane would never let me in the car with him while he's racing."

"Oh, because you know this kid so well," Rob interjected. "You just met him and he's violent."

"Rob, stay out of it. You hit him first, and now you're here lying to my mom."

"Christie, in this house, we treat people with respect. Now go to your room. I'm going to take Rob home. Your father is getting a much needed drink with Uncle George, so you'll be here by yourself. And I expect you to stay that way." She gave me a harsh look and then pointed toward the stairs.

I growled a little in frustration and just went up to my room. This was a disaster and I didn't want to deal with this tonight. Tomorrow, I'd see if I could get my dad on my side. Maybe if I promised to stop going to the races, they'd calm down and actually try to get to know Shane. In the meantime, I wanted out of this dress and into some leggings immediately.

***

I heard the front door close and I assumed my

mom and Rob left. It was nice that he didn't come in and try to talk to me. I could barely stand the thought of him in my house. Frustrated, I slumped onto my bed and tried to sleep. Maybe in the morning, everyone would calm down.

It was maybe five seconds after I closed my eyes when I heard a noise. It was a weird clacking sound near the front door. I ran to the hallway, and quickly keyed in the code to my dad's gun closet and grabbed my handgun. Then I went to the door and braced myself for whoever was on the other side. I slowly opened the door and pointed the gun.

"Easy, Barbie, don't shoot," Shane shouted, throwing his hands up.

"What are you doing here?" I asked him, lowering the gun. "You scared the shit out of me."

"Apparently, but I'm not going to lie, this is quite possibly the hottest you've ever looked."

I rolled my eyes and put the gun on the table. I wrapped my arms around his neck and gave him a light kiss. "I'm happy to see you, but I told you not to come here. If my parents see you, they'll flip. They already think you're corrupting me."

"You just came at me with a gun, and *I'm* the one corrupting you?"

"I'm serious, Shane." I felt bad enough about tonight and getting him hurt. I didn't want him in any more trouble. God only knows what my father would do to him.

"Look, I followed you. I wanted to make sure everything was all right. Then I saw your mom leave and I figured you might like some company. Was I wrong?"

"Where's your car?"

"I parked it two houses up."

"Yeah, that's no good. My parents know all the cars on the street. If you want to stay, I'm gonna need you to park around the corner and then jog back."

"All right, give me a minute." He left the house and I quickly put the gun away in the safe, glad I didn't have to use it. Then I rushed to my room, brushed my hair, and put on a pair of skimpy underwear on under my leggings. Now I just had to wait.

Shane knocked on the door seconds later. I let him in and practically pulled his arm out of the socket yanking him up to my room.

"So, I guess you want to get me in bed?"

"No, I just wanted to get you in my room before my mom gets home. She's dropping Rob off and he doesn't live far from here."

"So, I guess you *don't* want to get me in bed?"

"Shane…"

"No, I'm kidding. Okay, I'm being serious. How bad is it here?"

"Pretty bad. But I think I can get my dad on my side. I'm going to talk to him tomorrow."

"Is there anything I can do?"

"Yeah, just stay with me tonight."

"I can do that." He kicked off his shoes, shrugged out of his coat, then pulled me into a tight hug. "I'd love to do that."

We stood like that for a few minutes, no funny business, no sarcastic comments, just the two of us, almost not even daring to breathe out of fear it would ruin the moment. But of course, something did. It was the sound of my mom opening the garage door.

I put my hand to my lips, shushing him, then hit the power button on the tv. I flipped it to some fashion reality show and then brought Shane to my bed.

"For now, just lay with me here. I'm not ready for you to go," I whispered to him.

He sat down on the side of the bed and pulled me onto his lap. He stroked the side of my face with the back of his hand and then gave me a soft kiss. I wrapped my arms around his neck, embracing the peace that was now flowing through my system.

"I love you," he murmured into my ear.

"I love you too." We slid under the covers and I fell asleep in Shane's arms.

***

"You have *got* to be kidding me!" My mother screamed from the doorway of my bedroom.

I shot up out of bed, thankful Shane and I were both dressed. "Mom, it's not what it looks like." I felt embarrassed and a little terrified. What if she woke my dad up? What if they arrested Shane? I never should have let him stay over. No matter what I did, I put him in danger. I almost wanted to laugh. Who would have thought the nice Catholic girl who never did anything wrong was the bad influence? Well, screw it. I was done letting my parents rule my life.

"Oh, so you weren't fornicating with the

criminal under my roof?"

"No, we were just sleeping," I insisted.

"And you expect me to believe that?"

"Really," Shane interrupted and stood by my side. "We were just…"

"You can leave my home *now*."

"Mom, he isn't going anywhere." I took Shane's hand, and looked my mom in the eye defiantly. I needed to stand my ground before she tried to walk all over me.

"Christie Margaret, if he does not leave this house right now, I will personally go tell your father and he will *throw* him out."

"No, I'm not going…"

"Christie," Shane said to me softly. "I would never want to disrespect your mother in her home. I'll leave now and you two can finish this conversation." He slipped his shoes back on and grabbed his jacket. But when he got to the door, he stopped in front of my mom. "I just want you to know I care about your daughter and I would never put her in danger. It was foolish of me to bring her racing. I'll make sure it never happens again. But just know, I'll be around as long as she wants me because, right now, she's like oxygen to me. I don't do drugs, I get good grades, and I've never been arrested. Both of my parents are doctors, and I am fully prepared to join my uncle's firm as an engineer when I graduate."

"Shane, those are all very lovely things, but right now, I need you to leave."

"Whatever you say." He walked out of the room.

Mom turned to me and then rushed over to me,

yanking the sheets off my bed. She handled the bundle to me and then straightened her blouse. "Wash these. I won't have your sex sheets stinking up my house anymore." Then she stormed out of my room.

I dropped the sheets on the ground and followed her. "Mom, Mom, wait up." I chased her to the kitchen. She was probably going to her secret vodka stash. "Mom, stop."

"Christie, just go to the laundry room. I don't want to discuss this now."

"Is that because you need to self-medicate a bit?"

"I beg your pardon?"

"Seriously, we both know you keep the alcohol on the top of the fridge for moments like this. I don't think the PTA would approve of that."

"I did not raise you to speak that way to me." She shook her head at me and her usually perfect hair fell out of the bun as she shook with rage. "That boy is changing you and I don't like it."

"No, that boy is changing me for the better. I finally feel like the woman I'm supposed to be. I don't just follow orders because that's what I've always done. He's been helping me with my marketing project, he encourages me to do more than just become a wife and mother."

"And what is so wrong about being a wife and mother? You get home cooked meals every night, someone was always home when you needed them, I chauffeured you around wherever you wanted, and I helped you with your homework every night."

"And you smothered me. I'm old enough to make my own choices, and I don't want to be with

Rob anymore."

"So you have just decided to pick the one boy who would hurt us?"

"No! I picked the boy who cares for me and treats me well. Shane is such a good man and he makes me feel so amazing."

"I will not listen to your pornographic comments. Do you think I want to hear about how he makes you feel? Why is this filth coming out of your mouth?"

"Mom, we didn't have sex. He just slept next to me because he was upset about the fight."

"The fight that he started."

"Why do I even bother talking to you? You don't ever listen to anything I say."

"All right," my dad said as he walked in the room. "Christie, I don't appreciate the way you've been speaking to your mother and I am really upset about that boy sleeping over. For now, I think it's best if you go to school and then come home. No more EET activities, no more staying the night at Annabelle's, and no more Shane." He was stern, but not quite yelling yet. Maybe I could reason with him.

"Dad, you can't—"

"I can. I pay your school bills, I pay your car insurance, hell, I paid for your car. If you would like to continue with these luxuries, then you'll go back to being the girl that we raised. I'll give you a hint, she was respectful and obedient."

"This isn't—"

"You're right," he interrupted me again. "It isn't fair. But neither is the way you've been acting lately. You were almost engaged to Rob, and even he wasn't allowed to stay the night in your room. What made you think it would be all right to have that boy in here?"

"His name is Shane. Stop referring to him as 'that boy,'" I cried.

"You're right. That was disrespectful of me. Shane has gotten you into some trouble and luckily we were here to keep you out of it. Next time, I cannot guarantee that Uncle George will be able to keep it off your record. If Shane cared about you as much as you're claiming, then he would never have put you in that kind of danger."

"But I wanted to go."

"Christie, I'm done with the talking back. You have class tomorrow. I'm sure you have homework to do, so it's time to get back in your room and work on it." He wrapped his arm around my mother's shoulders and brought her into the family room, leaving me standing in the kitchen.

***

I had been sitting in my room, staring at the wall, for about two hours. There was no way out of this right now. Even if I wanted to keep seeing Shane at school, I wouldn't be able to see him after. At least not for a while. But not seeing him was going to crush me.

I gave Violet a call, maybe she'd have an idea. After all, she was the expert in forbidden love.

"Hey, what's goin' on, babe?"

I told her about Rob showing up, the fight, and

the situation with my parents.

"It just seems like every time I try to grow up, they force me to become this meek little ten-year-old. Like, I get I need to respect my parents and all that, but at what expense?"

"You're talking to the wrong person. Don't tell Annabelle this, but I still haven't told my parents about David. I'm afraid of their reaction, since he's so much older."

"So your advice is to keep seeing him and not tell them?"

"Oh, no. I'm all about you doing what I say and not what I do. I'd recommend just going a week or so for a break and then seeing how they feel about Shane. Maybe bringing him to dinner at your house so your parents can get to know him would help. Didn't you say his mom seemed to like you a bit more after dinner?"

"Yes! She stopped glaring at me. I wouldn't say she liked me, but at least it didn't look like she was trying to burn my skin off with her stare. That's a really good idea."

"Let me know how it goes!"

"I will. By the way, has Berneli found any luck with getting a job?"

"No. He's pretty much decided to spend another semester here. The school offered him this big bonus for one more semester and the schools near Elton Hall aren't hiring yet. If we're lucky, he'll be able to find something for the spring."

"Are you all right with that?"

"I don't really have a choice."

"I'm sorry. That really sucks."

"I know, but we're back to living things one day at a time. Next year, we may be long distance, but at this point, I don't actually think I have another option. I need him in my life."

I smiled, remembering when Shane said that last night. I couldn't give up on him just yet. Violet and I hung up and I sent Shane a text to meet up for lunch tomorrow. Then I started into my homework. I actually had a lot of it. After I turned in my marketing project, my professor decided she wanted me to do some follow up for her internship proposition.

After about twenty minutes of work, my phone went off, and I was surprised to see it was Mindy.

"Hey, slut, I'm at the coffee shop on Third. I need you to come over here to go over a couple things."

"Mindy, my parents and I had a bit of a fight, I don't think they're gonna let me out."

"I heard. I'll text your mom. I'm sure she'll let you out since I drove all the way here to see you."

"All right, let me get dressed."

Chapter 21

Turns out, my house arrest could be lifted if the right person begged enough. Now, I was sitting across from Mindy. We hadn't seen each other since the bridal store disaster, and now I was sitting across from her after getting in that huge fight with Rob. I couldn't help but think that this was a calculated conversation.

"Hey, you look good," I told her to try and break the awkward silence.

"Thanks. I tried this new diet that all the celebrities are talking about. It's supposed to make your hair shine, and your face glow."

"Well, this one actually looks like it works."

She nodded her head, and we both took a sip of our coffees and then sat there awkwardly.

"Listen, Christie, I talked to Rob last night."

"I figured."

"I'm really worried about you."

"There's nothing for you to be worried about. I just want to move on and be with Shane."

"I heard that too."

"And?"

"And, I just wanted to talk about it. Your college friends are probably saying you should stay with Shane and just forget Rob, but they also don't know your relationship. I think it's time you remember all the good times you had with Rob."

"Mindy, I just don't think that's necessary."

"Then there's nothing for you to be worried about, right?"

"Fine. Go for it."

"All right." She pulled her computer out of her bag and placed it on the table in front of us. Then she pulled up her Facebook. "Here, we're going to start with the pictures from when we all met Rob." Mindy showed me the shot of us at the alumni picnic lunch. All our dads were in college together, and they would get together every now and then. When we were thirteen, they decided to bring us with them. That was when I met Rob.

He was handsome, cool, and older. I almost instantly crushed on him, and come to think of it, so did Mindy.

"Next, here's your first date." She showed me the picture of our beach day. My parents wouldn't let me go out on a date alone, so we went as a group of friends. It still ranks as one of the best days of my life. We swam in the water, buried one of the other guys in the sand, and then headed to the boardwalk. Rob won me a teddy bear and gave me my first kiss.

"Yeah, that was a good day."

"It was. Rob didn't have eyes for anyone else that day. He told me that was the day he fell in love with you."

"What, why would he tell you that?"

"Because he's my friend too. He wanted to know if I thought you felt the same way. I told him you'd be a fool not to."

"I couldn't believe a guy like that was actually interested in me." I felt a little smile form on my face as I remembered how honored I felt and how special he made me seem.

"Me either. He was, well, he is the sexiest man I've ever seen."

"He was. Now, Shane is the sexiest man for me."

"Well, we have some more memories. Let's not cut this off yet." She then pulled up a picture from Valentine's Day a few years ago, before Rob's brother died. He had made me this home cooked meal, but it was a bit of a disaster. Everything was burned except the bread, which never rose, so instead it was all dough.

Rob felt terrible, but instead of freaking out, we ended up having a giant food fight. That was the night I lost my virginity. There was no fumbling around, or even uncertainty. I wanted him in that moment. But now, all I wanted was Shane.

"Mindy," I told her, closing the laptop. "These are all beautiful memories. But they're in my past."

"You can't just pretend like these things don't still affect you."

"I'm not pretending."

"No, what you're doing is leaving Rob because you don't like his attitude about his brother's death. Is that really the kind of girl you are?"

I stared at her in shock. It felt like she just

punched me in the face. "I was there for Rob. I was with him every night after it happened. I held him as he cried. And he—"

"And he still needs you. What kind of selfish person are you?" she asked harshly.

"I'm not selfish. I just don't want to be married right this moment, but Rob won't listen. He doesn't listen to anything I have to say anymore. I've tried to compromise, I've tried to get him to wait, but he won't. He is so focused on becoming the war hero that he's shut down everything that doesn't fit into his plan. Is it selfish to want the chance to make my own dreams come true?"

"When it involves shoving someone who loves you out of your life, then yes, it is."

"Mindy, I can't do this. You're supposed to be my friend and you're supposed to care about my feelings too. But lately, it seems like all you care about is Rob. Well, you know what? I'm sorry he fell in love with me. I'm sorry he picked me over you. But now you have the chance to be with him because I don't love him anymore. I didn't love him before Shane came into my life. If Shane weren't here, I still wouldn't be with Rob."

"How dare you say that! I haven't been pining all these years for your boyfriend."

"You have, and that's all right. Really, I give you permission."

"I don't need your permission. If I wanted Rob, I could have had him."

"Good, then go right ahead." I grabbed my bag and walked out the door, shaking in frustration. Part of me appreciated that she wanted to try and make things work between me and Rob. If I were in her shoes, maybe I would have done the same thing. But I would also listen when she objected. Right? Isn't that what tough love is supposed to be all about?

I got in my car and drove back home, confused. At what point did the people who know you best, become so clueless? What if they were right? What if at the end of all of this, I ended up unhappy because I ignored all of their opinions? I'd spent so much time fighting them that I never stopped to consider that maybe they had a point. There was a time when all I wanted to do was marry Rob. Was that really so bad? Yeah, I wasn't ready to give up on my dreams, but I assumed I'd have to. Rob was going to be away for basic training and then he'd probably end up going overseas. I could finish my degree and then maybe find a marketing job. If I got that internship, then I'd have some experience.

Maybe I'd have to reconsider all of this. I texted Shane and said that I couldn't meet tomorrow. I needed some time by myself to think. I always thought it was easy to figure out what you wanted out of life. But maybe that was because someone has always told me.

***

I spent the next two weeks ignoring Shane's calls, avoiding my friends, and focusing on my schoolwork. Things at home hadn't improved much. My mom and I were barely talking and I ate most of my meals in my room. I was desperate to try and

253

figure out what I wanted without the influence of anyone else. This seemed to be the only way I could figure out if what I was feeling was what I wanted. I couldn't get rid of the thought that Shane was just my rebellious stage. If that was true, and I pushed Rob away, then I'd be giving up quite possibly my entire future.

I was leaving the library when Shane finally caught up to me.

"Don't walk away. I know your schedule by heart. Your next class doesn't start for twenty minutes, so you can't run away. What the hell is going on?"

"Shane, listen, I'm just trying to work through some things and I needed to be alone to do it."

"Work through what? Last time we were together, you said you loved me. Were those just words to you?"

"No, I would never say them unless I meant them."

"Then, what? What is it?"

"I'm confused, okay? Everyone who has known me for years is telling me I'm being ridiculous. They don't understand how I could give up on Rob, just like that. Mindy stopped by. She reminded me how much I loved him. Now, I don't know what I'm thinking or feeling and I just wanted some time to try and figure it out. He was so important to me for so long and then you came into my life. You've taken my entire world and flipped it upside down."

"And what? Now it's too much for you?"

"I didn't think it was, but now, I don't know. That's what I've been trying to think about."

"So you've been spending time with Rob, then?"

"No, I've been spending time alone. I didn't want any outside influence or outside feelings. I just…"

"I get it. You just want to be alone. Let me know when you've made up your mind. I'll be waiting." He stroked my cheek and then walked away.

My mom always taught me never to cry in public. You smile and walk to the bathroom. If it's empty, you can have your nervous breakdown. But if not, then you go into the stall and take several deep breaths until you've relaxed enough to be seen. At that moment, I'd completely embarrass her. I didn't even have the willpower to stand up, let alone walk to the bathroom. I just sat on the couch next to the library as the gentle tears falling down my face turned into body wracking sobs.

People were looking, but I didn't care. I didn't care about any of it.

"Christie?"

I looked up and saw Jason standing there. I tried to swipe the tears away, but I couldn't get them to stop. He rushed over and pulled me into a hug, apparently not caring about the mess I was making on his shirt.

"Okay, so Annabelle told me something's been going on with you lately, and you don't need to tell me anything. Just, um, just try and take some deep breaths. Maybe think about that time we ran that ridiculous karaoke event without Annabelle. You forced me to sing Brittney Spears and I was so amazing, I got a standing ovation."

I sputtered, laughing and crying at the same time.

"I don't think they were cheering because you were awesome."

"Whoa, don't take that moment away from me. My moves were basically epic."

"You're right, Brittney will be calling you for pointers soon." I leaned back, wiping my tears, and smiled up at him.

"Ready to talk about it?"

"Um, not yet. I just need to work some things out, guy-wise. I'm trying to figure out what I want without getting influenced by everyone."

"I can respect that. With Annabelle, I basically had Violet and Kyle in my ear telling me that I should be with her. Eventually, their voices start to mingle and you can't tell which one is yours and which one is theirs."

"So how did you sort out the voices?"

"I fell into a weird funk. I kissed Annabelle, even though I was still with Janice, and then Violet threatened to kick my ass if I didn't shape up. She's tiny, but that girl is scary as hell when she's pissed."

"So I just need Violet to come here and threaten me?"

"Well, Annabelle can be scary when she wants. Maybe I'll call her?" He nudged me gently and smiled sweetly. "Listen, at the end of the day, I thought about who I'd want to spend a snow day with. Think about it, you're stuck in an apartment with that one person for, like, two days. With Janice, it was terrifying. We'd spend the first few hours together and it'd be great. But then she'd harp and criticize me, and then I'd succumb to whatever she'd want, whether I liked it or not. But when I pictured being stuck with Annabelle, I got excited. I wanted nothing more than to sit around with her, talking about the future, or boy bands, or whatever. I'd hold her, and if at any point we started to fight. I'd kiss her and shut her up before she had the chance because, with Janice, I wanted to end the fight, but with Annabelle, I just want her happy."

I nodded my head, looking at him in a new way. He was surprisingly more intuitive than I ever thought. "And that was why you decided to end it with Janice?"

"Yeah, I realized that with Janice, I was always looking for ways to make her happy. But that was because I thought I was supposed to. With Annabelle, I *have* to make her happy. It is like this inner desire I have and I'm not sure how to control it. It's like if she's happy, then I've done my good deed for the day."

"That's really sweet."

"Thanks, just don't mention it. I have a reputation to protect." He popped the collar of his jacket and I started laughing again.

"Oh, don't worry, I'll make sure everyone knows you're still a player."

"Appreciate it." Then he hugged me again. "If you need to talk about it, you can always call Annabelle. But I'm your friend too, so I don't mind it if you need someone to go blow off some steam with at the shooting range, or something."

"Actually, I may hit you up on that. It sounds like something that could help."

"Great. Let me know the time and I'll be there."

"Thanks." We said goodbye and I felt the power

return to my legs. I got up and went to the bathroom. I wiped my face and took my powder out of my bag to fix the red blotches that had broken out across my cheeks.

I thought about what Jason said. Who would I want to spend a snow day with? If Rob and I were stuck in my house all day, we'd probably watch movies, I'd cook for him, we'd have sex, and then we'd separate. He'd probably watch some sports and I'd clean up. It would be almost the same thing as my parents. And they were happy.

With Shane, he'd have me outside, engaged in an insane snowball fight. He'd tackle me into a pile of snow and kiss me fiercely. Then, he'd drag me inside and we'd have sex on the first surface we could get to. It would be passionate and erotic as he ripped my clothes off. Then, we'd probably spend the night arguing about something silly while we watched a movie. It'd be nice. But at the same time, how long could that passion last before it burned out? Wasn't there a saying about how people like this fight hard but love harder? Would that be my life?

I walked to class, even more jumbled than I was before.

Chapter 22

Luckily, Thanksgiving was coming, and I'd have a few days off and tons of time to be distracted. We always had an intense family meal with around twenty people all laughing and enjoying each other's company. It was one of my favorite holidays, but this year I didn't feel like celebrating. But I was tired of this funk, and I forced myself to get excited.

I put on a pretty green dress with a skater skirt, a bejeweled neckline, and perfectly ironed pleats. I did my makeup and curled my hair. I looked good, but there was still one thing missing, so I went to the kitchen and grabbed my lacy apron; the one that my mom bought me last year. She had a matching one, and had always insisted we'd look adorable cooking with them on. I thought it might be a peace offering if she saw me wearing it.

Sporting my apron, I grabbed the potatoes and started peeling. My mom walked in, took one look at me, and then grabbed her matching apron and put it on.

"Why don't you work on the pies, darlin'? Everyone always raves about your pies."

"Sounds good." I handed her the peeler and got the ingredients to make my crust from scratch. I listened as my mom talked about what was going on in her new charity event. She was so excited about being elected to plan the party.

"Will you be on the committee with me? I'd love to have some of your input."

I looked at her, smiling as I felt all the tension between us start to melt away. "I'd love to, Mom. That sounds like fun."

"I think so too, and we could really use your marketing assistance."

"Mom, I'm sorry about all the drama." I couldn't help but feel guilty for everything. Yeah, Rob played a huge role in this, but a lot of it still fell back on me.

"Shhh, not now, darlin'. You and I know that we come from a long line of dramatic women. Every once in a while, it just takes us over. I just want you to know how much I care about you and your future."

"I know you do."

"Good, now get to mixin'. Those pies need to be perfect. Mrs. Willimas is coming, and she insisted on bringing those awful lemon squares again. If the church's bake sale is any indication, she still hasn't figured out how to make them without cement."

"You got it."

Mom and I spent the next three hours cooking. My dad came in every now and then to check on us/steal pieces of food. But every time he did, every single time, he would drop a kiss on my mom's forehead. And then she'd lean into him, and for a second, they'd forget that I was even there. It was just the two of them. I loved seeing them this way. Sometimes, when I watched their nightly routine, it seemed to be monotonous. But then, maybe that was the point. They seemed to like it. Maybe that was their definition of romance.

I was deep in thought about what my definition of romance was when the doorbell rang. It was a little early for all of the guests to get here. Mom was a bit of a stickler about time and we should still have about two hours before anyone was due to show up. The table wasn't even set yet.

"Darlin', why don't you go see who that is?" Mom was in the middle of mixing together her stuffing, so I quickly grabbed a rag to wipe my hands off and went to the door.

Again, it was Rob standing there and my blood began to boil.

"What the hell are you doing here?"

"Seriously, after all of these years? We've spent Thanksgiving together forever. My mom sent me early to see if you all needed any help. She'll be here soon with some appetizers."

"That's great. Um, how have you been doing?" I asked him as I moved aside to let him in.

"I've been good. School is getting tough, since they are ready to let us out. But I love it. I can't wait to get out of the classroom and really start to experience life."

I looked up at him and the fire I once loved was back. "I'm happy for you," I said honestly. "All I've ever wanted was for you to be happy."

He looked down at me, smiling sweetly back, and I realized he didn't realize what I meant. "You know, happy in life. With whatever comes your way," I mumbled and walked toward the kitchen, afraid to be alone with him in case he acted on the feelings I saw in his eyes.

"Robert, it's so nice to see you here," my mother gushed as she gave him a little kiss on his cheek.

"Joy, it's lovely to see you, as always. My mom is going to be here in a little bit with the chicken, avocado rolls, and the meatballs."

"Fantastic. She makes the best meatballs. One of these days, I'm going to bend her arm into giving me the recipe."

"I have a feeling you'll get it soon. Just maybe not in the way you anticipated."

"Well, I hope so. Why don't you go and join Hank in the family room? He has the game on and I'm sure you're eager to check on the score. Christie and I have it all handled in here."

"If you don't mind, I was eager for Christie to try on the military ball dress. If she decides to go with me, we won't have much time to get a new one."

"Oh," she said and turned to look at me. "Did you decide to go?"

I looked from her to Rob, and then back again. After all the thinking, I really hadn't come up with anything. It was a choice between smooth sailing and braving the storm. "Actually, I haven't made a decision yet." I knew I was running out of time though, so I needed to figure something out fast.

"Well, why don't you try on the dress for him? To be honest, he has a point."

"I guess trying the dress on can't hurt." I took the apron off and then headed to my room. The dress was still hanging in my closet in the garment bag. I'd never even unzipped it to see what it looked like. So I walked into my closet and pulled it out.

I draped the garment bag on my bed and undid it. It was a beautiful red rose satin dress. I ran my fingers along the fabric, entranced by how silky it felt.

"Do you like it?" Rob asked from my doorway. He was leaning against the frame with a smile on his face.

"It's probably the most amazing dress I've ever seen."

"I love the way you look in red. I saw this in a shop while we were hanging out in the town near school. I called Mindy to get your size and bought the dress on the spot."

"But we were broken up then."

"We're meant to be, Christie. I figured you'd just need to get the cold feet out of your system."

He said that so matter of factly that I just wanted to scream. He didn't get it. And then it hit me. It wasn't that he didn't get it. I don't think he cared. "Rob, listen to me. I don't even know if I'm ready for all of this yet."

"I know. But it's what I want, so I'm going for it."

"Well, um, just close the door so I can put the dress on." I waved my hand at him, shooing him away. He nodded his head and closed it.

I quickly stripped out of the green dress and into the red gown. The straps were just off the shoulders and dipped down to a low back. I undid the side zipper and quickly stepped into it. As I stood in front of the mirror, staring at my reflection in the gown, I was stunned. It was perfect. I turned to the side and admired the way the dress flared out in the back. The train was dramatic, but not too long. It was breathtaking.

"Wow," Rob said from the doorway. He had opened it again, but I was too distracted by the dress to notice. "You are the most beautiful woman I've ever seen." He walked over to me, and wrapped his arms around my waist. I leaned back into his shoulder, closing my eyes, and remembered how good this felt. He gave me a little kiss on the cheek.

"Thank you. This dress…it's too much."

"No, for you, it's just the start of what I'd like to give you. Give me the chance, I'll give you the world."

"Christie, Rob," my mom called from the bottom of the stairs. "Come show us the dress. Carnie just got here with the appetizers and she wants to see how you look too."

"Come on. They're not going to be able to take their eyes off you." He took my hand and quickly spun me around so I was facing him. Then he dipped his head a little and kissed me.

"Rob, what…" I tried to say when he let go.

"Shhh, we should go show them."

He pulled me downstairs, where both of our parents were now waiting for us.

"Oh my god, look at her, Hank. Our little girl is

all grown up." My mom started to cry and my dad hugged her to his side, apparently too stunned for words.

"You did so well, Rob," his mother said. "You two make such an amazing couple."

"We aren't—"

"Christie, I think this dress was made for you," Mom insisted, cutting me off. "You have to wear it to the ball."

"Oh, I totally agree, Joy. This is the most amazing moment," Carnie managed through her tears. "Where's my phone, I need a picture of them." She rummaged around in her purse and pulled it out, pointing at us. "Oh my god!" she screamed.

I looked around at them. My mom had her hands over her mouth and there was the hint of tears in her eyes. I was confused and turned to ask Rob what was going on. He was on one knee, with a ring box open in front of him. There was the perfect ring with the sapphires, the antique band, and the two carat diamond sparkling up at me.

"Holy crap," I managed to say as I felt myself shaking.

"Christie, this last year has been hard for us. I know that we grew apart for a bit, and had some issues with that guy. But looking at you in my dress, I can't help but think back to all the plans we've made. If you want to finish school after we're married, then I'll support you. Whatever you want, I'll make it happen, as long as you say you'll be mine."

"Rob, I don't know what to say."

"I know, it's all so sudden, but this is when we've always said we were going to get engaged, and I wanted to show you that I'm true to my word. Here." He slipped the ring on my finger and smiled at his mom, who was videoing the whole thing.

"Oh, look at that, it fits just like that dress," my mom gushed.

Rob picked me up and spun me around. "We're going to have the perfect marriage. You just have to trust me."

"I do trust you," I told him. "But let me take this dress off. I, uh, I don't want to get anything on it." Rob let me go, even offered to come help me get out of it, but I turned him down. I needed to be alone. My heart was racing a mile a minute. He was right. We'd always talked about getting engaged at Thanksgiving because it would give us enough time to plan a June wedding, and we both wanted our parents there. Then how did I miss this? How was I so wrapped up in everything else that I forgot we planned this?

I sat on my bed for a minute and tried to control my breathing, but it wasn't happening. Every time I thought about marrying Rob, the panic came right back up. Then what Jason said popped in my mind. I thought about marrying Shane. It was almost automatic, as the calm quickly rushed away. We weren't anywhere near that step, but I knew with almost certainty that he'd never try and force something on me like this. He'd wait until we were both ready and then he'd plan something dramatic and meaningful.

I couldn't marry him, but I didn't know how to

say anything.

There was only one thing to do. I threw on a sweater, yoga pants, and a pair of boots and grabbed my purse. Everyone was probably still waiting downstairs, so I needed another way out. I opened my window and looked down. There was no way I could actually make it.

"Christie," my mom called, opening my door. "Is everything all right? Do you need me to help you get out of the dress?"

"No, I…I can't do this. I don't want to marry Rob." I started to panic a bit and it felt like the bridal store all over again. I wrapped my arms around my stomach, trying to mimic what Annabelle had done as it became harder and harder to breathe.

"What are you talking about? This is what you've always wanted."

"But it's not."

"Listen, Christie, I think I've been dealing with this rebellious phase quite well. But it's time to be done with it. That boy downstairs is your future. He will provide for you, love you, and give you the life you deserve."

"But I won't be happy. Sure, it'd be fine and I'd check all the boxes, but I don't want fine. I want passion, fire, excitement, and I don't care if it fizzles out. I'd rather have a couple years with Shane than the rest of my life with Rob. If I marry him, I'd be settling."

"Why? Why does that make you settling? What about a strong military man is settling?"

"It has nothing to do with the military. Rob and I

267

just aren't meant to be."

Mom sat down on my bed and patted the seat next to her. She took my hand in hers and held it tight to her chest. "Darlin', there are times when I wish I could understand what goes on in that pretty head of yours, but I don't, so you just listen. I know what you need, and it's time to listen to me. Rob is your future, so marry him, and the rest will sort itself out."

"And if I don't?"

"Christie, I'm not going to force you to marry Rob. But I'm not going to support you or your decision not to. So that's your choice."

"You're not serious?" I begged her, feeling betrayed. Here she was again, choosing Rob and his feelings over my own. "How can you say that to me?"

"Because I'm tired of these melodramatic games and your father will take my side. So, put that pretty green dress back on and let us celebrate this moment." She let go of my hand and started toward the door.

"Mom?"

"Yes, darlin'?"

"Did you know he was proposing today?"

"Of course. I've known for a couple months now." She closed the door and I sat frozen.

So the entire time I was getting to know Shane, she was convinced I would get back together with Rob. But not just back together—engaged with Rob. She watched me struggle with my decision between the two boys. Instead of being my mom, she just bided her time until Thanksgiving.

I needed to get outta here. I went to my dresser and grabbed some of the spare cash I kept for emergencies. There was about five grand there. Then I quickly packed a bag. I threw some clothes in there, my laptop, and all of my notes and school books. This would do for now. Maybe I could sneak back in another time and grab my comic books. The case that held them was way too heavy for me to carry out of here quickly.

Now to get out of here. Everyone was probably waiting down the stairs, so I couldn't go out that way. Then it clicked. There was a balcony that led to the garden in our backyard. If I climbed down the stairs, I could run around to the front of the house and hop in my car. It was a good thing I left my purse in my room last night. This definitely would be a lot harder without a car.

I ran over to my parents' room, and down the balcony. Then I booked it to the front of the house, but my plans were quickly dashed. There was a car that was blocking my car in, my car was blocking my mom in, and I didn't have a key for my dad's car. I went into the garage and tried to look and see if he had an extra set of keys. The only ones I found were for his motorcycle.

I bit my lip as an idea quickly ran through my mind. I hadn't been on a bike since that one time with Shane, and I'd never done it by myself. I looked at the door to the house and then at the ring. What choice did I have? I grabbed the keys and took off on the bike before I could second guess anything else.

I rode, feeling the wind flow through my hair

269

and the rush that came from going fast. It made me think of Shane and the first time I was on the back of his bike. I shifted gears and went faster, pushing the bike even more as I went down the highway.

I reached Shane's parents' house and stopped on the side of the road. But as I was getting off the bike, I tripped and felt my ankle twist and my hands scraped the pavement. I hobbled over to the door and started knocking frantically.

"Yes?" Mrs. Choi asked when she opened the door. "Oh, Christie, I didn't know you were coming over today."

I held up my left hand, showing her the ring finger, and I immediately started to cry.

"It's all right, honey." She pulled me into a hug and stroked my hair as I cried into her shoulder.

"Mom, who was at the door?" Shane asked, and then stopped in his spot as he looked at me. "What's going on?"

"Shane, I think Christie here needs a moment to get it all together. I'm going to take her upstairs, and I think you need to get her some food. Go grab a plate and bring it up to my bathroom, please." She draped her arm around her shoulder and started to lead me up the stairs. But I couldn't get there. I cried out as I tried to put my weight on my hurt foot.

"Christie," Shane shouted, bending down to me. "Are you all right? What happened?"

"I just fell over getting off my dad's bike."

"Wait, you rode a motorcycle here?"

"Shane, why don't you pick her up and bring her upstairs? Then go get the food. You two can talk later. Right now, I think she needs some care for that ankle."

He bent down and brought me up to the most amazing bathroom I've ever seen in my life. It was about the size of the guest room in my house. It had a dramatic Jacuzzi bathtub, a raindrop shower, a vanity with perfect lighting, and an elaborate chair. Shane sat me down on the chair and then knelt down in front of me.

"Maybe you could not be down on one knee right now?" I showed him my ring and looked down.

"You said yes?" He turned, walked out the door, and kicked the railing several times, slamming it with his fists. I grabbed his shoulders, trying to balance on one foot but he flew from my grasp. I should have known there would be no calming him down.

I shook my head and started crying again.

"Christie, I—" he started to say but we were quickly cut off.

"Shane, please get the food," Mrs. Choi ordered.

"Right," he responded to her. Then he stroked my cheek again. "I'll be back."

Mrs. Choi watched him leave and then knelt down in front of me. She started undoing my boot and slowly took it off.

"So, I want to tell you a story. Now, Shane doesn't know about this, so I need your word that you will not tell him."

"I promise," I murmured to her.

"Before Mr. Choi and I came to the United States, I was a lot like you. I was in a relationship with this boy. His father and my father were business partners. They were training Seo-Juh, well, that was his Korean name, but he goes by Paul now. They were training him to take over one day. They'd decided it was the perfect merger. There was just one problem. Paul had a problem being faithful. So I ended things with him. But when my father found out, he told me that I'd be cut off if I didn't marry him. I never even got a proposal."

She stopped her story and then started wrapping my ankle with an Ace bandage she pulled out from under the sink.

"What did you say?"

"I said yes. Then I went to my room and applied for school in the United States. Once I got my acceptance letter, I got my visa and left my family. I tried to explain to my mom about Paul's problem, and you know what she told me?"

I shook my head.

"She said that my father cheated as well. It was a part of life and I'd just need to get used to it. But I decided I didn't want that life. So when I came to the United States, my parents stopped talking to me. They wouldn't finance my education, and they didn't come to my wedding to Mr. Choi. In fact, they've never even met Shane."

"Was it worth it?"

"Yes. There isn't one day that goes by that I regret my decision to leave South Korea. I had to work two jobs to support myself in school, but now I am a respected doctor, with a beautiful house, a loving marriage, and a respectful son."

"Sounds amazing."

"It is. But my sister married Paul. She has a beautiful house in South Korea, two amazing children, and as far as I've heard, she and Paul are happy. Do you understand where I'm going with this?"

"I thought I did. But your sister kinda confused me a little."

"My point is, you have to decide what makes you happy. Maybe the reason Paul cheated was because I didn't make him happy in the way my sister does."

"Your son makes me happy. These past couple weeks I've been trying to figure out what I wanted. I thought that my family wouldn't push so hard if they didn't know what's best for me. I thought I needed to listen to them about Rob. But now that I could have him, all I feel is fear and panic."

"And when you saw Shane? How did you feel?"

"I felt calm begin to resonate through me. Rob is trying to force this marriage on me because he thinks it will happen eventually, so he figures, why wait? But Shane, I don't think Shane would force anything on to me. He values my opinion and listens when I speak. It's a nice change for me."

"Then he's your choice?"

"I don't think there ever was a choice. It was always him."

Chapter 23

Mrs. Choi cleaned up my hands and gave me some Tylenol for the pain in my ankle.

"All right, I'm going to get Shane and see about that food."

"I'm right here. You doing all right?" Shane asked from the door of the bathroom.

"Yeah, I just don't really know where to go from here."

"Okay, well, I'll bring you downstairs. I have a plate set up for you there, and I called one of my friends to meet me here. We need to take the bike back."

"Wait, why?"

"It's your dad's bike. If I wanted to find my daughter, I'd report the bike stolen and let the cops find it, therefore, finding you."

"Oh shit. I never thought of that."

"Don't worry about it. I'll take care of it. Just stay here and I'll be back in a little bit."

"Thanks, Shane. Your mom has been really great to me."

"I think she is warming up to you."

He kissed my forehead, and then picked me up, bringing me to the kitchen table. Mrs. Choi already had a pillow propped up on a chair for me.

***

Shane got back about an hour later, looking grim. He took a seat next to me on the couch.

"How did everyone seem when you dropped the bike off?"

"There weren't any cars there. I guess they're out looking for you."

"I told them I was fine."

"I know. They probably just want to make sure that you are."

I nodded my head and bit my lip. This was a disaster.

"So, tell me what you want to do."

"I don't know. My mom told me she wouldn't support me anymore. I mean, I have a scholarship that will take care of school, but I have nowhere to live. Yeah, the marketing internship pays, but I haven't gotten it yet."

"Okay, why don't we worry about all of that tomorrow? It's been a stressful day, and everyone probably just needs a little time to calm down. I doubt your parents are going to completely write you off because of this."

"I hope not."

He wrapped his arm around my shoulder and we leaned into the couch. Mrs. Choi walked into the room and smiled at us. Shane moved to get up, but she stopped him.

"No, stay where you are." She sat down on the loveseat across from us. "Christie, I want you to know that you are welcome to stay here or at Shane's apartment whenever you want. But tonight, I'd like you to stay here. I'd love to spend the night all together. Mr. Choi is doing something with the surround sound in the basement, and we have a tradition where we spend Thanksgiving night watching movies."

"That sounds nice."

"Perfect, why don't you come help me get some snacks, and Shane, please go make sure your father doesn't electrocute himself." I was tired of being carried around. I needed to try and walk, or at least hobble a little bit.

We went into the kitchen and fell into a silent rhythm. We made popcorn, poured chips into bowls, mixed lemonade, and dumped candy on a platter. It was nice at first, but then it reminded me of earlier today with my mom. The difference was that I finally felt free. I had no secrets from Mrs. Choi, and it didn't seem like she hated me anymore. I brought the snacks downstairs and tried to focus on forgetting about my day so I could enjoy the night.

***

We ended up watching an old western. Apparently, Mr. Choi was obsessed with them since they helped him learn English. It was actually why they decided on the name Shane. That was Mr.

Choi's favorite old western of all time. Mr. and Mrs. Choi went to sleep after one movie, and we headed up to Shane's old bedroom. It was bright green with awards, trophies, and pictures all over the walls.

"Who would have thought that the street racing thug was a science fair champion?"

"I'm in school for engineering. What did you expect?"

I laughed a little and came to a trunk at the end of the bed. "What's in here? Your porn collection?"

"Nah, Barbie, I wouldn't leave that out in the open. Mom would have found that in two seconds."

"So what's in it?"

"Are you sure you're ready to look into my secret life?"

I looked at him, starting to get a little creeped out. "Now I'm a little scared."

"Nope, you walked down this path, you have to keep going." He knelt in front of the desk and rapped on it like a drum roll. Then Shane slowly unlocked the latch and whipped it open. I looked over his shoulder and breathed a sigh of relief.

"Comic books?"

"Yes. I have a bit of an obsession. Captain America is basically the most epic character ever."

"Well, Captain America is an engineered soldier with way too much of a moral code. Now, if you want epic, then Wolverine should be your favorite character. He can't die even if you cut his head off."

"I've never been more turned on by a woman in my entire life."

"I'm full of surprises."

"Are you trying to tell me you're a closet comic book nerd?"

"I'm trying to say that your collection looks a little light. Maybe you should stock up on the lesser known superheroes, like Aquaman or Mrs. Marvel."

"Keep talking dirty to me. It's getting me all sorts of excited." He got up and wrapped his arms around my waist.

"Oh, no, we're just going to sleep tonight. Your parents have been very kind to me and I'm not doing this here. We can wait until we go back to your apartment tomorrow."

"But we've gone, like, three weeks."

"So you can go one night longer."

We laid down on Shane's bed and continued to talk about comic books before we drifted off to sleep.

***

"Where are we going?" I asked Shane as he drove in the opposite direction of his apartment.

"It's a surprise."

"You and your surprises are getting old. Just tell me."

"Actually, it brings me joy to watch you get so aggravated. The flush in your cheeks is very becoming." He ran the back of his knuckles against my cheek and I batted his hand away. "Yeah, girl, I like it when you're feisty."

I rolled my eyes and crossed my arms in front of my chest.

"Relax, we have a bit of a drive ahead of us."

"Good, I was not done with our discussion about female Thor when you fell asleep last night."

"Your argument was just so dull, I couldn't help it."

We talked the entire way, continuing to bicker about the comic book world I've always been too ashamed to discuss with practically anyone else. It was so comfortable and I couldn't help but think I'd made the right decision. The one time I'd corrected Rob about something comic book related, he'd quickly shut down and grew grumpy. Any other time I'd tried to bring up something related to superheroes, he'd grown frustrated and angry. Shane, on the other hand, thrived on the argument.

Eventually, we pulled down a deserted road with beautiful trees leaning over the road, creating an arch for us to drive under. There were still some leaves on the branches, so the colors were still breathtaking. A sharp wind came up and surrounded the car with stray leaves, making us feel like we were being transported into a fall wonderland.

A few more turns and we pulled up to a wood mansion in the woods. There were no neighbors in sight and no other cars around. There were massive bay windows with a red double door in between them. Just behind the mansion was a giant lake fit with a pier. It was like a fairy tale house, or quite possibly where a serial killer takes his victims when he wants to keep them alive for a long period of time.

"This is amazing," I breathed as Shane took our bags out and walked us to the front door.

"This is my parents' cabin. They usually come

here for holidays, but I asked them if we could come here for a couple days. I figured that if we put some distance between you and your parents, everything could calm down. Plus, I think there are a couple things on your list we haven't finished." He kissed me gently and nuzzled against my nose sweetly.

I smiled at him, and then panicked. "Wait a minute...the lake? I'm not jumping in there."

"Oh, yes you are!" He dropped the bags and threw me over his shoulder, running like a mad man toward the pier.

Before he got to the end, he set me down on my feet and started taking his clothes off. "Are you going to join me?"

"No way in hell. The water is probably freezing."

"Haven't you ever heard of a polar plunge? People jump into freezing water all the time. Besides, the house is right there. We'll jump in, go underwater and then run into the house."

He was standing there in his boxers, muscles flexed, and I just had to. I don't know. Maybe it was the lack of control I'd felt yesterday that made me do it. Whatever it was, I started stripping too. As I got to my underwear, Shane walked over to me, taking them off for me and I slid his boxers down.

"Come on, let's go skinny dipping," I said and took his hand.

Together we both jumped into the water. It felt like little knives stabbing me all over and I had to fight to breathe. But Shane's hand was strong and he pulled me up above the water.

I took a deep breath and went to run back to the pier. But Shane yanked me back to him and gave me a kiss.

"All right," he said in between shivers. "Let's get back into the house."

We scrambled to the pier and hauled ourselves out, grabbing our clothes. Shane pulled the keys out of his jeans pocket, and quickly let us into the house. He led me to the bathroom just inside and grabbed two towels from the linen closet inside of it. I wrapped him up tight and he pulled me into a hug with my own towel. We stood like that, absorbing each other's body heat.

I turned my head and kissed him, begging for passion, but he pulled away suddenly.

"Not just yet. I'll grab our clothes from the front door and meet you here."

"Last night you couldn't wait, and now you're telling me to hold on?"

"There's something I need to say to you first, and it doesn't feel right for me to say it when you're naked, and I might not be able to get it out because you naked is one of the most distracting things on the planet." He quickly bolted from the bathroom and returned with our bags.

We quickly got dressed and Shane brought me to the living room couch. He knelt in front of me and gave me a little kiss.

"All right, so I'm not proposing marriage, but I am proposing something. Okay, um, here it goes." He took a piece of paper out of his pocket and then looked up at me.

"You wrote it down?"

"Shut up. I was nervous, okay?"

"Sorry, I'm going to be quiet now."

"That's unlikely." He raised his eyebrows at me and I rolled my eyes at him. But when I returned my gaze to him, all the joking from Shane's face was gone.

He took a deep breath and started. "I vow to make love to you often, but love you always. I vow to support you even when you're being crazy, well, especially when you're being crazy. I vow to never let you drive my car, but to always make sure you get where you need to go. I vow to hold you when you cry, when you laugh, and when you make sarcastic comments. I vow that if one day we do get married, I won't ask until you're ready, and after that, I vow to never let you give up on our adventures. As much as I'd like to see you barefoot and pregnant with my child, I want to see you take on the world first. Unless you want a baby sooner than later, and I'm down to practice. Basically, I vow to be, not just the man you need in your life, but the man you want in your life."

I didn't know what to say and the tears took over. That was the ultimate non-proposal I'd ever heard, and quite possibly the most amazing thing I'll ever hear. He understood me down to my core and appreciated all of my ridiculous quirks. But it was more than that. The speech was so Shane. He didn't try to be anyone else or to act all fancy. I know this came from the heart and I know he worked on it by himself.

"Shane, I want you to be the man in my life too. And as much as I hate your surprises, I hope they never stop."

He sat down on the couch next to me and kissed me, pressing hard against me. He pulled away again and took my face in his hands. "Look, I know if things don't work themselves out with your parents, it's going to be hard for you, but I'm not going anywhere. You can move into the apartment with me. I make enough from racing and the internship to support us if you don't get your own internship. Besides, I'd love to see you bare ass naked cooking me dinner every night."

The smile on my face fell. I wanted to be happy. These were all the things I'd wanted, but now I was getting them because of the awful circumstances my parents put me in. It wasn't fair to him. I stood up and paced a little.

"As much as I'd love to do that, you don't have to do this. I mean, it's not your fault that my parents cut me off. I don't want to be a burden, and you helping to support me would definitely be—"

"My choice," he said, cutting me off and standing up in front of me. "Christie, didn't you hear what I said? I didn't come up with that last night. I've been working on that for the last three weeks we've been apart. You needed me to ask you to be my girlfriend, so I decided to do this vow thing so you'd understand exactly how crazy I am about you. Yeah, this thing with your parents sucks, but that doesn't mean I still don't want these things."

"Are you sure?"

"I'm positive."

"Will you buy me a lacy apron?"

"Yes."

"Then I'd love to."

Shane kissed me, wrapping his arms around my waist. I melted into his arms as he picked me up and brought me to the bedroom around the corner. He placed me down on the bedspread and quickly started taking my shirt off.

"Didn't you just insist I get dressed and now you're undressing me again?"

"Yes, I never said this relationship wouldn't be complicated." He slid my shirt up over my shoulders and I reached to quickly strip his shirt off too, so I could feel those muscles I was drooling over earlier.

I purred as he kissed my breast through my lacy bra. He reached behind me, unclasping it, and tossed it to the ground. His strong hands quickly took a hold of me as he teased my nipples with his teeth. I arched my back, pushing my breasts deeper into his hands. Moaning, I dug my nails into his back and he let out a growl.

"Christie," he snarled, before covering my mouth with his, passionately kissing me as he slid his hands around my back, pulling me tightly against him.

I wrapped my legs around his waist and he slammed me down against the bed, tearing my leggings off.

"What, no underwear?" Shane asked, smiling at me.

"I don't like to wear it. Are you disappointed?"

"Right now, nothing could disappoint me. I have you back and you love me."

"And you love me."

"I do."

"Then kiss me."

Epilogue

I got the internship, but lost my parents. Since moving in with Shane, they refused to talk to me. Though, I guess I should consider myself lucky that they gave me a half hour to come back in the house and pack some of my stuff. I wrote my parents a letter every week, updating them on my life. Every letter got sent back to me, 'return to sender.'

At first, it devastated me. How could they write me off when I was trying to be true to myself? But they were determined I'd made the wrong decision. It was hard, but Mrs. Choi was an amazing surrogate mother for now. She worried that I wasn't eating healthy enough, she asked about my grades, and gave me a job filing in her medical office on the weekends. It was liberating to be more independent. Well, as independent as a woman who cooked wearing only a lacy apron for her boyfriend could be.

I thought it would be difficult to live with a guy permanently. But things with Shane were better than ever. We went to the track on Saturdays, spent

Sundays completing our new couple bucket list, and focused on school during the week. However, the best part, Shane and I fell asleep together every night. Most nights, he fulfilled my every desire, and I worked hard to remind him how he was my king of the night.

Life wasn't perfect, but I was happy, and it was my choice.

***

Three Years Later

We all stood at Violet's graduation party, watching her give a speech about how grateful she was that we all took the time to celebrate with her. But she didn't get to finish her speech because Berneli interrupted her. He stood up and wrapped an arm around her shoulder.

"Listen, everyone, I have known this woman for the past four years and, as her favorite character likes to say, "you have captivated me, body and soul." Looking at all of the people who love her and me, I cannot contain this anymore." Berneli dropped to his knees and took her hand.

"Love, we have a lot to look forward to in the next year. Things are going beautifully with my university position, and you have that journalist position. Our apartment is beautifully decorated thanks to Christie and Annabelle, and Mom's restaurant is a hit. But to make life perfect, I would like to ask you something. Do me the honor of being my wife."

I watched tears fill Violet's eyes as she nodded to him, extending her hand so he could put the ring on her finger. I smiled at her, and tried to keep from crying myself. I know I didn't want to get married early, but it suited Violet and Berneli. The hopeless romantics would make a beautiful couple.

Annabelle and I let their families hug them before we freaked out. I turned to look at Annabelle when I heard her sniffle. Jason quickly offered her a tissue and pulled her into a tight hug. They'd be moving in together as she started graduate school and he began a position with a prominent cyber security company. They talked about marriage, but Annabelle said she wanted to establish her own career before she became a Mrs.

"So, when I propose, I'm gonna give you a ring pop. You don't need the big ring, right?" Shane asked me.

"Listen, to me, you spazzy man. If you think you're getting off without buying me a beautiful ring, you've got another think coming. I have needs and those needs involve diamonds."

He smiled at me and wrapped an arm around my waist.

"Huh, it's a good thing I won the race last week. I guess I could spend maybe two or three hundred dollars."

I turned to look at Shane and saw the goofy look in his eyes. "I will call your mother if you even think about that."

"I'm not afraid of her." He kissed the tip of my nose and leaned in to whisper in my ear. "But if it makes you happy, I might consider a simple two carat solitaire. I wouldn't want to take away from the beauty of your face. Then, when we got married, I'd present you with an elaborate wedding ring. The kind that stops people in their tracks. This way, you can be the princess you always wanted to be, but only when you want to. The rest of the time, you can be whoever you want to be."

I leaned into him, knowing that in a few hours, I'd be going back to our apartment, and starting my job at the marketing firm. Trent moved out of the area and we never heard from him again, and Finn was just a ghost from the past. Funny what can happen in just eight semesters.

Acknowledgements

Thank you to all the readers of the Elton Hall Chronicles. Remember to follow your heart and if you doubt it, ask your best friend. She'll tell you what you need to hear even if you don't want to.

About the Author

Always the avid reader, Sarah Fischer found it frustrating that there were so few books following the struggles and joys that a typical college student faces. While recovering from surgery, she decided to write one. *Elton Hall Chronicles: First Semester* is based on real events that happened to Sarah and her friends over the years. When she isn't unveiling long held secrets or working as a government drove, Sarah likes to go to the movies with her husband and spend time with her three furbabies.

Facebook:
https://www.facebook.com/sarah.elizabeth.129

Twitter:
https://twitter.com/SarhAlexander7